Coffee

KUNG
FU

Coffee

KUNG
FU

KAREN BRICHOUX

NEW AMERICAN LIBRARY

New American Library
Published by New American Library, a division of
Penguin Group (USA) Inc., 375 Hudson Street,
New York, New York 10014, U.S.A.
Penguin Books Ltd, 80 Strand,
London WC2R 0RL, England
Penguin Books Australia Ltd, 250 Camberwell Road,
Camberwell, Victoria 3124, Australia
Penguin Books Canada Ltd, 10 Alcorn Avenue,
Toronto, Ontario, Canada M4V 3B2
Penguin Books (N.Z.) Ltd, Cnr Rosedale and Airborne Roads,
Albany, Auckland 1310, New Zealand

Penguin Books Ltd, Registered Offices:
80 Strand, London WC2R 0RL, England

First published by New American Library, a division of Penguin Group (USA) Inc.

First Printing, June 2003
10   9   8   7   6   5   4   3   2   1

Copyright © Karen Brichoux, 2003

(NAL) REGISTERED TRADEMARK—MARCA REGISTRADA

LIBRARY OF CONGRESS CATALOGING-IN-PUBLICATION DATA:

Brichoux, Karen.
    Coffee and kung fu / Karen Brichoux.
       p. cm.
    ISBN 0-451-20902-8 (alk. paper)
    1. Young women—Fiction. I. Title.

PS3602.R5 C6 2003
813'.6—dc21

                          2002031534

Set in Weiss
Designed by Erin Benach
Printed in the United States of America

PUBLISHER'S NOTE
This is a work of fiction. Names, characters, places, and incidents are either the product of the author's imagination or are used fictitiously, and any resemblance to actual persons, living or dead,
business establishments, events, or locales is entirely coincidental.

For Christa
Yodel on, evil elf maiden

Acknowledgments

Three kowtows to BJ Robbins, agent extraordinaire, and to Ellen Edwards at NAL, who didn't realize she was signing up to work with a stubborn mule, poor woman. A generous helping of thanks to Jerri Corgiat and Natalie Collins for their wide shoulders and wise (or otherwise) comments, and for plain, old-fashioned friendship. And dipping farther into the barrel of debt, thanks to Janeanne Houston and Andrew Currier—siblings beyond compare—who listened to more whining than mortals should have to endure. Even more thanks to my parents, who supplied me with plenty of Big Chief pads, pencils, and the idea that a girl shouldn't be afraid to switch horses in midstream. And last of all (because the most important people are always listed last), thanks to Dave, who knows how it feels to step out of the tropical sun and into a dark theater that smells like damp foam rubber seats. I love you, man.

Chapter
1

*I*n the movie *Magnificent Bodyguards*, Jackie Chan sells the evil Mountain King his fists in order to protect his friends. Selling a body part that is still attached to your body. It's a funny concept. I wonder if it's possible to sell part of yourself and not your whole self?

I'm trying to smooth the grammatical errors out of an amusement park brochure when Carol brings two cups of coffee to my cubicle.

"I heard you had a date last night," she says as she moves a stack of paper off my spare chair.

I take a sip from the cup of coffee she's set on my desk. "Who'd you hear that from?" We both know she's the one who set up the date, but she's fishing. I don't want to tell her that I didn't show. It would sound like cowardice.

Or maybe I just don't want to talk about my personal life at all. I give this office nine hours out of every day. Nine, not eight. The half-hour lunch break is a joke. You can't even walk to the nearest coffee shop, eat, and be back in half an hour. Last spring, I sat outside the front door to eat my lunch. I wanted to be in the sunshine and fresh air. The boss called me into his office and asked me to use the lunchroom. Something about sanitation. Something about what the clients would think. I asked if I could skip the two fifteen-minute breaks. Take an hour for lunch. He said no. *"The law is the law and the law says I have to give you a break every four hours. Sorry."* So now I stare out the lunchroom window while eating mustard and bologna on wheat, but it isn't the same.

"Oh, c'mon, Nicci. How'd it go?" Carol asks, sitting down in the chair. She isn't going to leave.

"I didn't go."

Her face turns pink. Not the little-girl blush, the blotchy, angry kind. "You just stood him up?"

"No. I called the number you gave me. We talked."

"You just talked." It's not a question.

"It wouldn't have worked, Carol."

"Why not?"

I lean back in my chair and shrug. "I don't know. It didn't feel right."

"You didn't even meet him. How could you know if it felt right or not?"

I don't think I should tell her that I asked him if he had ever watched a Kung Fu movie. He said he didn't like foreign films.

"He's a vegetarian," Carol is saying. "He likes animals, movies, going out to eat. . . . In fact, he sounds exactly like you."

"I'm not a vegetarian."

"You know what I mean."

I take my glasses off and set them on the desk, neatly crossing the ear pieces. In *Snake & Crane Arts of Shaolin*, Jackie Chan slams crossed chopsticks onto the café table to indicate that the conversation is over. I doubt Carol will get the hint.

I rub my eyes. "Likes and dislikes aren't everything," I say. But I know that if he'd said he liked Kung Fu movies, I probably would have shown up. Just to see.

"His favorite movie is *Die Hard*," Carol says. "You like action movies. He likes action movies. I just don't understand how you can sit there and tell me likes and dislikes don't matter. Every time I want to watch *Pretty Woman* I have to catch Bill and tie him to a chair."

"You'd have to tie *me* to a chair," I say without thinking.

"See? See? I wish you'd given it a chance."

I sigh. "I'm happy, Carol. Really. I'm not all that interested in hooking up with anyone right now."

This is an outright lie, of course. Everyone is always interested in hooking up with someone. Sure, we like to pretend that we aren't really looking, but we're all looking just the same. We're not exempt from evolution. And evolution tends to produce animals whose main goal is perpetuation of the species. So, yeah, we're all looking. It's just whether or not the looking should turn into the hassle of mating and trying to get along with another human being for the rest of your life.

Carol sighs. "No one can really be happy when they're on their own."

"Why not?"

"How could you be, with no one to talk to? No one to share your life with?"

As if you could do this with any warm body. I've noticed that a lot of people seem to think any warm body who shares your hobbies is a good enough warm body to share your life with. In the lunchroom, the other women like to talk about soul mates, but I'm not sure they know the difference between soul mates and the early stages of being bed mates. That euphoric period when you don't need to sleep, don't need to eat, you just live on love. It lasts about two weeks. If you're lucky, two months. From there on out, it all goes downhill. The guy who was "the one" becomes "the sonuvabitch who slept with my best friend." But hey, you probably both liked mountain biking.

"You know?" Carol asks from the other side of my cubicle. She's still waiting for an answer to her statement.

"Yeah." I really wish she'd leave.

"I know this other guy—"

"Maybe some other time."

"He's cute. He works in Bill's office. Something to do with computers, you know?"

"You know?" It actually means, "Are you listening?" I'm listening, but I want to finish this brochure, leave early, and go to the grocery store. I'm out of TP at home and I need something other than refried beans for supper. And maybe *Shaolin Wooden Men* will be in my mailbox. I finally found a subtitled version on-line last week.

"Some other time," I say out loud. "Not right now."

Carol purses her lips. You can see the little wrinkle lines she's going to have when she gets old and her lips move into permanent pucker mode. The corners of her mouth are going to hang down in soft rolls of parchmenty flesh. I hope she and Bill are still fighting about movies. But I doubt it. Bill put his hand on my knee the first night I met him. He didn't pat it. He squeezed it. I don't know about Carol, but I wouldn't want to spend the rest of my life mating and trying to get along with a man who squeezes other women's knees.

"You're being deliberately difficult, you know?" she says. "I'm just trying to set you up on a date, you know?"

"I know. Thank you, Carol." Maybe I should tell her that I'm in the Witness Protection Program. Or that my last boyfriend was a stuntman who died in a fiery balloon crash and I'm still in mourning. I doubt either excuse would work.

Carol stands up and twitches her pantyhose. "I hate these things," she says as she smooths her skirt back into place.

"Try knee-highs," I say, already thinking about that dangling modifier in the third paragraph of the brochure.

"I need the control top or I wouldn't fit into this skirt."

"Oh." I glance up. She's looking at me. Her lips are pursed again.

"Are you sure?" she asks. "About the guy in Bill's office? He's recently divorced. No kids. Cute, too."

And used to be some other woman's soul mate before he started squeezing her friends' knees.

"No thanks."

I moved to Boston after the president of the limestone and ivy buildings that passed for a college handed me a piece of paper with "Nicole Bradford" printed on it. It was a fancy piece of paper. Cream heavyweight. My name in loopy Old English Bookplate. But all the calligraphy in the world couldn't help me turn an English lit BA into a job. After floundering around as a temp in my college town, I moved here. Of all the cold, gray cities in North America, I moved to Boston.

I didn't just stab my finger at a map, I *chose* this city. Because of all the cold, gray cities I could have chosen, *this* one has people on the streets. Not as many as I'm used to, but a lot. That sounds funny, considering that I'm living in one of the largest cities in the country. But there's something about cold cities that keeps people and businesses from spilling out into the streets, setting up boxes of shoes, cabbages, fish, cigarettes. . . .

Okay, I'm not making any sense. I grew up in the Philippines and lived in Manila while I went to high school. Manila is giant, humid, filthy, neon, and so damn alive you take in the life with every breath. With every breath you catch a whiff of the charred corn from a cookfire, a passing jeepney's exhaust, the odor of the person's body next to you on the bus, fresh flowers from the corner shop, burning rubber, new shoes, and the hot, smokey scent of squid cooking. . . . The smells might not be pleasant, but if you could plant them, they would grow. And every possible inch of the city is covered with people. Sitting on the curbs, setting up shop on the corner, passing out sweepstakes tickets on the steps of a department store, milling around a TV playing the latest soccer game.

Manila is not cold or gray or dark.

So why am I here? I'm a coward, I guess. Clutching my calligraphied diploma, I picked a cold, gray city where I could disappear into the crowd and no one would ever notice.

When I was eighteen, I moved back to the United States with my parents. They were retiring after twenty-some years of living in various cities throughout Asia, and they decided to retire when their last bird—me—left home to go to college in the U.S. My parents were missionaries, but I always said they taught English (which was true) because I didn't want to say the word "missionary." Aside from the connotation of the Great White Father going out into the world to bring the White Light of God to the brown or black masses, I didn't want to be a missionary kid. I didn't want to be from another country. I wanted nothing more than to be exactly like all the other college freshmen who had spent their lives in the heartland of the USA. The proudest moment of my eighteen-year-old life was when another student at my college said, "You're a missionary kid? I didn't know that. You're nothing like the other MKs. You act just like someone from around here."

"Got a light?"

The voice wakes me up from my memory daydream. I'm on the bus which will drop me off within walking distance of my Watertown apartment, and the woman next to me is holding a cigarette in front of a toothless smile.

"Sorry," I tell her. "I don't smoke."

"I didn't ask ya if you smoked. I asked if you had a light."

I shake my head. She sidles across the aisle to a man in pinstripes and shiny shoes. He slaps his paper against the NO SMOKING sign, then goes back to reading the business news.

Leaning my head against the clammy window, I watch the buildings crawl by. All that effort to be just like everyone else and now I find out homogeneity is only skin deep. Because I'm not sure where I want to be from. I'm not sure where I fit.

No big surprises here. Nicci's confused again.

What brought this little problem to my attention was an on-line shopping expedition for a classic Jackie Chan movie. During the last five minutes of my half-hour lunch, I finally tracked down *Fearless Hyena* in Cantonese. The voluntary buyer reviews all said the same thing: Amazing fights, but a lot of cheesy humor that has nothing to do with the plot.

Cheesy humor. The stuff that makes living fun. But I guess even movies have to be goal oriented.

Outside the bus, a horn blares. Everyone is hurrying to get somewhere they don't really want to go. Rushing toward today's goal. Furious if another human being gets in their way. On a bad day, the guy who has to put his foot on the brakes might even pull out a gun. And he was only going home to watch a sitcom on TV.

Shanghai Noon isn't really a Kung Fu movie, but it has this marvelous horse that sits down, stays, and gives Jackie a horse laugh at the appropriately funny moment. As a kid, I spent hours in my room writing stories about horses. Racehorses, cow ponies, horses with ridiculous names like Queen and Golden Cloud. I never named the horses in my books Bob, Freddy, or Peaches. But if you were a horse, would you rather be called Bob or King of the Wind?

Even though I wasn't able to have my own horse, I did take riding lessons when I was a junior in college. The instructor thought it was hilarious when I fell off. She nearly doubled over laughing. I thought it was funny, too, until I realized that she got more enjoyment over my falling off than when I finally mastered the up-and-down sway of the dressage trot. I didn't go back.

Carol eventually talks me into going out with a guy from the bigger cubicles down the hall. I'm not sure how she knows so many men, and I wonder if she'd be able to set me up with a woman if I were a lesbian. Maybe Carol is the matchmaker from *Dragon Lord*. Helping young boys land potential mates. Lucky for Jackie, the matchmaker liked to hang out in odd places and had nothing better to do than follow young boys around to see what girls they were interested in. Maybe that's what Carol is doing whenever she comes into my cubicle with a cup of coffee. Maybe she's following me around.

Kevyn (with a *y*) is about six feet tall and looks like Russell Crowe. That is, he looks like a young Richard Nixon. He's about ten years older than I am—somewhere in his late thirties.

"So you're . . ." he trails off.

"I guess so." Maybe he forgot my name.

"Wow! That's so tight." He grins.

"What is?" I keep a straight face. The only people I know who use the word "tight" are my nephews. Maybe Kevyn with a *y* doesn't know how old I am.

He looks confused. "It's nice to meet you, I mean."

"Same here." I look around the coffee shop.

"So do you want to see a movie or something?"

"Okay." I spot the grinning guy behind the counter. He obviously finds all this amusing, because he's watching Kevyn and me as he scoops coffee beans for a customer. And he's listening to our conversation. Eavesdropping without shame. I try not to smile.

"Any movie you'd like to see?" Kevyn asks. "There's a new movie out with Julia Roberts and Richard Gere."

"Another one?" I ask, still looking at Grinning Boy. He's looking back at me.

"Yes. I liked *Pretty Woman*, didn't you? It was tight."

"What was?" I ask again. When Kevyn's mouth opens and closes several times, I realize I'm acting like my riding instructor. It's not Kevyn with a *y*'s fault. He's just trying to fit in with what he thinks I am. He's trying. And I'm laughing.

"Look, I'm sorry," I say. "You probably came all the way down here—"

"No problem. I work in the same place as you."

"I know. But something's come up. I'm not going to be able to go out tonight. I tried to call Carol—"

"You can't go out tonight?" Kevyn asks. He almost lets a genuine look of relief slip, then he pastes something bland and concerned over the crack.

"No, something's come up—"

"No problem. To tell you the truth . . ." He trails off again, but I know what he didn't say. I'm not what he was expecting. Too odd, too brusque, not girlie enough.

You can always tell the men who want a woman who acts like they think a woman should act. They want Miss Melanie Jones from the third grade. She smiles, she laughs, she listens, she scrapbooks, she wants one-point-eight kids, maybe even two-point-four, a minivan, a nearby Baptist church, and a three-bedroom house. And she likes movies with Julia Roberts and Richard Gere, and loves the man who will go to them with her.

Kevyn looks uncomfortable, like he doesn't know if he should shake my hand, give me a hug, or just leave. He swallows. I watch his Adam's apple bob up and down, and take pity on the poor man.

"Maybe I'll see you at work sometime," I say, tucking my hands in the back pockets of my jeans. I've found that it always makes people more comfortable if you don't have any loose appendages hanging out there, requiring some form of etiquette. And putting your hands in your back pockets rather than your front ones causes your elbows to stick out and solves the problem of whether or not you need a hug.

"Sure. Maybe. Take care." Kevyn starts to leave, then turns back to me. "I'm sorry."

I raise my eyebrows. "For what?"

He waves a hand. "For this. For wasting your time."

"And yours. At least we'll be able to tell Carol to bug off, right?" I grin, but his return smile wobbles off to one side.

"Right. Take care."

"You too." I watch him push through the glass door with the steaming cup of coffee painted on the inside. A twinge of guilt surfaces at how relieved and happy I am to hear the shop bell ring in his wake.

"You two have a fight?"

I turn around to find Grinning Boy talking to me. Stepping up to the glass counter, I pretend to look at the endless varieties of coffee. He's about my age. Has brown eyes. And the name tag on his green apron reads: MICHAEL.

"No fight," I say, still looking at the coffee beans in their faux burlap bags. "Someone at work set us up. Thought we'd hit it off."

"Guess you didn't."

"Guess we didn't." I look up at him and smile. His head is tilted slightly to one side. I'm expecting faux concern.

"Want a cup of coffee?" he asks instead.

"Sure."

"Customers rave about my cappuccino," he says, leaning his elbows on the top of the glass case. Below his rolled-up sleeves, his arms are roped with tendons, veins, and muscle. Not a weight lifter's arms. A working man's arms. Like you might see on the docks.

For years, I lived with my parents in the belly of the prehistoric animal created by the Philippine Islands. Surrounded by a distant reef, the possible ports on our island weren't deep enough for the big ferryboats, so the government built a dock. Like a finger, a mile-long pier stretched out from the island until it found the deeper water the ferries needed. Every morning, just as the sun broke free of the ocean, a line of shallow-bottomed fishing boats pulled up alongside the pier, bumping barnacle-encrusted mahogany pilings with their prows. *"Hup!"* someone would yell and narrow, wooden gangplanks would slide up from each boat to the pier. Then the impromptu market would begin as box after slatted box of fish, crabs, mussels, and even the occasional shark would be hand-carried up the plank to the eager buyers above.

The men who carried those boxes could have picked up the world. And they had never seen a set of weights in their lives.

I stop staring at Grinning Boy's arms.

"Just plain coffee with cream," I say out loud. He might make the best cappuccino on the planet, but it would still be a six-dollar cup of coffee. Besides, with the money I saved by avoiding the latest Julie and Rich movie, I can buy another Jackie Chan DVD.

He doesn't even blink. "What blend?"

"Blend?"

"Of beans."

I blink. Blend? I buy my coffee in a can. Already ground. If I want to have a ceremony, I make tea. "You pick," I say, but I feel . . . what's the word? *Gauche.*

"Coming right up." He twirls around on the balls of his feet. The move is so graceful, I forget my embarrassment and just watch. He doesn't waste an atom of energy. Every twitch is pure music. An acrobat in a green apron.

He sets the coffee on the glass counter. I start to hand him some money, but he closes my hand over the bills. His fingers are long and warm, and he has a dusting of powdered coffee bean on his knuckles.

"My treat. If you'll sit with me on my break."

I look up from his knuckles to his brown eyes. The irises are so dark, I can see my reflection. For one heartbeat, I watch myself, then I turn our clasped hands over and let the money go. "Thanks. But I can't. I'm sorry."

He smiles and my reflection disappears. "Another time," he says, taking the money and stepping over to the cash register.

"Yes. Another time." I snap a plastic lid over the top of the coffee cup and push open the glass door. The bell rings.

*I*n *Half a Loaf of Kung Fu*—the dubbed version—Jackie complains to the Beggar Master, "It's my Kung Fu. It's just no good except for laughs." Sometimes I wonder if my life is only good for laughs.

It's been two weeks since my "date" with Kevyn. Down at the Common, the last of the orange and yellow leaves are starting to fall, and I'm grateful for the heated air of the bus after standing in the autumn wind. Summer stayed late this year, and the weather went directly from shorts to coats, without passing sweaters. The bus driver sighs as I try to swipe my T-card without taking off my heavy gloves. Exasperated, he takes the card from me and does it himself. I say thank you, and this surprises him so much he almost smiles.

Today is going to be a lousy day. Carol wasn't happy with me when she found out I'd aborted the date with Kevyn. Now she's punishing me by making me go shopping with her for the office party's Halloween decorations. I hate shopping, but on the list of possible punishments, shopping is preferred over the full-scale interrogation I was expecting.

I've only been a copy editor at Graphics and Design since

last February, but Carol says the holiday parties at the office are "a blast." Since the parties aren't exactly voluntary, I'm not sure if she's being enthusiastic or sarcastic. In any case, she's in charge of decorating for the Halloween party tomorrow night. And I've been volunteered to help.

It's a costume party. I found this out yesterday evening as I was leaving the building. The boss stepped into the elevator just as the doors were beginning to close. He smiled, asked me how things were going and if I was fitting in. I smiled and said the obligatory, affirmative things that any employee says in these situations, even when they've already been with the company for nine months. Then he asked me if I intended to be a call girl for the party on Friday. This is not the kind of question you want to hear from your boss in an elevator slowly creaking toward the ground floor. My eyes must have been five times too big, because his face turned red, and he began to stammer that someone had said something about all the copy editors going as—and here he swallowed hard—pimps and call girls.

"Oh," I said, "it's a *costume* party." Then I realized what *that* sounded like, and mumbled something about not having a costume yet, but that I definitely wasn't going as a call girl, and hadn't heard a thing about the pimps. We were both relieved when the elevator doors swished open.

But just try and find a costume the day before Halloween. Every office in the city is having the not-so-voluntary costume party. Or at least it looks that way, judging by the large number of female duos shopping for fold-out pumpkins and swags of ghosts. I pick up a jointed skeleton that looks as if it's been passed over the last few Halloweens.

"What about this?" I ask Carol, who's rummaging through the poster-board images of baby ghosts and black cats with orange bow ties.

She looks up. "What about it?"

"We could get a bunch of them and make it a sort of Dia de los Muertos theme."

She stares at me.

"Dancing skeletons, candles, All Saints' Day," I helpfully add.

Carol shakes her head. "Too weird." She pulls up a picture of a baby witch with a green face and a nose wart. "What do you think about this? It's cute."

"Sure. Whatever." *Cute.* It's not something I associate with Halloween.

Thanks to three hundred years of Spanish occupation, the Philippines is predominantly Catholic. Although the U.S.-style Halloween is catching on, the majority of people troop to the cemeteries to light candles at the graves of family members. Being a tropical country with heavy rain and clay soil, bodies are placed in stacked cement boxes above ground—much like the cemeteries in New Orleans. The candles flicker from as high as twenty feet and litter the ground below like lighted confetti. It's beautiful and haunting. But not cute.

"We could put these pictures up all around the conference room, then hang swags of ghosts and bats," Carol says.

"Okay."

"And this light for the table. What do you think?" She holds up a ceramic figurine of a scarecrow complete with fiber-optic "straw" in place of the traditional corn shuck. The scarecrow's arms stick out at odd angles—a confused, straw-stuffed bicyclist who doesn't know if he's turning right or stopping—and he's giving a sideways leer to the safety-orange jack-o'-lantern at his feet. A white electrical cord dangles from the back of this ceramic monstrosity. Carol finds an outlet on a nearby pillar and plugs it in. The scarecrow's eyes light up, the jack-o'-lantern glows, and the "straw" changes colors.

I paste on a smile. "It's okay," I say. "But why not just carve a pumpkin?"

"Yuck. Too messy." Carol drops the light into the shopping basket. After we add some "cute" poster-board baby ghosts and witches, and countless packages of swags, she decides we have enough decorations. Standing in line with eight other female duos who also have shopping baskets filled with poster-board pictures and swags, we wait for the tired cashier to ring us up.

"What was wrong with Kevyn?" Carol asks. She's looking at the racks of gum and candy bars, and her voice has the same tonal quality as if she'd just asked me whether I preferred wintergreen or peppermint.

"Nothing." I feign interest in a mop witch.

"If nothing was wrong, you'd have gone out with him."

I thought I'd managed to avoid the interrogation. Now it's happening in a line at the local hobby-and-craft store. And with sixteen pairs of ears straining to hear every word.

"He's not looking for someone like me," I say at last.

"Bullshit," Carol says.

Four or five pairs of eyebrows skyrocket toward the ceiling. I try not to notice.

"He's a man," Carol continues. "You're a woman."

Around us, heads nod and wag.

"Yes," I say, "but I'm not interested in the one-point-eight, the minivan, and the suburbs."

Different heads nod and wag.

"Neither is Kevyn."

"Bullshit."

This time, no eyebrows go up, but I swear the line of female duos is constricting into an atom, each duo forming an electron and circling around Carol and me—the positively interesting nucleus.

Before Carol can protest, I offer a wise and discerning argument about Kevyn's heartfelt desires. "He's in his late thirties and has 'have my baby' tattooed on his forehead," I say, trying to keep my voice too low for the spinning electrons to hear.

Carol's mouth opens and shuts, and I swear there's the tiniest hint of wistfulness in her eyes. "Maybe," she says. And I realize that Carol is probably in her late thirties, doesn't have any kids, and is married to the knee-squeezer.

"What costume are you wearing tomorrow?" I ask.

Her face smooths out into a smile. "I haven't decided. Either a witch or Frankenstein's bride. It depends on what Bill is going to wear."

A sigh goes up around us, and the duos step back into line.

"Bill's coming?" I ask.

"Sure. Families and significant others. Didn't you see the flier?"

"No." This is a surprise. I thought the party was only for people in the office. Now I feel even more uncomfortable.

In today's world, office walls are painted plain beige or else have that nubby gray or blue material. No way to merge with the wallpaper. Ugh. That leaves hanging out by the punch bowl. Looking pathetic. Double ugh.

"Have you found a costume yet?" Carol asks.

"Yes." I'm still picturing the punch bowl. My palms are damp and my heart rate's up.

"Well? What is it?"

"Wait and see."

Looks like I'll be hunting for a costume to rent after work.

Standing in front of the mirror that hangs on the back of my apartment door, I realize that I don't make a good flamenco dancer. First, I have short hair. I mean, really short. Cropped close to the head short. Next, my hair is red. Flamenco dancers are supposed to be dark-skinned, fiery-eyed, *morenas*—brunettes.

And I'm a perfect tribute to my Anglo-Saxon forebears. At least the golden orange dress moves well and hides that stubborn little bulge under my hipbones that no amount of jogging seems to help. The skirt is a bit too long, but with the help of some masking tape and heels it ought to work out all right.

At least it seemed like it would work out all right when I was standing in front of my mirror. It's an hour until the party, and I've already used an entire roll of masking tape. The heels of my shoes keep catching in the taped-up hem. Then the skirt drags along the floor like a badly colored wedding gown. I'm paranoid about damaging the costume and having to pay for it with next month's grocery budget.

"I just love that dress," Carol says for the fifth time as she brings me a cup of coffee.

"Thanks." I would like to finish editing the ad for a local used car dealer before the party, but after seeing the wistfulness in Carol's eyes yesterday, I don't have the heart to say so. I lean back in my chair and take a sip of coffee.

"So you went with the witch?" I ask. She's just finished putting on her costume. Unlike me, she was smart enough to change in the bathroom. I've been a redheaded flamenco dancer all day.

"Bill hadn't decided by the time I left this morning, so I just grabbed the witch." She's radiating the forced good cheer of a PE instructor, but I don't think she knows it.

"Is everything all right?" I start to ask, but Dracula pops into my cubicle before the first two words are out of my mouth.

"C'mon, ladies. Let's party!" He gives an un-Dracula-like whoop and bounds off down the hall chanting, "Party-party, party-party."

I can hardly wait.

"Ed. From down the hall," Carol says. She leans forward. "I think he just broke up with his girlfriend."

"That explains it, then."

She frowns.

It's an "all hands on deck" kind of party. And it looks exactly like I expected a mandatory party to look. Some people mill about in confusion. Some batten down the hatches, fiddling with food and punch and keeping busy. Most look like condemned prisoners about to walk the plank. Dolly from sales brought her five kids. They're dressed as Munchkins and are about as annoying as the originals, but without the singing. Ed flits from woman to woman pretending to hunt for a jugular. The women titter, then lean in to discuss his love life when his back is turned.

Through it all, around it all, Carol is the witch-goddess of serenity. She hands out cookies, rescues a Munchkin from drowning itself in the punch bowl, introduces Ed to a nervous-looking blonde. . . . If the boss were smart, he'd ditch his stuck-up assistant and hire Carol. But the assistant has Pamela Anderson–sized breasts—highly visible in the red swimsuit and body stocking—and the boss is drooling. He's wearing a chest wig and a pair of red swim trunks over his pants. David Hasselhoff, I presume. After being shrunk by aliens. Kevyn came as himself in a top hat. He's standing by the punch bowl, which leaves me the frosted, pumpkin-shaped cookies.

Unfortunately for the bulge below the hip bones, the cookies are really good.

Sometimes I feel as if I'm caught in a Kung Fu movie. Somewhere between the tough-guy stuff and the comic relief. But if this were a movie, the bad guy would come busting through the doors about now and murder some venerable old man, giving the hero a burning need for revenge. Nothing that exciting is going to happen here.

The door swings open and in walks Bill, dressed as Frankenstein's monster. Seeing her husband, Carol smiles a big smile that wobbles when Bill crushes her in a rib-breaking bear hug. Movement by the punch bowl. I glance over and see Kevyn step around the edge of the table. He's frowning. Carol struggles a little, then she's free and rubbing her side, playfully slapping Bill's shoulder while pretending to laugh. Bill squeezes her again. At the look of near-panic on Carol's face, I pick up the hem of my dress and head to the rescue. But before I can move, Kevyn is there, pumping Bill's hand. In the process, he manages to put his smiling self between Bill and Carol. The three of them obviously know each other. Then Bill wanders off toward the appetizers, and Kevyn leans down to ask Carol a question. She shakes her head. I've almost reached them when I feel someone watching me. I look up. Over a mini-hotdog dripping barbeque sauce, Bill is giving me the knee-squeezing eye. I do the only thing an Anglo-Saxon flamenco dancer can do.

I escape to the bathroom.

After washing my hands, I strike a flamenco pose in the bathroom's full-length mirror. I look like a little girl who's wearing her big sister's clothes after stuffing herself with frosted pumpkin cookies. A little girl hiding out from the big, bad wolf in the office restroom.

I am definitely the comic relief in my movie of life.

I drop my arms and lose the flamenco posture. Being the comic relief isn't a big ego boost. I look ridiculous, I feel ridiculous, and all I want is a bowl of cellophane noodles and Jackie Chan on my TV. The decision to skip the rest of the party isn't a difficult one.

But as I step out of the bathroom, I run into Bill.

"There you are," he says.

"Yup. Here I am." *And here I go.* I try to step around him, but he catches my shoulder.

"I haven't seen you since you came over for dinner that one time." The time when he squeezed my knee.

"Nope. I've been busy. Listen, I'm supposed to meet some—"

But Bill has moved forward a step. He smells like someone who fell into a keg and never dried off. I take a step back. He steps forward. I take a step back. He steps forward. I hit the wall. He reaches out and touches my hair.

"Isn't really right for a flamenco dancer," he says.

I laugh. It sounds too high, and that pisses me off. "Nope. Look, I've got to go—"

Bill's hand falls to my breast. "This is pretty nice, though."

Sorry, Carol, I think, as my knee collides with Bill's groin.

He doesn't make a sound. Just a little *oomph* of pain before sliding to the floor.

I grab my coat off the rack. By the time I hit the elevator, I'm running.

It's snowing. Not fluffy, white, Christmas flakes. Spitting ice chips. I look back into the warm lobby. The security guard at the front desk is watching me with that bored disinterest people get when their job is to watch other people. It's forty-five minutes until the next bus. I can stand out here and freeze or I can go back into the lobby.

I turn and walk toward the coffee shop, the golden orange skirt dragging behind me, wiping out my tracks.

My hair is wet and my nose is running by the time I reach the painted glass door. It never occurred to me that the shop might not be open, I'm just glad it is. The bell rings as I pull on the door. Except for two homeless men sitting at a back booth, I'm the only person in the shop. I swipe a gloved hand under my nose before I remember the pack of tissues in my pocket.

Grinning Boy's head and shoulders push through the swinging doors that lead to the back of the shop. He looks around, then sees me. He's not grinning today. He's not frowning, either. Just looking.

"Hi," he says.

"Hi." I shove my hands and the used tissue into my coat pocket, and walk toward the counter.

He wipes damp hands on his apron.

"Did I catch you washing cups?" I ask.

"One of the grinders clogged." He still has the plastic name tag that says MICHAEL, but now he also has a round bleach spot on the apron strap that goes over his right shoulder. "Black coffee with cream?" he asks.

"Sure."

He moves slowly and without the acrobat's grace. As if someone kept him awake last night, talking about unpleasant things. I dig out my wallet and try to sort through the rumpled dollar bills without taking off my gloves. My hands are still shaking.

I'm not a weak person. Not physically. Not emotionally. But I've never been felt up by a friend's husband before, and I'm still shaking. I set the wallet on the glass case and tug my gloves off before trying to take the money out again. This time I get it right.

He's warming the cream over a burner. I want to tell him that he shouldn't bother, but I can't make myself call his name. Michael doesn't fit. It may be what's printed on his name tag, but it isn't him. I don't know what is, so I keep my mouth shut.

After pouring the warmed cream into the coffee, he sets the cup on the counter. Steam rises between us. I hand him the money, but when he reaches out to take it, I catch his hand.

"Why did you ask me to sit with you on your break the other day?" I didn't know it until now, but this is something I've asked myself in that heartbeat between being awake and falling asleep. Something I've asked myself for two weeks.

He looks at me, and I can see my reflection in his eyes. The second hand on the clock above the counter stops, but I can hear the two men in the back booth whisper to each other.

A nickel escapes our clasped hands and clatters onto the glass. The second hand ticks. He takes the money from my hand and picks up the nickel.

"I was lonely," he says.

Lonely. No one is ever lonely. They're bored. They're sad. They're depressed. They're horny. But never, ever lonely. Being lonely means no one likes you. Being lonely means you don't have any friends. Being lonely means you're . . . alone.

"Oh," I say.

He rings up the sale, separates the two rumpled dollar bills from the change, then shuts the cash drawer. Our public transaction is complete. There's no excuse to continue interacting. If I say something now, it moves past public and becomes private.

"My friend's husband groped me outside the bathroom tonight. At our office party."

For two clicks of the second hand, he's still, then he pours a cup of coffee and lifts the partition section of the counter. We walk over to a booth by the window. The homeless guys are quiet. One is asleep, his head leaning against the back of his seat. The other is watching us with the bored disinterest of the security guard at the office.

The coffee has cooled enough to drink before he says anything.

"Are you all right?"

"Yes." I'm beginning to be embarrassed. He must think I'm short a few brain cells, bursting out with something like that. It's not the sort of thing people talk about with strangers.

"Did he hurt you?"

"Only my pride."

He nods.

"I didn't ask for it," I add. I'm feeling defensive. When a guy feels a woman up, people always seem to assume that she was giving off "please feel me up" signals.

"I know," he says.

The air between us stretches and goes still. From the back booth, I can hear the sleeping man snore. I ask the question that's been bothering me.

"Should I tell his wife? I mean, it seems dishonest. Not telling her. She's my friend. I just don't know if I should . . . tell her." I pick my coffee up a little too fast, and it sloshes out over my fingers and onto the table. I wipe it up with a paper napkin from the booth's dispenser.

"It can go either way," he says. "Either way, she won't thank you."

"Oh." I look up from the wet napkin. He's staring out at the snow, his chin cupped in one hand. I wonder if he's ever had to say something to a friend. Or if he's the one who wasn't thankful.

"I always thought loyalty would be easy," I say when I can't bear the silence and my silent questions anymore. "Cut-and-dried. You don't rat out your friends. You stand beside them through thick and thin. Easy."

"Like a movie," he says, still staring out at the snow.

"Yes." I drink the last of my coffee. The clock on the wall says I have just enough time to make it to the bus stop. "I have to go," I say.

He looks at me as I stand up. I look down at him. For the first time since I came to this city, I feel like I've actually talked to someone. I take a deep breath and say what I want to say before I lose my nerve.

"I wish I'd taken that break with you."

His eyes widen a fraction, then he smiles.

Chapter 3

The Young Master is a movie about loyalty. Broken loyalty between a master and student, unselfish loyalty of one brother to another, and ultimately, the loyalty that comes from forgiveness. The theme of loyalty isn't just in *The Young Master*, it's the hinge that swings most Kung Fu movies.

The hem of the flamenco costume isn't too messed up. A little soap and water and a blast from the hair dryer will fix it. I wish I could say the same for me.

I know Grinning Boy—I still can't call him Michael, not even here in the solitude of my apartment—is right. No matter what I say to Carol, and that includes saying nothing at all, she'll be hurt and angry. But is that a good enough reason to take the easy way out and not tell her? What if she already knows Bill's a philandering piece of shit, but hasn't admitted it to herself?

And why does this have to be so hard?

It's almost as if Bill's groping really *was* my fault.

I'm not hungry, so I decide to go to bed. Before crawling between the blankets, I turn my tiny jack-o'-lantern until it faces the window. The flickering grin reflects off the glass and the icy snow, and sheds a guiding light for any lost spirit needing to find its way home.

Lying in bed, looking up at the glowing shadows on the ceiling, I wish someone would light a candle for me.

By Monday, I'm a mess. I still don't know what I'm going to do. The snow has melted, and the weather has backpedaled to sweater season. On my run, I break a sweat for the first time in weeks.

I love my morning runs. It's the one time when this city feels alive. I can smell bread baking and the sour smell of garbage from a passing truck. Two delivery men are arguing in the alley behind the newspaper kiosk. As I pick up a paper, the news seller in the kiosk leans out and adds his opinion to the argument. Loudly. With meaningful gestures.

In my apartment, I toss the paper onto the table and grab a cup of coffee before stripping and stepping into the shower. As the hot water beats on my head and back, I realize my shoulders are still in knots. I don't have that many friends in the city. Carol is the only person who actually qualifies. Now I'm about to ruin it. Damn Bill, anyway.

At the office, I can't concentrate on the used car ad. When I hear Carol's voice in the hall, my hand jerks on the computer's keyboard and types a string of meaningless numbers.

"Hi," Carol says. The word is normal and noncommittal. She walks in, sets a cup of coffee on my desk, then sits down.

"Hi." It comes out more of a croak than a greeting.

"You didn't come back to the party?" Her gaze slides away to the corner, and she has a white-knuckled grip on her mug. Through her fingers, I can see a dazed, purple cat surrounded by frazzled bubbles. *Today is the first day of the rest of this miserable week,* reads the mug.

Amen.

I swallow before replying. "No." I haven't really made a decision about what to do, what to say. But looking at Carol's face, seeing the dark shadows under her eyes, it all seems very simple. "Carol, I've got something I have—" I begin.

"Bill told me about what happened," she interrupts.

I blink. "He did?"

Coffee splashes into her lap. Twin tears slide down her face, leaving slug tracks on her cheeks. "How could you?"

Of course. Of course. Stupid me. It never even occurred to me that Bill would lie. Tell a story with a hint of truth, just enough to sound right. *She came on to me in the hall outside the bathroom. I was drunk. I did something I shouldn't have. I'm sorry.* And Carol—who takes everyone at their word and never looks beneath the surface—would believe him.

"Here I was trying to set you up with all these men, and the whole time you're . . . you've . . . you want Bill." She holds a wad of tissue to her mouth.

"No," I say. I'm not sure what to tell her. It would be naive to think she would take my word over Bill's. But the part of me that hates injustice has to try. "He was drunk, Carol. He put his hand on my breast outside the bathroom. I kneed him in the groin. I left." End of story. But I'm not stupid enough to think the truth will matter at this point.

Carol is staring at me as if I've sprouted a nose wart, like the one owned by the baby witch that still hangs on my cubicle wall. She leans in close. "I always thought you were an honest person, Nicole Bradford. Loyal. A little mixed up, maybe, but honest. Instead, you are such a . . . *liar.* Stay away from my husband." She bounces up out of the chair. Her heel catches in a loose carpet thread and she falls against my desk. "Fuck you," she says to the carpet. And to me.

Especially to me.

* * *

Being accused of attempted adultery is a new one for me. I spend the rest of the day in a fog, moving from used car ad to sailboat rental brochure to upscale restaurant premiere. If anything makes it past me while managing even to *approximate* grammatical correctness, it's an accident. I skip lunch. I skip both breaks. I'm considering skipping going home altogether when Kevyn knocks on my cubicle wall.

"Hey," he says as I try to focus on his face.

"Go away." It's rude, but I don't need a lecture from Carol's knight in shining armor. I ignore him and keep working.

Everything is quiet. So quiet, I think he's left.

"I believe you."

I type another string of meaningless numbers as my hands jump on the keyboard. I look up just as Kevyn sits down. "What did you say?"

"I believe you. Bill's a jerk. And a drunk. He's picked on women before during office parties."

Now I'm confused. "So why does Carol—"

"Because Carol never found out before. This time, she went looking for Bill and found him on the floor by the women's bathroom. He called you a bitch. I guess after he sobered up, he said what she wanted to hear."

I laugh, but it tastes bitter. "She wanted to hear that I came on to her husband?"

"She wanted to hear that it was someone else's fault. Anyone's."

"Great." I lean my elbows on the desk and cradle my head in my hands. "What are the chances I'll be able to stand working here after today? Carol knows everybody."

"She's not talking about it."

"Just to you." The words come out as sarcastic as I feel.

Kevyn sighs. "Look, I know this is going to sound pretty

weird, but I think Carol knows it wasn't your fault. She just can't deal with the situation at home. She's making up her world as she goes along."

I lift my head and look at him. He's staring at the carpet. I remember him putting his body between Carol and Bill. "Are you going to be there to help her pick up the pieces when she finally catches Bill in the act?"

He smiles a sad little smile.

Kevyn's visit doesn't make me feel any better. I finish the restaurant's opening ad, then pack up for the day. Outside, the weather's turned cold, and the clouds hang heavy in the sky. In *To Kill with Intrigue,* Jackie stumbles through the icy dark, searching for his lover while being taunted for a fool by a witch. I don't need the witch. I have my brain. And it's telling me I'm the worst kind of fool.

My usual bus never comes. Neither does the next. A guy next to me mutters something about an accident blocking crucial streets. I tuck my hands into my armpits and stamp my feet, but I'm numb by the time I decide to hell with it and walk down to the coffee shop. Being emotionally self-sufficient isn't any comfort when you're cold.

The coffee shop is packed. I recognize a number of the regulars from my bus. Two guys rush around behind the counter. Neither one is the one I want. I wait in line until I'm in front of the register and the blond cheerleader standing behind it.

"Is . . . Michael here?" I have to swallow to get the name out. It tastes wrong, sounds wrong. But I don't think she'll know who I mean by "Grinning Boy."

She turns to one of the guys. "Hey, Brad. Is Michael here?"

Brad nods, then bellows into the back room. "Mikey! Miguel! There's someone here to see ya!"

"He'll be right out," the girl says to me.

Obviously. I smile. "Thanks." My palms are sweating inside my gloves. I stand stupidly in place until the girl makes a show of looking around me. After apologizing, I move over for a crinkled woman who wants a refill.

My nerves are guitar-string tight. I nearly break when a man in his early twenties pushes through the swinging doors to the back. He looks around, then at Brad. "Who?"

"Over there." Brad points to me.

I frown as the man walks over to me. Michael? Only if—in another life—he's a member of Los Lobos. This guy is a good six feet tall, two feet thick, and has black hair that hangs down to his waist. "Can I help you?" he asks.

I start to say that he's the wrong Michael, then I see the bleach spot on the right shoulder strap of the apron. I bite my lip.

"A couple of times . . . there's this guy . . . I guess he was wearing your name tag," I stammer out.

Michael—Miguel—raises his eyebrows. By now, Brad and the cheerleader have joined him. "What does he look like?" the cheerleader asks.

"Brown hair, brown eyes, about this tall . . ." I raise my hand to a few inches above my head, then let it fall. There are three males behind the counter. One is Michael, the other two have brown hair, brown eyes, and are about this tall. The blond cheerleader doesn't count.

I try to smile, but it slips a bit. "Never mind," I say. "Maybe he doesn't work here anymore." Which is ridiculous. He was here the other night.

Michael shrugs and goes back into the kitchen. The girl turns to a new customer. Brad smiles and says, "Sorry we couldn't help you."

"Yeah, thanks." The bell over the door rings as I go back out into the cold.

Everyone has seen the spooky movies about ghosts who appear when they feel needed. Sad ghosts wandering the world, trying to make up for their sins by doing good works. In *Spiritual Kung Fu*, five ghosts tease, torment, and ultimately teach Jackie the five-fist style so he can defeat a vengeful murderer. So what was Grinning Boy? Some kind of ghost? But that isn't right. A ghost doesn't stare out the window at his own ghosts.

At least now I know why I wasn't able to call him Michael.

He isn't Michael.

What do I call him? Why do I care what I call him?

I'm still standing in front of the coffee shop when it starts to snow. Gray snow from a gray sky falling between gray buildings. The month before Thanksgiving is a gray month. All the leaves are gone, the snow can't decide if it's ice or rain, and the trees are like so many gnarled, black fingers reaching for the sky. If you turn around, all you can see is metal, cement, and death. On Thanksgiving, the Christmas lights will transform the black trees and snow-covered streets into fairyland avenues of color and sparkle. But November is gray.

Maybe it's because November drew Thanksgiving in the holiday lottery. October barely drew Halloween, with its costumes, candy corn, and caramel apples. December drew Christmas—a gold mine of twinkling lights, glass ornaments, foil wrapping paper, and blown credit cards. November got ripped off. What kind of holiday is it when you're supposed to celebrate genocide by stuffing yourself? I'd be gray, too, if I were November.

I end up taking the Green line. Which means I walk. A lot. My fingers can't feel the key when I push it into the lock on my apartment door. Inside, the gurgling radiator has—blissfully—overheated the place, and the phone is ringing.

It's my sister.

"Where have you been?" she asks when I pick up the phone. "I've been trying to reach you all weekend."

"Here."

"Oh." Kristie is the outgoing type. The type that makes friends easily and for life. Sitting alone all weekend in a no-bedroom apartment is beyond the scope of her imagination. "I guess I should have e-mailed you," she says, as if I haven't just caught her in the I-tried-to-call-you lie.

"Probably. Did the kids like trick-or-treating?" Kristie has the two-point-four. I mean this literally. She's about three-and-a-half months along with what promises to be another bouncing baby boy. Her third. Matt walks around with a paternal-stud grin on his face and feels her stomach a lot. At family shindigs, everyone rubs her stomach and makes those cooing noises people make after they join the post-baby crowd. It seems like an invasion of personal space to me, but Kristie's the kind of girl who thinks it's great when complete strangers walk up to her in the mall and rub her belly as if she were a lamp and had a genie inside rather than a half-formed human.

"I couldn't believe that Jenna Cummings," Kristie is saying. "She passed out caramel apples. Can you believe it? She obviously didn't think about what a pain it would be. Imagine trying to keep caramel apples away from the kids until I could get home and cut them open."

I collapse onto my futon couch. "The kids or the caramel apples?"

Kristie huffs. "The apples, of course."

"I don't get it. Why couldn't the kids eat the apples?"

"'Why . . . '?" She trails off in amazement. "Haven't you ever heard of razor blades in caramel apples?"

"Sure, but don't you know the woman who made them?"

"Of course. She's our neighbor. But even neighbors can be psychos."

"Oh, right. Gotcha." I lean over and begin untying the laces on my snow boots. My feet are nearly thawed by the time

Kristie finishes giving me the last jot and tittle of the nephews' Halloween experience.

"What about you?" she asks, after taking a breath. "Don't tell me you sat around watching old movies?"

"I should have," I say, without thinking. Now Kristie won't let it go. I give her the Nicci-vision version. I leave out Carol's accusations in the cubicle, and turn Bill's attempted seduction into a *Saturday Night Live* skit. Kristie thinks the whole thing is hilarious. Of course, Kristie would probably have screamed righteous murder outside the bathroom and spent the rest of the party basking in everyone's heartfelt sympathy. Did I do that? No, I had to clobber the guy between the legs and run away so he could have the opportunity to frame me.

I don't feel like doing the hindsight 20/20, so I change the subject. "How's Grandpa?"

"Fine. He misses you."

This is another one of those things people say on the phone—like lying about trying to call all weekend. Kristie would never say it if we were sitting across the table from each other, but it's okay to lie when I'm on the other side of the Rust Belt and connected by fiber optics. And it *is* a lie. Grandpa Bradford and I have this understanding. When we're apart, we're apart. When we're together, it's as if we've never been apart. I'm his favorite granddaughter. He's my favorite person in the world. But cards, phone calls, and missing each other aren't part of the relationship. No one else in the family understands, so they say things like "he misses you" to indicate that he's alive and grouchy.

"You know how it is with older people," Kristie is saying. "They like to have young people around."

"I guess," I say, but I'm rolling my eyes, remembering Grandpa's repeated escape attempts whenever my nephews are within hearing distance.

Kristie is in the kitchen. She's banging the cupboard doors and running water into the sink. "Are you going to Mom and Dad's for Thanksgiving?" she asks.

"Of course."

"Bring someone this year."

This is a surprise. I make a funny, choking noise that Kristie interprets as a question.

"Because Mom is worried about you. She thinks you're too alone up there. Not fitting in well. That sort of thing."

"So bringing home a complete stranger will give her an added confidence boost?"

"You know what I mean." In the background, I can hear Nathan or Philip screaming. Small boys under six all sound alike when they go for the maximum decibel. Kristie mutters something to the screamer, but nothing happens. "Look, I gotta go. Remember what I said about bringing someone. Think about it, okay?"

Think about what? "Sure. Fine. Thanks for calling."

I hang up the phone and let my head fall back onto the couch. No one likes to hear that their mom is standing in the wings, wringing her hands. It's bad enough that I'm worried about me, I don't need the added pressure of parental anxiety. But maybe that's what parents do. It doesn't mean I should go out, dust off the nearest Salvation Army bell ringer and take him home to Mother.

A small voice says I'd rather dust off a man in a green apron who has coffee grounds on his fingers, but I squish it. In a way, I'm glad I couldn't find him today. Okay, I know that sounds stupid. But I have this fear I never admit to anyone: I'm afraid that I can't make it on my own.

In high school, there's this unspoken assumption that if you don't have a boyfriend or a gaggle of giggling friends to hang out with, you're not important. The girls who have boyfriends and friends know that they're happy, healthy, productive members of society. The girls who sit alone in the cafeteria and stand with their arms crossed over their bodies in PE are not. They wish they were. They try to be. But the ranks of the happy, healthy, and productive are closed tight by seventh grade. If you think this is so much bullshit, just look at the teen movies. They're all about the unhappy, unhealthy, and unproductive bursting through the ranks and snaring the Most Popular Boy or Girl through sheer force of hidden personality—and maybe the help of a snazzy dresser. Pure fantasy. Because the MPB or MPG would never bother to step around a bug, much less date it.

I was a fringe person in high school. I didn't walk around with a Girl Scout troop of friends, but I had friends and I even had the occasional serious relationship. Very normal. College was the same. I didn't like parties, found most of the men to be immature morons, and spent the majority of my time in the library with a couple of equally studious friends. I tried having a relationship with one of these friends, but there didn't seem to be much point. We studied, we ate, we talked. The same things we did before we started going out except now we crashed in the same bed rather than on separate couches. I haven't seen him since graduation. Not even a phone call. And I haven't missed him once.

So, why am I afraid? Because I'm afraid of my happiness depending upon the number of friends I make or on a man. I want to be comfortable with me. With my own skin. I want to make it on my own. I want to be alone and feel happy anyway. And I thought I was doing okay.

Until now.

I stand up and put a full teakettle onto one of the burners of my two-burner stove. I'm warming up, so I take my coat off. Soon I'll have to adjust my thermostat—the window—to let some cold air in to counteract the steaming heat from the radiator.

After spooning some jasmine tea into the teapot, I lean back against the counter and wait for the kettle to boil. Being self-sufficient only works when you're sailing on glass. When a storm comes up, you can't take in the sails and hold the tiller at the same time. You need someone. Maybe that was what Grinning Boy was for me the other night. Someone to hold the tiller while I dragged in the sails and did a damage assessment. The trouble is, once someone holds the tiller, you get used to working with a partner. And when the next storm comes and you're going it alone, you feel even more helpless and lonely.

Lonely.

I might as well admit it.

Chapter 4

$\mathcal{T}$he week plods like an old racehorse put out to pasture. I go to Carol's cubicle to try and talk to her. She pushes past me as if I don't even exist. I can't help feeling angry. Not just at Carol. At me. Because even though I didn't do anything wrong, I'm starting to act and think as if Bill's drunken lechery *was* all my fault. I don't try to talk to her again.

On Thursday, the boss calls and asks me to bring the sailboat brochure down to his office for a meeting with the client. Yes, sailboats. Probably the reason for my sails and tiller analogy. The final mock-up of the brochure is back on my desk for editing. I shove everything into a folder, and start the long trek past the little cubicles identical to my cubicle, the bigger cubicles, and, finally, the offices. Within sight of the boss's corner office, I trip on a bulge in the carpet and go sailing into the arms of a man stepping out of the elevator. The folder keeps on going until it encounters a potted palm. The man and I stand in front of the elevator like two tango dancers waiting for the music to start.

"I'm sorry," I say, too embarrassed to look past the perfect knot in his silk tie.

"Not a problem." He doesn't make the usual silk-tie kind of jokes, like "It was my pleasure," blah, blah. We step back from each other, two bemused tango dancers who have just realized the band left an hour ago.

"There's a bulge in the carpet. I should have remembered," I say. Still embarrassed, I wrestle with the palm fronds, forcing the plant to give up its folder prize. Some of the papers fall out and drift to the floor. He picks them up and hands them to me.

Suddenly, he laughs. "When I was a kid, the second-to-last step on our stairs had lumpy carpet. On her first prom date, my sister's heel caught on one of the lumps and she landed on top of her date. Six years later, she tripped on the church carpeting and fell on the groom."

I look up past his tie. He's got dark hair and blue eyes. Light blue. The color of a flame as it licks wood.

"The same guy?" I ask.

"The same guy. Dad still hasn't fixed the lump on the stairs. I've tried to tell him that if *I* ever fell on my date, she'd end up with a broken rib. Maybe even in a wheelchair. But he's still hoping."

I slide the sailboat brochure back into the folder. He's probably right about breaking his hypothetical date's rib. He's got a good three inches on six feet and shoulders that would block out the sky if he were falling on you. I try to think of something clever to say, but nothing comes to mind. It's always been like this around gorgeous men. I can't tell if they're really talking to *me* or if they're just responding to the fact that I'm female and the only other person in the room.

"Oh," I say at last, giving up on finding something better to say.

One corner of his mouth twists up. "Are you on your way to the meeting about my brochure?"

"Ah," I say. Then, before he thinks I only speak in tones, I add, "So you're the owner of the sailboat rental?"

We start walking toward the boss's office. He's telling me about the business, and I should be listening. But I'm only the copy editor after all, not the sales department, and I've just discovered that he smells good.

My mom has one of those paperback *Guide for Girls* from the fifties or sixties. In it, some sage attempts fifties hipness by dropping such gems of wisdom as "don't be caught outside without makeup" and "learn a little something about sports and cars so you can be a good listener." Please. Somebody kill me now. But nowhere in that book is there any advice about how to act when one of the beautiful and productive people notices the bug that landed on them.

Literally.

Despite my semiconscious state, I manage to say intelligent things during the meeting. One part of my brain is going through the routine of assuring the customer that Graphics and Design—me, in other words—made this brochure much more attractive to potential customers than the brochure produced by the idiots he hired last time. The other part is obsessed with the way the customer smells and sounds.

Everyone has heard of animal magnetism. Some people might actually have experienced it. I'm not one of those people. Sure, I read the study about the male graduate students who went without deodorant for a week, and then handed their unwashed T-shirts to the female graduate students, thus proving that some women are more capable of handling smelly laundry. Actually, the women supposedly *liked* the smell of the T-shirt worn by the unwashed man with whom they were most genetically compatible. Yeah. Right. Some of those guys snuck a few squirts of Right Guard. I'm sure of it. What male wants to find out he's not genetically compatible with the local girls? Or worse, have the girls find out?

But none of this helps me understand why my heart and my semiconscious brain are holding hands and skipping along singing a merry little tune because the silk tie next to me remembered his aftershave.

His name is actually Robert Cole—Rob, if my boss isn't just doing a hearty salesman act. My part in this meeting is over, and I'm doodling on my notepad. If I'm not careful, I'll be drawing hearts and flowers. The graphics designer is trying to convince Rob-of-the-silk-tie that a sailboat made out of a crescent moon is a perfect logo for a company named Dream Sail. Rob leans back to think. The boss leans forward and tells me I can shove off.

Actually, he says something polite and bossly, like, "You can go if you want, Nicole. I'm sure you have a lot on your plate today." Translation: *Get back to work and stop wasting my money drawing doodles in your notebook.*

I say something equally polite, gather my papers, and stand up.

Then a strange thing happens. Rob stands up—the boss and everyone else in the room pops up in his wake—and walks me to the door. He steps outside with me, and shuts the door in the boss's gaping face.

Okay, here's a guy who's had his way in life way too much. But my heart and brain are too busy skipping to pay attention.

"Would you like to go out for a drink sometime?" he asks.

My heart and brain stumble. This is different than sitting and sniffing and doodling while your imagination takes an imaginary trip down the Yellow Brick Road. This is real-world serious. I look at the perfect knot in his tie. And say the first damn thing that comes into my head.

"Are you married?"

He actually takes a step back. "No-o." He draws the word out. "Why?"

I tap the knot in his tie with the corner of the folder. "The knot in your tie. You can't tie something that perfect looking in a mirror."

He reaches up to touch it, and then he laughs. A nice laugh. The deep kind that comes up from the stomach. "My tailor does all my ties. I just do my best not to mess the knots up when I take them on and off."

"What? No valet?"

"I could use someone like Jeeves." He waits, looking at me. I'm drowning in blue eyes. Dancing flames over wood. "Will you come?" he asks.

I'm wondering if I can dust him off and take him home to Mother. But I take another gem from the *Guide for Girls* and play hard to get.

"I don't drink." This isn't a moral thing, it's a caloric thing. I'd rather have three hundred calories of chocolate than three hundred calories of wine. Besides, my being difficult gives Robert "Rob" Cole a reason to shrug, laugh, and walk back into the office if his offer isn't for real. Let's face it. I'm feeling a little insecure after last week. If the guy wants to go out with me, I want him to *really* want to go out with *me*. Customers have asked me out before, usually because they ask out anything with breasts. That kind of situation is easy. Cut-and-dried. I say "no." This time, I want to say "yes." I'm just being careful.

"Fishing for dinner?" he asks, but it's a joke. And he hasn't moved toward the office door.

I relax and smile. "On my salary? You bet."

Back in my cubicle, I wish I could change my mind. I'm always like this about something as formal as a date. Rob must have guessed. He hasn't given me any time to back out. Unless I can come up with an excuse in the next four hours.

I take some personal time so I can catch an earlier bus home. I'm in what my mother would call "a tizzy." This sort of thing happens when you remember—three hours before he's supposed to pick you up—that the only thing in your closet other than jeans, boots, sequined T-shirts, and office clothes is that little black dress you wore to your friend's wedding. Three years ago.

I confess, I'm not a fan of playing dress-up. And shopping for clothes ranks up there with visiting the chiropractor—I don't do it unless I have to. But I don't think I can greet Rob wearing jeans, boots, and a T-shirt with blue glitter that spells out Byte Me. He might get the wrong idea. Plus, I think Rob has the impression that I'm older than my actual age of twenty-six. And I'd like to keep it that way. Not that he's so very old. Mid-thirties, maybe.

I'm pulling off my coat before the apartment door is all the way shut. If the dress doesn't fit, I'll be making a flying leap for the next bus heading toward a mall. Stripped down to my undies, I drag out the black dress and put it on.

It fits. In fact, and I'm not making this up, I've lost weight, because the dress fits better than it did when I wore it to Ginger's wedding. It must be the jogging.

I've always had a take it or leave it—usually leave it—attitude toward organized exercise. It's my high school PE teacher's fault. She rejoiced in giving us fitness tests: How long could we hang on a bar? How many sit-ups could we do in a minute? How many sprints, push-ups, that sort of thing? Guaranteed to make anyone avoid putting on a pair of Reeboks except when there's a pot of boiling oil hanging overhead. But last year, my mother found out she has diabetes. Just like her mother. There's nothing like the threat of a life-altering disease to get you up and pounding the pavement every morning.

Now I've just discovered a pleasant side effect.

After a shower, I'm prepared to tackle the fine art of playing dress-up. The little black dress requires a thong. I've read the articles in *Glamour* and *Cosmo* where women claim thongs are comfortable. Compared to what? Water torture? Having your fingernails pulled out? Wearing a thong is the same thing as deliberately giving yourself a wedgie. But it's either the wedgie or visible panty lines, and Lord knows, we wouldn't want anyone to know we wear underwear. Then there's the matching bra guaranteed to give me cleavage by shoving my boobs together. I suck in a breath, and my breasts heave like a Victorian damsel's. Okay, I've properly altered the landscape, now I can move on to stockings and other stuff.

Compared to bras and thongs, silk stockings are like ice cream for the body. I only have a few pairs—I don't like them enough to go without food—but on the rare occasion when I need ice cream on the body, I put them on. I remember watching an old World War II documentary where some women managed to get a few rationed silk stockings. At the time, I didn't understand the joy on their faces as they bent down to put the stockings on right there in the street. But once you've worn silk, nylon/spandex feels like sandpaper.

Okay, foundation and landscaping are in place, so I step into the black dress and pull it up. The thong promptly pulls up, too. Zip. Wiggle, wiggle. I reach up under the hem of the dress, pull the thong back down, rearrange the stocking that became twisted somehow, more wiggling . . . there. All ready. With fifteen minutes to spare.

Except I'm barefoot.

I dig around in my closet, hunting for the black linen heels that go with the dress. They're dusty, and a spider has been living in the right toe. I wipe them off, put them on, and promptly twist my ankle.

I've never mastered the jaw-dropping pelvic gymnastics of the high-heeled authority strut. The boss's assistant sometimes saunters by in her five-inch spikes. She makes it look easy. I make three inches look like a death sentence.

Five minutes to go. I spend the full five walking around the apartment trying not to break my nose. When Rob knocks on my door—my building isn't exactly high security—I can feel a bead of sweat slide between my pumped-up breasts. But the effort pays off. I barely wobble walking toward the door.

Rob is wearing a smile and a double-breasted silk suit that makes me feel like a chicken beside a peacock. Not that it's flashy, it just screams "made for the guy I'm hanging on." My dress moans something about hanging on a Nordstrom's sales rack with its twin sisters.

"You look great," he says, without a hint of mockery. Or flattery. And he hands me a single red rose.

I'm a sucker for roses. Especially fragrant ones. Most longstem roses sold in the U.S. come from Central America where they're grown in terraced fields in the highlands. They're large, perfectly shaped, and smell as much like nothing as you can get. Maybe I'm spoiled.

About five hours north of Manila, there's a mountain city called Baguio. With its pine trees and cool air, it quickly became a resort city for the very rich and the U.S. Air Force. At its heart is an open-air market, which probably only takes up a city block, but seemed like more when I was a child. Strawflower necklaces hang in spicy ropes above racks of strawberries and blueberries—fruit impossible to grow in the humid lowlands. Just past the souvenir stands are the flower sellers. Buckets and buckets of roses stretching toward the sky and spilling out onto the sidewalk. Pink roses of every shade, yellow roses, red roses, white roses. Some in tight bud form, some in full-blown glory, all lacing the air with the delicate scent of growing, flowering things. The scent that no designer fragrance has ever captured but wishes it could.

This rose smells like the roses in the Baguio market. I bury my nose in it, close my eyes, and breathe in memories. "Thank you," I say to Rob. And I mean it in more ways than he could possibly understand.

Rob looks around. "This is a nice place," he says in that neutral tone that means he's lying in order to be polite. I happen to like my eclectic mix of oriental blankets, wall hangings, carvings, and junk, but my nose is still buried in the rose, so I forgive him. I put the rose in a bud vase and set it on the window sill. When I turn around, he's looking at my videos and DVDs.

"Are these yours?" he asks.

Great. Here we go again. I guess I was too busy wiggling and tugging to remember this part.

"Yes," I say.

"I had no idea you liked violence," he says, grinning. "Promise you won't hurt me?" He's making a joke. I force a smile.

The only people who think Kung Fu movies are violent are people who haven't seen one. Or else they've seen the U.S. action movie equivalent. But the genuine Chinese or Hong Kong Kung Fu movie is pure opera, and based on folk stories and legends that were popular hundreds of years before Jesus was born. Good versus evil. Love versus hate. Justice versus injustice. Kung Fu movies explore the very depths of human emotion. With comedy and highly choreographed hand-to-hand combat thrown in, of course.

Rob runs his finger along the line of movies on my shelf. "You've got a lot of them," he says. "Don't you have any real movies?"

I can tell he doesn't mean to be judgmental. It's just a normative statement that popped out and judged me anyway. After all, Kung Fu movies aren't *real* movies. Not like the latest Julie and Rich fiasco.

Why is it that people feel they can pass judgment on the way you live your life if you choose not to live your life exactly like everybody else? I don't decorate in peach and blue with color-coordinated artwork. I don't decorate at all. If something catches my eye or makes me feel happy, I find a place for it. And every guy who's ever seen my movie collection has run a finger along the boxes on my shelf, shifted his feet, then looked me up and down.

I tell myself that likes and dislikes don't matter, and suppress the urge to wiggle and tug on my dress. I start to put my coat on. Rob reaches out to help me, and we thrash around in confusion for a minute until my hands appear at the end of the sleeves.

"Thanks," I say, and he rubs the back of his neck and laughs.

Rob drives an SUV made by a luxury car company. The maneuverability, height, and parking capability of a pickup truck, but with leather seats and a CD player. Under my long coat, I can feel the little black dress creep up my thighs as I take the giant leap for mankind from the sidewalk to the SUV. Scrunching into the leather seat, I wonder how I'm going to get the dress back to decent levels before someone takes my coat off.

We decide on Italian, and Rob calls ahead to make a reservation. But the restaurant isn't like any Italian place I've ever been to. It has valet parking. Inside, it's dark, and filled with the musky scent of garlic and olives, bread baking on a smokey fire. My stomach starts to growl, but I suck it in and force it to shut up. This time, when Rob reaches over to help me with my coat, I'm ready. No thrashing. He turns to give my coat to the maître d', and I make a quick swipe at the hem of my dress, twitching myself away from indecent exposure.

The maître d' is a tugboat of a man, and like a tug, he guides us through the maze of tables. At a two-seater near the back of the restaurant, he bows and smirks before pulling out my chair. I almost sit all the way down before remembering the procedure. The maître d' mutters something disgusted-sounding, then leans over to give Rob an oily smile and equally oily wishes for a pleasant dinner.

I look down. The tablecloth is white linen, and a row of gleaming forks stretches from the side of my plate to the edge of the table. I swallow and clutch my fingers together in my lap, desperately trying to remember *anything* I might have been taught about place settings with more than two forks. I'm clueless.

"Are you sure you don't want some wine?" Rob asks. The waiter beside us bobs toward me.

I start to shake my head, then remember I have a voice. "No, thank you. Just water."

The waiter rolls his eyes, but seems pacified when Rob orders something appropriate.

After he leaves, Rob and I sit and stare at the candle in the center of the table. Once or twice he looks like he might say something, then he swallows it. After a few more embarrassed moments, I give up pretending and laugh.

"Am I going to need all these forks?" I ask. "Because I haven't got a clue which one is which."

Rob bites his lip, then pretends to lean secretively across the table. "Neither do I. Just pick one up and look authoritative."

And suddenly, everything is okay, wedgie and all. By the time the waiter comes for our order, I'm comfortable enough to make up the no-wine caloric difference with pasta carbonara and bacon.

Once jogged out of his silence, Rob is witty and talkative. I pork down on the pasta, and do a lot of listening about sailboats and college football while the dim lights, creamy food, and, yes, even the row of forks turn the dinner into a fairy tale. When I excuse myself to use the restroom, I can't believe the woman in the mirror is me. Flushed, pouty-lipped, and girly-looking. It must be the little black dress and the push-together bra. They say clothes make the man. Maybe they can *remake* the woman. Cinderella all over again.

Rob pays the bill, waving aside my weak protest—weak, because I don't have enough room on my credit card to pay for the after-dinner coffee, much less for my dinner. Outside, it's raining. A spitting, damp, pathetic rain where you're too embarrassed to use an umbrella until you're too wet for it to do any good. The valet holds the door for me, and I refrain from asking him for a boost. He'd probably just put both hands on Cinderella's ass and give her a push into the carriage.

"Do you feel like doing something else? A movie or something?" Rob asks.

The dashboard clock says it's past eleven. Cinderella shouldn't push her luck. "I have to work tomorrow," I say. "I'm sorry."

"No problem."

We're quiet on the way back to my apartment. I'm feeling mellow and full of pasta, and I'm enjoying watching the puddles of light swish over us as we drive under the streetlights. Rob drives with precision. Hands at the six and nine, moving in and out of traffic as if he were an Indy driver and the rest of the cars were little orange cones.

I'm a lousy driver. I know a lot about cars, but I hate parallel parking. And in this city, that's the only thing there is. At least on my street. Then there's that head-on collision with a tree that I haven't lived down. I was eighteen, newly licensed, and swerved to miss a small, black dog. The cop who came to the scene frowned while the entire neighborhood swore up and down that they'd never seen a small, black dog and that I must have been drunk or speeding. I was neither. Two weeks later, I saw an old lady on her porch, petting her black poodle while she watched the tree-cutting crew saw up the broken limbs. That's when I sold my car and moved somewhere with reliable public transportation.

Rob pulls up in front of my building. Light from heaven shines down on the empty, almost-never-empty, parking spot next to the front door. I think I hear angels singing the "Hallelujah Chorus." He parallel parks a perfect eight inches from the curb. I'm still blinking when he opens the door and stands there to help me out.

"Are you blessed?" I ask, ignoring the urge to reach up under my coat and yank the black dress into place.

"Blessed?"

"By the parking gods?"

"Oh." He grins. "I've never had any trouble finding a parking spot. Is that what you mean?"

"Yeah."

We stand there in the rain that doesn't quite need an umbrella. I should probably ask him up for coffee, but that's too big a step for me to take. Especially in wobbly heels.

"Thank you," I say instead.

He nods. "Can I call you?"

"You could. If you had my number."

"What makes you think I don't have your number?" He winks, his grin devilish. And charming enough to have charmed my number out of the boss's Pamela Anderson look-alike.

"Because I haven't given it to you."

That stops him in his tracks. I don't like having my phone number tossed about like a piece of trash. Just a quirk reinforced by the psychotic pizza man who kept calling me up at two in the morning wondering why I'd ordered an anchovy pizza and not been there to pick it up. I hate anchovies. I really hate getting the phone company to give me a new number.

"I'm sorry. I should have asked."

I shrug. "No big deal. I would have given it to you tonight."

He nods, grins again, and touches his forehead in a salute before turning to leave. Just as I start to say, "Good night," he comes back and kisses me.

*I*n *Snake & Crane Arts of Shaolin*, Jackie places his trust in a friend only to be stabbed in the back. Literally. As he cradles his bleeding shoulder, the smile on his face is both sad and secretly amused as he realizes the stupidity of trusting a traitor merely because he said he was a friend.

The next ten days are more like riding a bullet train than a plodding horse. Thanksgiving is less than a week away, and all tasks and conversations at Graphics and Design have "imminent vacation" stamped on them. Everyone is pretending to work until they can legitimately stop working and go home to put the turkey in the oven.

Rob calls me every day. Sometimes just to say hello, sometimes to find out if I want to further our restaurant tour of the world. Last weekend, he invited me to his apartment for a meal cooked on his stove. "Apartment" is not the word I would use to describe Rob's place. What *I* live in is an apartment—and it would fit in his bathroom. His highly chromed bathroom. But everything in Rob's . . . apartment is chromed, angled, or glass. All that shiny, coated steel and see-through stuff—plus the eye-to-eye view of some of the city's tallest buildings—made me feel naked and cold despite Rob's spicy food. But I did my best to look comfortable. I don't think I was successful. Since then, we've spent all of our time together on neutral ground—the park, restaurants, even a football game. I can't shake the feeling that we're two tango dancers waiting for the music to start. Hesitant and sweaty until the first note gives us our cue.

We don't talk about movies.

I'm wrestling with a travel brochure that has a bad case of too many colorful sunsets when Melissa knocks on my cubicle wall. Melissa is the boss's assistant. The one who went to the Halloween party as a *Baywatch* lifeguard. Only the augmented boobs aren't part of a costume. They're real. Just like the not-so-subtle riding lessons she's taking from the boss behind office doors.

Meow.

I don't actually have proof that Melissa and the boss are getting it on. Except for the phone call I made to the boss's office about a month ago. Melissa answered all breathy and gasping. The boss panted something about my calling back in fifteen minutes. He thought I was on hold.

They could have been moving a file cabinet.

Yeah, right.

"Hi," Melissa says. "Can I talk to you?"

"Sure." I point to the other chair. "Have a seat."

Holding her two-inch pink nails out straight, she picks up the dictionary from the chair, then sits down and cradles Webster's hard work in her lap. She taps one nail on the cover, and I can imagine old Noah swooning as her breasts shiver in time with each *tchak*.

The tapping stops. "I guess you know I gave Rob your phone number," she says.

"Ye-ah." It comes out sounding confused, but I'm not sure what to say.

"Rob says you were angry."

Now I really don't know what to say. And I'm not sure if that gnawing in my stomach is jealousy because I'm picturing Rob leaning over Melissa's desk or hunger pains. It's almost noon. I'll go with the hunger pains.

"Not really angry," I say after a minute. "But isn't giving out my phone number kind of against company policy?" I'm trying to find a nice way to say, *"You gave out private employee information. I could have you fired."* Not that the boss would fire her. She knows it, too.

"Oh, sure." Melissa waves a pink-tipped hand. "But this was Rob."

And that makes it all okay.

"I've had a lot of trouble with obscene phone calls," I say, turning my usual sarcasm into a little white lie. "I'd be really grateful if you didn't let anyone else have my number."

"Wow! Heavy breathing or phone sex?"

I blink. Melissa looks as if she'd find an obscene phone call exciting. Like passing an accident on the highway.

"Mostly just threats," I say. "Something about frying anchovies on my face."

"Ooo. Kinky." She looks down at her watch. "I'd better go and try to look like I'm working. At least until lunch. I absolutely *love* working at a place where I get an hour for lunch, don't you?"

An hour? I try not to stare as she stands up and shimmies. I guess shimmies are worth a half an hour at Graphics and Design.

"I wouldn't know," I say. But she's already doing the high-heeled authority strut down the hall and doesn't hear me.

Last night, Rob took me on a carriage ride around the park. It was wonderful, but I didn't get back to my apartment until late.

So late that I slept in and didn't have time to pack a lunch this morning. I eye the mealy apples, egg sandwiches, and minicartons of sour milk in the Vend-a-Crap machine, and try to convince myself that this is better for me than potato chips and a Snickers bar. I'm forking money into the machine when Carol and Dolly (of the five Munchkins) from sales walk into the lunchroom. I smile at them. Dolly looks down, but Carol raises her eyebrows and glares until I feel the smile melt. Something clicks, and I look up to see that I've pressed the button for an egg sandwich when I was aiming for milk.

And the day's only half over.

I sit down at a table on the opposite side of the room from Carol, and unwrap the egg sandwich. As the rest of the non-CEO types trickle in, I lose sight of her. Ed and a new temp hire sit at my table. She's cute and blond and starry-eyed. He's in love.

"Egg sandwich today?" he asks.

I make a face. "Pushed the wrong button."

"Can you believe her nerve?" Carol says loudly. "Smiling at me like that?"

A tortured hush descends on the lunchroom, then someone giggles, and things return to normal.

The egg goes rotten in my mouth. Kevyn told me Carol wouldn't say anything. Kevyn was wrong. She's been keeping everything inside, letting it fester over the last two weeks. And now something's going to blow.

I set the sandwich down and begin to carefully wrap it up. Ed gives me a funny look.

"Is it bad?" he asks. "They'll give you a refund if—"

"Hey! Simone!" Carol calls from across the room.

The cute blonde beside Ed perks up and waves.

"Watch out for that bitch across from you," Carol continues. "I caught her with my husband. Next thing you know, she'll be after Ed over there."

The blonde is confused. She looks at me and shrugs. I try to smile, but it hurts. The entire lunchroom is deathly silent.

Metal chair legs screech across the tile floor.

Everyone watches Melissa stand up and shimmy her tight, little skirt into place. The spike heels click rhythmically as she walks over to the Coke machine. Nails held out at right angles, she feeds quarters into the slot. *Thuck, thuck, thuck, thuck.* A pause while everyone breathes. Then *thuddle-thwack*, the plastic bottle falls down from the slot and into the dispenser. Melissa bends over and takes the Diet Coke out of the machine. Tapping the sweating bottle against her cheek, she turns toward Carol's table.

"Your husband would screw anything that was female. It wouldn't even have to be a *human* female," she says to Carol.

And then she smiles.

The room hisses as forty-odd pairs of lungs pull in air.

Carol is out of her seat. She shakes off Dolly's restraining hand. "I'm sorry," she says to Melissa. "Aren't you the woman who trots after the boss like a bitch in heat?"

This time, the deflating balloon noise of forty-odd pairs of lungs losing air is mixed with titters.

Oh, shit. When I said things were going to blow, I didn't think it would be full-scale nuclear war. I push back from the table.

"At least I'm not flat-chested and perimenopausal," Melissa says as she leans back against the Coke machine and twists the cap off her Diet Coke.

"I'm flat-chested because there isn't any silicone under my skin." Carol steps around the table. She's only a few feet away from Melissa.

"Your husband doesn't seem to care *what's* under the skin, so long as it's big."

"Bitch!" Carol starts forward, but now I'm in between her and Melissa.

"Carol . . . don't," I say in a whisper. "This isn't you."

But Carol's eyes are wide and wild. Her anger is only pudding skin over a hot bowl of fear. She knows her life is falling apart.

I can see all this in the nanosecond before her hand flashes out and slaps me across the face. The crack of skin against skin echoes through the silent lunchroom. She leans in close to me.

"You worthless, lying whore," she whispers in my face.

I look into her angry, scared eyes until she drops her gaze, then I leave. I bump into Kevyn just outside the door.

"How's it going?" he asks.

Let the boss fire me. Today I'm taking an hour for lunch.

In *The Young Master*, Jackie is unfairly accused of losing the annual lion dance contest. He takes the blame and the punishment because he wants to protect his brother—the real culprit. Being loyal is noble when you have a choice. I'm not getting any choice.

After signing out of the building, I blindly walk the streets. So now Carol has convinced herself that she caught me in the very act of seducing Bill. Perfect. In another hour, every person in the entire office building—all the way down to the substitute security guard—will think that Nicci Bradford had her best friend's husband up against the wall outside the women's bathroom. And him so unwilling and all. I wish I could find Bill and spit on him. If I knew how to spit. I'm angry enough to try anyway.

When I was eight years old, one of my friends scribbled all over Kristie's favorite Nancy Drew mystery. Kristie swore I had done it. I swore I hadn't. My parents believed Kristie. I was too old to spank, but they let me know how disappointed they were that I had taken a purple marker to a book that didn't belong to me and then lied about it. After shedding hot tears at the unfairness of life, I gave up trying to explain and took the blame. But I couldn't sleep at night. Being called a liar hurt so much my chest ached and I developed a hacking cough. A week later, Kristie caught my friend in the act of turning Nancy Drew's face green on the cover of Kristie's second-favorite book. That was the first and last time my father ever apologized to me. The cough magically disappeared.

My chest hurts now, and I cover my mouth as TB-style hacking chokes me.

A hand thumps me on the back, nearly sending me into the gutter. "Try ta breathe," says a voice.

I look through watering eyes and see one of the homeless men from the other night in the coffee shop. The one who stayed awake. He smiles at me. His teeth are too big for his mouth.

"You're Ethan's friend," he says. "I thought I knew ya." He rubs his bare, blue hands together. "Nice guy, that Ethan."

"Ethan?" I try to ask, but my throat is hoarse.

He frowns. "Weren't ya the one at the coffee shop t'other night? 'Bout two, three weeks ago?"

Ethan.

The name fits.

"That was me," I say. "You were in the other booth."

He smiles the horsey smile again. "Yep. Me and Arthur." He leans forward and taps his temple. "He's looking for Camelot."

"Not the Holy Grail?"

"Nah. What good's a cup when ya want some place warm to sleep?" He laughs, then holds out his hand. "I'm Jimmy."

I shake it. "I'm Nicci."

He leans back into the building and sticks his hands into his armpits. "You were looking mighty down just a minute ago."

I start to deny it, then give up. Jimmy's eyes are too blue, too alert, too much like my grandpa's. "My best friend just accused me of jumping her husband. In front of the entire lunchroom."

Jimmy laughs. "Bet he's one of those hands-on types, huh?" he says when his eyes stop watering.

"A real knee-squeezer. First thing he did when he met me."

Jimmy doubles over again, laughing until he coughs. "Some guys . . . they're like bees. Have to try every flower before they die."

"Some women, too," I say, but Jimmy shakes his head.

"Nah. Women do it for power. Men do it because they're curious and haven't figured out that one woman's about the same as t'other on the outside. It's the inside that's different. And it takes a lifetime to figure out the inside of one woman."

"Maybe." I'm not sure I agree that women use sex for power, even if Melissa seems like a good example.

"Sure enough."

A gust of wind snaps the hem of my coat. Jimmy shrinks harder against the building. "Ethan lets us in at night," he says. "But during the day, he ain't got no say."

Time skips a beat.

"He's still working at the coffee shop?" I ask. Not that I ever really doubted it, I've just let myself start believing that he isn't there anymore.

"'Course he is. You haven't been to see him lately, huh?"

"No." Something grabs on to my chest and tries to tear my rib cage apart, but I dismiss it as leftover pain from the coughing.

Jimmy is rubbing his hands again.

I pull off my gloves. "Will these fit? I get to go back inside in a few minutes, so if these fit . . ." I don't want to offend him, don't want to look like some over-moneyed bitch tossing an alm at the beggar in order to soothe her conscience. I just want his hands to be warm.

He stares at the gloves.

They're fuzzy red-and-yellow plaid with fake shearling on the inside. And there's a small burn on the left one.

I swallow.

He reaches out and takes them, puts them on. They fit. "Thank you." Dignity oozes from him. "These are nice." Then he reaches out a hand and touches my face. "You're a lot like my daughter would be," he says, and I can feel the trembling in his fingers. "When I look into your eyes, I can see the soul of God."

Dropping his hand, he smiles his too-big smile and walks away.

As I watch Jimmy turn the corner, I realize that my problems with Carol are . . . well, not insignificant, just not the end of the world.

One repeating plot in Kung Fu movies is the appearance of the wise old man disguised as a beggar, a fool, or a drunk. It's up to the hero to discover what is hidden beneath the outward disguise. Although this motif appears in medieval European folktales, the modern Anglo-American has buried it deep inside a nursing home. If the grocery store magazines are any guide, we're all obsessed with youth and beauty. But the forgotten fact lost between the lipstick and alpha hydroxy ads is that age does make a difference. What seems important at twenty isn't important at seventy. And without the wisdom of age to temper the short-sightedness of youth—

But I'm starting to sound like a selection from the *Book of Proverbs*.

I bury my numb fists in my coat pockets and walk back to the office.

* * *

I said I had realized that Carol's accusations weren't the end of the world. That didn't mean I was prepared for the looks and the whispers. Kevyn drops by and shoves the dictionary onto the floor.

"I'm sorry," he says as he sits down. "I really did think—"

"I know." I carefully set my blue pencil into the hold-all on my desk and give up on the rest of the afternoon.

"It's just—" he begins. He stops and sags back into the chair.

"She's really unhappy," I say when he doesn't finish. "I'm as good a target as any."

Kevyn looks up. "Yeah. And Bill's being a prick." He doesn't elaborate, but he doesn't have to.

"Why doesn't she just leave?"

"Her mom's a hard-assed Catholic." He shakes his head. "A little of it has rubbed off, I think."

"Oh." Something else I didn't know about Carol. "What about the no-kids thing? Isn't that a problem?"

"Carol says it's her fault."

I watch Kevyn for a long two minutes. His face is rumpled, and thin with unhappiness. "What do you think?" I ask.

He smiles. "I think Bill's a low-budget, lying loser and that Carol should dump him before he takes away the only thing she has left."

"What's that?"

"Her dignity."

Chapter
6

*A*s I'm riding the bus home from work, I remember what
Kevyn said. In some ways, I feel as if *my* dignity has been
stolen from me. The substitute security guard actually looked
up after I signed out and he saw my name. Even the bus driver
seemed to give me an extra-long glance of disinterest, but that
might have been because I'm not wearing any gloves on a day
when the high was below freezing.

The apartment seems even more empty than usual. Maybe I
should get a bird or a gerbil or something. Something that will
make noise when I open the door so I can pretend it's happy to
see me. But I've never liked the idea of keeping a living thing inside a cage. All they ever do is pace back and forth, back and
forth, looking for a way out or a jungle or fresh meat. Back and
forth.

I've been across my apartment three or four times before I
realize what I'm doing.

So people are whispering. So what? I didn't do anything.
Isn't that what's important?

I need a Kung Fu movie marathon and a can of potato
chips. I feel like sulking. At least that's what Kristie calls it when

I go off, wrap myself in a blanket, and munch my way through an entire can of Pringles while watching Jackie Chan solve all the world's problems. I call it rejuvenation. What else can I do when I can't fix the problems myself?

I've just dragged my hidden stash of Pringles from behind the useless serving platter Kristie gave me last Christmas—"for parties"—when Rob knocks on the door.

I know it's Rob because he likes to tap out songs. He started with "Shave and a Haircut" and moved on to "Jingle Bells." This time it's "Deck the Halls." I guess Thanksgiving doesn't have any popular ditties. Another reason for November to feel cheated.

"Hi," he says when I open the door. He has a bag from a local movie rental in one hand and Chinese takeout in the other. "I heard you had a bad day and thought you might like some cheering up."

What's a girl to say?

I say, "Where'd you hear that?" But I already know.

"A little bird."

A big-breasted little bird, no doubt. I step over and let him in.

"I'm sorry about that bitch. What's her name?" he asks as he walks in.

"Carol. And she isn't a bitch."

He shrugs. "Whatever you say." He sets the food down on my table and hands me the bag from the movie rental. "I got you a Kung Fu movie," he says. "The guy at the store said it was really popular. Even won some awards."

I already know which movie he means. It was a foreign film darling in the U.S., a ridiculed joke throughout Asia where the average moviegoer couldn't understand why anyone would get so excited over a movie that so obviously patched together bits and pieces from other movies. But I give him a big smile. "Thank you."

We sit cross-legged on the couch. I do my best to help him understand the principles behind eating with chopsticks, but he gives up too soon and goes for a fork.

"How can you eat like that?" he asks.

"One of my friends grew up in Hong Kong. She taught me."

"No, I mean with your food so close to your face."

I shrug and watch the movie.

Despite what Rob said, I'm not exactly licking my plate. One of the principles of chopstick etiquette is holding your rice bowl near your mouth. I know this. And I know that nearly two billion people—maybe more—use the same chopstick etiquette every single day. But now I feel self-conscious.

Little things—a comment, a word, a gesture, a sound—little things are what make the world go round and what make the world grind to a halt. A seemingly harmless question from a dinner companion. A comment from across a crowded lunch-room. A hand catching another hand over a glass counter. Little things change how you feel about yourself whether you want them to or not.

I get up and put my bowl and chopsticks in the sink.

"These are weird special effects," Rob says as I sit back down beside him. "How do they do that? CGI?"

"Wires," I answer.

"Weird." He slips an arm around my shoulder and tucks me in close. Usually, this would be fine, but tonight I'm not feeling a lot of love for my fellow man. I don't pull away, however. I may not be feeling all warm and fuzzy, but that's no reason to be rude.

Fifteen minutes later, Rob is bored with the movie. Boredom is streaming from his pores. Like sweat. Like the bored sweat I felt the one and only time I went to a gym and rode the stationary bike. Pedaling madly and going nowhere. He starts to draw tiny circles on my shoulder. The circles get larger as the movie goes on. Halfway through the one decent fight, his fingers begin to stroke me from my elbow to the top of my head. Back and forth. Rhythmic finger pacing. I'm not surprised when his hand finally clasps the back of my neck and he leans over to kiss me.

Rob is a good kisser. He knows the lips are an erogenous zone and he takes full advantage of that. I like kissing him. But this time I can tell things are going to move into the naked, on-your-back stage, and I'm not sure I'm ready to go there. Sex changes things. Really changes things. Like the switch from public transaction to private communication, sex moves a relationship from casual to proprietary. Not in every case, of course, but it's definitely the case here.

Even as Rob's fingers begin to draw circles on my breast, I'm still trying to figure out why I feel so hopeless and sad about this shift in our relationship. But he's good with breasts, too, so I don't stop him. Then he's pushing my sweater off, unbuttoning my shirt, and tugging down my bra. His mouth is hot on my nipple. Somewhere in the background, the hero of the movie is talking. He's telling the heroine he's dying, but he will live on because she is his life.

My brain goes numb. I'm a lump of sweet dough and Rob is the master pastry chef, working over my body with the same skill and precision he uses to drive his SUV. I feel every tingle I'm supposed to feel, gasp every gasp, moan every moan . . . and my brain is still numb.

He sits up and pulls off his shirt, then his fingers are unbuttoning the fly on my jeans and he's taking everything off. He kisses me some more, and I'm spread naked along the futon when he stands up and turns it into a bed. He doesn't say anything, doesn't talk, just kneels down in between my legs and begins to rub his thumbs in circles on the inside of my thighs. It feels good. I'm already wet and now I'm wetter. My body knows it's in the hands of a master and it takes over from my brain, wipes out the ambiguousness of the whole thing. But not before my brain reminds me about diseases, unwanted pregnancies, and a—

"—condom," I say.

"Taken care of," Rob says. And he pushes inside me just as my orgasm hits.

I have another before he finishes. Then he rolls off and lies close, his arm across my stomach. The television screen is nothing but snow. Rob nuzzles my hair. I'm watching the black-and-white fuzz and wondering what happens next. Not what happens in the next minute or hour, but in the next few days, weeks, months. Rob's arm is across my stomach, but it's my chest that feels the weight pressing down, making it hard to breathe. I can tell he's asleep now, so I slide out from under his arm and wrap myself in the blanket from the foot of the bed before turning off the television.

The sudden darkness increases the volume of Rob's breathing and the whisper of the passing cars below. Outside my lone window, I can see snow swirling around the streetlight. As my eyes adjust, the apartment turns from black to gray—enough light to make tea. Wadding the blanket around my shoulders, I concentrate on the familiar ceremony and block out the noise of Rob's breathing. Tea. Nothing but tea. From a square, golden tin, I spoon a tiny amount of loose leaves into my clay teapot.

I take a bus, several different colors of T-lines, and walk four blocks to reach a shop scented with tins and jars and cans that last saw the light of day on an Asian loading dock just so I can buy this particular brand of tea. It's the only jasmine tea I've found that uses whole *Jasminum sambac* flowers to flavor the green tea. Although most people have heard of Arabian Tea Jasmine, *sambac* is also called Sampaguita, and is the national flower of the Philippines. As I pour the boiling water over the loose leaves and flower petals, I can smell the vine that crawled past my childhood window and up one side of our wood-and-hollow-block house. Hundreds of white flowers untwisting in the moonlight, covering the green leaves with snow, hovering like scented moths in the tropical night.

Tea leaves swirl up into the water, then settle onto the bottom. Unlike black tea or that horrific stuff that passes for iced tea in cafeterias, green tea should be a light caramel color. Too many tea leaves and the brew will be bitter, setting your stomach on fire. Ginger, the friend from Hong Kong who taught me that chopsticks weren't for sticking things, once quoted me some Chinese wisdom about bitter tea. I can't remember what she said exactly, but it runs along the lines of "tea made too strong can cause stomach pain, constipation, and yellow teeth, which would be a sad thing for the young person." I'm not sure if the last part only refers to the yellow teeth or to the whole list of ailments, but either way . . . let's just say I don't make strong tea.

Careful not to trip over the trailing ends of the blanket, I carry the teapot and porcelain drinking cup to the window sill. Rob snuffles and rolls over when I pull a chair up to the window. I hold my breath, and he goes back to sleep. Tucking the blanket around my toes, I sit with my feet on the sill, drink tea, and watch the snow fall past the streetlight.

Somewhere around the dregs, I feel tears drip from my chin.

"What are you doing for Thanksgiving?" Rob asks after swallowing a mouthful of croissant. "Because I'd love to have you meet my parents."

I pick at the flaky pastry and ignore the gnawing in my stomach. "I'm sorry," I say, while feeling guilty that I'm not. "I've already promised my family that I'd go out to see them."

"You're flying?" He polishes off a second roll.

"The bus."

"Long trip?"

"About a day. I asked for Wednesday off six months ago."

This is the part I dreaded. The part where everything turns into a discussion. The part after mating. The getting along part. The going along part. The "let's make plans" part.

"I could go with you," Rob says. "We could take the SUV, leave Tuesday night, stay in a motel with a real bed." He wags his eyebrows and flashes the come-hither grin.

I try to smile back. "Inviting yourself, are you?"

"Sure! Why not?" If he's noticed my lack of enthusiasm, he hides it perfectly.

I shake my head. "I'm sorry. I mean, it would be okay with my parents—great, actually—but I don't think I can foot a motel."

"Who's asking you to?" He leans across the table and kisses me. My toes curl into the floor. His kisses should come with a warning label. "Besides, I might want to stay in one of those places with the pay-to-bounce beds," he says after he's kissed me into oblivion.

"Okay," I force my stunned lips to say.

He sits back down and picks up another croissant. "What are you doing today?"

I take a bite of my roll and the gnawing disappears. Maybe I was just hungry. "What day is it?"

"The day after the best night of my life."

The gnawing starts up again, but I smile anyway. "Ha, ha. And here I thought you didn't make silk-tie jokes."

Rob looks confused, so I answer his question before he can ask me another one. "I'm not doing anything, I guess. I might drop by the library to return some books."

"Want to come sailing?"

I look out the window. The snow has turned to slush and the sun is out, but it still can't be much over forty degrees outside. "Isn't it kind of cold?"

"That's when you really feel alive."

He's right. I'm swaddled up in so many clothes I look like the Michelin Man, but I love the feel of the deck rising and falling, the sound of the wind snapping the canvas, and, best of all, the fishy-salt smell of the ocean. I lean against the side rail with my back to the wind and wait for my cheeks to stop stinging. Rob is standing at the wheel, his legs braced against the pitch and roll, his hair tossing wildly above the blue ear warmer. For the first time since I've met him, I can tell he is completely satisfied with life. Sailing is his Kung Fu movie. It buoys him up, makes him happy, defines him. He throws his head back and laughs.

And the heaviness in my chest disappears.

"Do you like it?" he calls over his shoulder.

"I love it!"

"You're not seasick?"

"No." I laugh, walking up to stand beside him. "Should I be?"

"No, thank God." His eyes aren't just dancing out here on the ocean, they're on fire with raw joy. I feel myself begin to respond to that joy. I can't help it.

"Do you want to have a go?" he asks, patting the wheel.

I start to shake my head, then change my mind. Keeping one hand on the wheel, he draws me in front of him, keeping control until I catch the rhythm. It's like riding a horse. My hands can actually *feel* the boat shivering and straining and snapping its jaws at the waves.

"Do you like it?" Rob asks again, his chin resting on my shoulder, his arms around my waist.

I like it so much I can't speak, so I nod. Rob pushes my hood aside and nibbles my ear with his cold lips and warm breath. "I've always wanted to make love on a boat," he whispers.

I laugh. "And you haven't?" Yeah. Right.

He starts to deny it, then says, "Maybe once or twice."

"Must be a little tricky, unless this thing has auto-pilot."

His hands warm my breasts through the sweater, jacket, and parka. "That's what the anchor is for."

With the boat protected by a spit of land and riding peacefully, Rob follows me down the steep ladder to the cabin. The bunk is impossibly narrow, and I'm trying to figure out the logistics of having sex on a two-by-four while I take off the parka. Behind me, I can hear Rob unzip his coat. Then his hands are on the hem of my sweater, pulling it up while it pops and crackles with static. Even in the sheltering cabin it's still chilly with only a jersey camisole for warmth. Rob's hands wrap around me from behind and cover my breasts with heat.

"You're not wearing a bra," he says against my neck, his mouth hot and wet on my skin.

There's no need to answer. I'm not sure why I didn't wear a bra. Maybe because I knew something like this would happen. Maybe because I wanted it to happen. Maybe because this time I wanted to have an active part—no matter how small—in deciding where and how it would happen. I don't know, and right now I'm not thinking too hard about it.

Rob's hands slide down over my stomach. He unfastens my jeans and pushes them down low onto my hips so he can smooth his hands over the skin that stretches across my hipbones. Then he pushes lower, down between my legs where I'm hot and wet, and he strokes his fingers back and forth until my pelvis jerks involuntarily against his hand. I nearly fall, only to be caught back against him by his arm around my waist. He keeps thrusting his fingers between my legs, and I come, groaning, nearly fully clothed and standing in the middle of a sail-boat's galley.

"I've always wanted to do that," he says, and he lets me go. I lean against the cabin wall and gasp for air, watching him kick off his shoes and push his jeans down over his thighs. Wearing only a T-shirt and boxers, he sits crosswise on the berth, his feet sticking out into the room.

"Do what?"

"Make a woman come in her clothes." He grins and folds his arms over his flat stomach.

"And you haven't?"

His grin widens. "Maybe once or twice."

I've never been around a man who is so supremely sexually confident. It makes me nervous, but at the same time it's liberating. I just turn myself over to him and enjoy the ride. It's never been like this before. I've never been like this before.

I'm not sure that's a good thing, but again, I'm not thinking too hard about it.

I bend down to untie my shoes and toe them off. Hooking my fingers through the loops on my jeans, I push them and my undies all the way down to the floor and step out of them. I pick up my wet undies and toss them at Rob. "Here you go."

He catches them reflexively and laughs, his laughter dying as I strip out of the camisole.

"I hope you have some condoms?" I ask, and he reaches into a side drawer and tosses me a brand-new box. I open it and toss a package back at him. "Put it on."

"Feeling dominant?" he asks, but he takes his T-shirt and boxers off, and rolls the condom on.

"I wondered how two people would fit into this bunk," I say, leaning over and running my fingernails up the bottom of his bare foot. "I think you've solved the problem." I climb in over him and straddle his thighs, so close my breasts are practically in his face. Bracing one hand against the wall, I reach down to guide his penis with the other, and run the latex-covered tip around the wet lips he just finished touching so thoroughly. His back arches.

And maybe Jimmy was right because it does feel like power.

But do I want this kind of power?

I ignore the question and sink down into his lap, taking him in as deep as I can. His hands make fists in the muscles of my buttocks. It hurts a little, but a good kind of hurt. I pull up, the walls of my vagina sucking hard, then sink down again. His mouth clamps down on my breast, sucking equally hard. I can feel myself tighten around him, and I can't stop. I'm moving up and down faster now, fighting against his hands, which are clenching around my hipbones, trying to make me go slower. But he can't stop it now. Can't slow it down. It's too much for both of us. I feel the groan he buries in my breasts and the sound sends me over the edge.

Too much. Too much.

We pull apart, gasping for air.

Beneath us, the boat rocks to the rhythm of the waves.

Chapter 7

D runken Master is a story about appearances and unexpected outcomes. An old man easily defends himself from three young toughs in a restaurant. What the toughs see is an aged, teetering, drunk. Easy victory. What the toughs get is a skilled, strong, Kung Fu master. And unexpected defeat. Perhaps the moral of the story is: *Appearances can be deceiving*. It's an old theme and has a variety of manifestations. *Don't judge a book by its cover. Still waters run deep*. That sort of thing. Which is great, unless you happen to be one of the toughs who is fighting the old drunk.

I'm lying on my futon and psychoanalyzing myself. Rob dropped me off after saying that he had a few things to take care of before Tuesday, but he'd call me, blah, blah, blah. The usual plans that get made when casual becomes proprietary.

What happened on the sailboat wasn't me.

Not quite true.

What happened on the sailboat was me doing something I might fantasize about. But it wasn't me. It wasn't *all* of me. It was the "close my eyes and think about an unlikely scenario while doing the one-handed hip-hop" fantasy me. Emphasis on *fantasy*. I think I left the real me crying in front of the snowy window.

But when Rob touches me, I get all shivery and happy and . . . it feels *good*, so I forget everything else.

I roll over and hug my pillow. This is dumb. I don't usually lie around psychoanalyzing myself. I know myself too well to be impressed with the drivel I can think up.

Only this time, the psychoanalysis is my stomach's fault. It's been gnawing away at something ever since I got up out of the sailboat berth to put my clothes back on. Ever since I got up this morning. And I listen to my stomach, because it doesn't have a brain for thinking up drivel. The problem with listening to my stomach is that it can't talk. It can't even do telepathy. So I have to pinpoint the cause of the gnawing in order to make it go away. Am I hungry? Should I take the next bus instead of this one? Is the guy following me a psycho? But I can't just lean down and say, "Hey, Stomach. What's your problem?"

So I'm lying here trying to figure things out, but nothing's happening. Maybe because the mechanism for figuring things out is too busy enjoying the shiver and wetness that happens when I remember what it felt like to put Rob inside me and rock up and down until we came. And how it's going to happen again Tuesday night.

Maybe I'm just turning into a nympho.

I throw the pillow across the room and go for a run.

After three miles, I jog up the stairs and see a dark shadow standing outside my door. I tense before I figure out that it's Kevyn. How he got my address is a mystery. A mystery with long, pink nails.

"I need to move to one of those buildings where people have to be buzzed in," I say. "I hear it keeps out the riff-raff."

He doesn't smile. "Carol's in the hospital," he says instead.

I lean against the wall for support, and breathe in and out for a bit. "What happened? Where . . . ?" I manage to croak.

"Can we go inside?" Kevyn asks.

"Oh. Sure." I open the door and hope the room doesn't smell like two people had sex in it last night. Kevyn walks in and sits down on the couch. He's had ten birthdays since yesterday. I gulp a glass of water and put the teakettle on the stove before sitting down across from him.

"She's in the hospital?" I prompt, when Kevyn keeps on staring at the threadbare patch of rug in front of him.

He blinks but doesn't look up. "Yes. Bill . . . the bastard." There's no heat in the word, only exhaustion. "Carol's parents are . . . were taking a cruise over Thanksgiving. So they had an early holiday dinner last night. Carol went to the bathroom, and caught Bill and Alena's friend together."

"Alena?"

"Carol's younger sister."

It's funny how people can work together, talk to each other every day, eat lunch, drink coffee, do things together five days a week—and yet not know even the tiniest private detail about each other's lives. Perhaps this is the new alienation. If you don't really know someone, how can you care when they're laid off and those children you never knew existed go hungry? Or when the woman from down the hall simply stops showing up at work?

"She's in college," Kevyn continues. "Alena, I mean. Her friend, too. Bill tried to make up some shit about the kid wanting to learn how to give a blow job. The kid ran out. Carol started screaming at him . . . then she just . . . collapsed." He sucks in a breath.

"You were there?"

"Her mother called me."

Maybe I'm the only one who doesn't know private details.

Kevyn seems to hear my thoughts. He shakes his head. "Carol and I grew up together. On the same street. We've been . . . friends . . . forever."

But never more than friends. Poor Kevyn. I remember the wobbly smile he gave me at the coffee shop. Carol has probably been trying to set him up with someone for years. And he goes on the dates just to make her happy.

Depressing.

"Can I go and see her at the hospital?" I ask, after he's been silent for a long time.

He looks up from the carpet. "I don't think so. Not yet."

Then he starts to cry.

The teakettle whistles.

I get up to turn it off before sitting back down beside Kevyn and handing him a box of tissues. He holds the box in his lap while the tears drip down onto the tissues.

"I'm so helpless," he says through lips twisted in an attempt to hold everything back. "So damn helpless. And I have no rights. None. I want to be there. *Be* there. But I don't have any right to be there."

"Bullshit," I say as I rub soothing circles on his back. He hiccups. "Bullshit. She needs you. She needs a friend who loves her. And she's going to need all the help she can get picking up the pieces."

He blows his nose and stares at the tissue box. The teakettle is still making little whistling noises as the steam escapes.

"I can't help her pick up the pieces for Bill," he says finally.

This surprises me. "She'd do that? She'd go back to Bill after he . . . after all this"—I fumble for the right word—"*humiliation?*"

"I don't know. I just don't think . . . don't think I can."

But he's already been doing it for years. People can stand anything once it becomes the normal thing.

I pat his shoulder and keep my mouth shut.

* * *

"I hear she finally got what was coming to her," Melissa says.

I've been lulled into a trance by the swish and thump of the copier, and her voice makes me jump.

"What?" I ask, blinking over at her. Today she's wearing black leather and blood red nails. A silk blouse clings to the curves of her chest before disappearing into the leather miniskirt.

She raises her eyebrows at my question, then moves to stand a little closer, bringing her exotic perfume with her.

"Carol. She walked in on Bill getting a—" Melissa waves a hand up and down in a vague gesture filled with meaning. "Serves her right for being stupid enough to stick with the cheating bastard. I mean, one time would be enough for me. Just a hint"—she skids one flattened hand across the other—"and *bam!* End of story. I can't believe Carol was such an idiot. She deserves it."

I stare at her. "I don't think she deserves it at all. No one does."

Melissa's eyebrows climb higher this time, disappearing beneath the smooth, blond bangs. "Wow!" She pats my shoulder. "You're amazing." Her voice is one hundred percent pure cane sugar. And what she's really saying is: *You're such a little fake, you liar.*

But I'm not. I admit, I might have felt a twinge of vindication. After all, no one likes being lied about and accused of husband theft in front of the entire lunchroom. But that doesn't mean I wanted *this* to happen to Carol. And speaking of what happened—

"How'd you find out about it?" I ask Melissa. I keep my voice casual and feign great interest in tapping a handful of papers into a neat stack.

Melissa shrugs, and silk drags across her pouting breasts.

Everything about her is pouting right now. If I looked down, I'd probably see pouting toes. She was hoping I'd have a more interesting reaction to her news.

"Oh, here and there. Kevyn came to tell me she wouldn't be at work for a while. He obviously needed sympathy, so I gave the poor guy a shoulder and some tissues. They've been friends for years, did you know that?"

Shit. I'm not sure which one makes me more disgusted. Melissa, for taking advantage of someone's agony for the sake of a little gossip, or Kevyn, for being a gullible twit.

I shrug. "Yeah, Carol said something about that once."

Melissa's pouting toes begin to tap. "What I really can't believe is how nasty she was to you. About Bill, I mean. You were her *friend!*"

Bending over the output, I gather all the copies together. "He was her husband," I say as I inch toward the hall that will take me down to my cubicle. "Relationships can be complicated."

The toe stops. "Speaking of relationships, how are things going with Rob?"

The question isn't a simple query. There's a dark, sweaty, tangled-sheets quality about it.

I stop inching. How could she . . . ? I blink.

Melissa looks like an angel. Beneath the fluorescent lights, her blond hair creates a hovering halo over a face that would make Max Factor swoon. Pink lips, shining eyes, hands practically clasped to a bosom heaving with love and goodwill toward her fellow humans . . . Maybe Kevyn isn't so gullible after all. Last Friday—before the sailboat—I might have said something. Now I'm hunting for hidden meanings.

"Fine," I say.

Her smile spreads to show the edges of perfect teeth. "Has he taken you sailing yet?" This time the meaning isn't very hidden.

Has he fucked you on his boat?

Teeth? Fangs.

I shrug again and smile. "Of course he's taken me sailing," I say, doing the happy ingenue routine. Her shining eyes narrow a bit. "After all," I continue, "he rents sailboats for a living, doesn't he?"

Melissa opens her mouth to say something, but I turn and walk down the hall toward my cubicle, ending the conversation. It's only after I drop the neat stack of copies onto my desk that I realize I'm shaking.

Sitting down, I rest my head in my hands.

I'm a fool. A complete and utter fool.

This is Rob's first account with Graphics and Design. He couldn't possibly have a history of taking copy editors out on the water for a romp below decks. But Melissa? Could he and Melissa . . . ? Is she one of the "once or twice" Rob helped come in her clothes? And if she isn't . . .

But that's worse. Because if she and Rob never . . . then that means Rob told her about . . . us. The sailboat.

Oh, God.

I drop my forehead down to the surface of the desk. I *thump* my forehead on the surface of the desk. Once. Twice.

Oh, God.

I'm trying to tell myself that Melissa only guessed. She finds obscene phone calls exciting, after all. A little imagination about a guy who owns a fleet of sailboats and even I would come up with sex on board.

What I'm trying to tell myself doesn't fly.

Deep down inside, down in that cobwebby part of myself where even I don't go all that often, is a tiny truth. I don't mean a *true* truth, but the kind of truth people use to justify their existence. My truth says I'm smart. I'm different than all the fools out there because I'm too smart to be fooled.

Melissa just turned a spotlight onto my cobweb-covered truth.

And I'm scared.

Why can't people be what they appear to be?

After work, I ignore what Kevyn said and go to the hospital to see Carol. The smiling volunteer gives me her room number, and I ride the elevator to the fifth floor, leaving my stomach down by the reception desk.

When the elevator doors swish open, I step out and see an older version of Carol buying a cup of coffee at a vending machine across the hall. I swallow. "Mrs.—" And I realize I don't know Carol's maiden name. "Uh . . . Are you Carol's mother?" I finally ask.

She looks up and gives me a puzzled look. "Yes."

"I'm one of Carol's . . . friends. Nicole Bradford." And I try not to feel like a viper when her face lights up and she takes my hand to lead me down to Carol's room.

Outside the door, I hesitate.

"How is she?" I ask.

Carol's mother sighs and smiles at the same time. "The doctor says she needs rest, but that she can go home tomorrow. There'll be therapy, of course, but . . ." She trails off. "I'm sure seeing you will cheer her up."

I'm not. But I let myself be led into the room.

"Carol?" her mother says in the hushed voice people use when they're standing around a hospital bed. "There's someone here to see you." She gives me a little push toward the bed.

Carol is sitting up and looking for all the world as if she's at the office. Magazines are piled across the blue blanket, and she has a copy of the latest *Vogue* open in her lap.

"Hi," I say. And cringe, waiting for the explosion.

"Nicci," Carol says. She closes the magazine and sets it on

the swinging table beside the bed. With nothing to do, her hands begin to twist. I can feel them around my neck.

"I'm sorry," I say. "I probably shouldn't have come." I start to turn, but Carol's voice stops me.

"Nicci. Don't go. Here." She shoves some of the magazines to the foot of the bed, clearing a space beside her. "Sit down."

And get within choking distance.

I sit down.

Carol is silent, staring at me.

My throat is full of sixty-grit sandpaper.

"I was wrong," Carol says. Her face is stiff, and each word is so quiet I can feel her mother straining to hear from the opposite side of the room. "On Halloween. And after." Then her shoulders slump and the dam breaks. "I'm so sorry. I just couldn't believe he would . . . and yet I think I knew the whole time. And the son of a *bitch*. *My* friend. My own goddamn *sister's* friend, for Chrissake. Oh, God, Nicci. I'm so sorry I didn't believe you."

I grab up her twisting hands and tuck them between mine. "It's okay, Carol. I understood . . . understand what was going on. He was your *husband*, after all. Someone you should be able to trust. If it had been the other way around, I probably wouldn't have believed me either."

I'm not just saying this to make her feel better. I'm saying this because I'm scared I'm a fool, too. About Rob. Damn Melissa and her perfect teeth.

As I wait for an outbound bus back to Watertown, I realize that I haven't gotten around to calling my mother about Rob coming with me for Thanksgiving.

Sitting on the bus as it crawls toward my stop, I realize I'm not going to call Mom until I have a talk with Rob.

From gullible twit to shrew. Forget Kung Fu comic relief, I'd be great fodder for a Shakespearean play. One of those tragi-comedies.

As if he knew I was thinking about him, Rob is waiting for me at the Watertown Square bus stop. "Hi," he says after I climb down from the marvel of public transport.

"Hi." I waste a moment wondering how long he's been waiting for me.

"You're late," he says.

I nod. I'm wasting another moment wondering how long he would have kept on waiting.

He shrugs. As if he's heard me. "I know I said I wasn't going to be able to see you until tomorrow . . . but I missed you." He grins.

I'm analyzing every word and facial twitch.

Foolishness has degrees of nastiness. If Rob came to my apartment, took me out to dinner, and had sex with me on Monday, then did the same thing with Josie on Tuesday, Cheryl on Wednesday, Jane on Thursday . . . If that were true, I would be angry, but I would feel less foolish than I do right now. Right now I'm wondering if he tells Melissa the details. Or worse, if I'm merely the latest in a long string of women who have been to the same restaurants, heard the same whispered words, and, ultimately, been fucked in the same places. Because right now, the nastiest fool I can be is another warm, breasted body in a long line of warm, breasted bodies. An object. Nothing more, nothing less. An object to be teased and tempted until he knows I'll let him give me an orgasm without taking off my clothes. Just like all the others.

I have to know.

But I don't know how to ask.

Rob's grin has turned worried. We're alone, standing on the

curb and facing each other. The wind catches my coat and tosses papers and pigeons into the sky.

"Do I know any of the once or twice women?" I say at last. It's a lousy question and it doesn't even begin to touch my fear.

"'Once or twice women'?" he asks.

"On the boat? Once or twice?" I say, not being very helpful. My face feels hot.

"Oh. Got it." He frowns a little. "Why?"

I shrug.

"No, you don't know any of them." He's looking me right in the eye. "Once was my high school girlfriend. Twice was when I was half drunk and I'd just bought my first boat. There have been a few others, but no one you know."

My face is in flames, but I don't look down. He's a little angry and is trying—maybe without knowing it—to intimidate me into feeling bad for asking. He can't know why I'm asking, so I cut him some slack.

"Why?" he asks again.

"Someone asked me if you'd taken me sailing yet."

He looks confused. "Yeah? So?"

"She didn't mean above decks."

Pieces begin to click together in his brain. "Melissa. Last Friday, I had another meeting. I said something about taking you out on the water. She twisted 'taking you' into a joke and I laughed." He frowns. "I just laughed, Nicci. I had no idea . . . I mean, I *hoped*. Shit, every guy *hopes*. But I didn't . . . I wasn't trying to . . . shit. Is that what you thought? That I was taking you sailing just to get laid? To cut a notch on the bunk?"

"No," I lie. Scuffing a shoe along the curb, I try hard not to feel as stupid and naive as I feel. "She was just pissed about something else," I say at last. "She knew it would bug me. And with everything else . . . I'm sorry. I've never liked it when a guy asks about former boyfriends . . . lovers . . . whatever."

"I don't give a shit about that," he says. "Ask all you want. I just don't like it when you think I'm trying to bullshit you."

"Are you?" It just pops out. Because he still could be . . . bullshitting me. I could still be a fool, believing all his excuses. Just like Carol and Bill.

He's staring at me. "What's going on?"

"Just . . ." I don't want to tell him about Carol. "Stuff."

Another bus pulls in. People jostle us with pointy, frustrated-commuter elbows.

"I get it," he says. "This is about the woman . . . what's her name. The woman whose husband grabbed you outside the bathroom." He laughs and puts his arms around me. "Come on, Nicci. Don't worry about that. You're not that stupid."

I go into his arms, but the deep, cobwebby part of me has a new truth.

It says I'm a fool.

Chapter 8

I wake up wet with Rob warm at my back and his fingers between my legs. He reaches across me to shut off the alarm on the clock radio the motel so kindly provided, and picks up a condom on the way back. Then he's inside me. It takes a long and lazy time for us to come this way, but the motel bed is soft and I don't want to get to my parents' place too early.

And I think I really am turning into a nympho.

My parents live just across the invisible but tangible border between the Rust Belt and the Bible Belt. A small Ohio town that only appears on the train and bus schedules. It's a solid place, filled with good old-fashioned family values like sexism and racism. A foreigner is someone from the next state over, and everyone knows everyone else's begats unto the fortieth generation. Conversations with men my grandpa's age usually begin with some variation of "Well, I know Richard (or Earl or Pete or Vernon). His great-great-grandfather came here in 1844. He married that Wilshire girl"—a number of heads nod at this stage—"and they had fourteen children. Eight of 'em boys." And so on. The first question the matriarchs ask at church potlucks is, "Have you met any nice, young men up in the city?"

I've never lived here by choice. It was home base when Mom and Dad came back to the U.S. for "furlough"—the missionary version—but it's never been home to me. It's merely the place where my parents live now and the place where my dad's parents have lived forever. Grandpa Bradford is the last living grandparent I have. But I'm sure Mom and Dad will stay here after he's gone. Small towns in the Bible Belt are places you fall into and never leave. Once your forty begats are recognized, you become a fixed part of the scenery and that's that.

"Nice," Rob says as we pass brown fields lined with brown trees. "It's so . . . wide open."

"An ocean of land," I say. "It's prettier when it's green." I'm not really defending the place, but I feel like it needs defending because it is beautiful in the spring.

"Sure." He sounds doubtful. We drive in silence for a bit, then he turns on the radio. Country music moans through the car. Someone got drunk and cheated again. I turn the radio off.

"How much farther?" he asks.

"A few miles." The brown fields look familiar now.

"So did you live here a lot?"

"No."

He laughs. "I didn't think so."

Funny. In college, it was life-and-death important that I look and act like someone who'd never been more than three states away from home. Now I feel a happy tingle because I don't meld well with the brown landscape. Psychologists say that crucial development happens between the ages of eighteen and twenty-five. Does that involve 180-degree flips in personality?

"Turn here," I say to Rob. He turns onto the gravel road that skirts the edge of town and slows down to a crawl.

"There's still time," he says.

"For what?"

"For one last screaming orgasm before we have to sleep in separate beds for three nights."

The nympho tingle is back.

"Too late," I tell him as a red mailbox comes into view. "We're here."

"Darn." He laughs and turns into the driveway.

Three dogs, a cat, and two nephews bound out to meet us. I get out of the SUV before I lose my nerve.

"Aunt Nicci! Aunt Nicci!" the nephews scream. I haven't even shut the door, but they're already wrapped around one leg. The cat is climbing the back of my coat and Rusty, the blindish, brownish bulldog, is happily pretending my other leg is an attractive, blind, brown, female bulldog.

"Rusty! Stop that!" I say to the dog. "Hey, guys," I say to the nephews after Rusty figures it out.

The boys stare up at me as I disentangle myself from the cat, set her on my shoulder, and give her a scratch under the chin.

"Rusty was humping your leg," Philip, the youngest, says.

"Yeah," I say, "but don't let your mom hear you say that."

"Yeah," Nathan says with the importance of a five-year-old. "Don't let Mom hear you say 'humping.'"

"Humping, humping, humping," Philip says loudly.

I sigh. "Great, Phil. Just get us all in trouble, why don't you?"

I've never understood why adults talk to kids as if they were stupid or something. Kristie, my mom, Dad, Matt . . . whenever they talk directly to Nathan or Philip, they add a high, squeaky tone to their voices. I almost expect them to bend over and say something like, *"Is oo little baby-kins hoongry? Does oo little baby-kins tummy-wummy need some food?"* Ugh. One time—I think I was about Nathan's age—my parents and I were visiting a supporting church and enduring the typical potluck when a sweet, grandma type leaned over me and asked those exact same questions while pinching the hell out of my cheek. I reached up, grabbed *her* cheek, pinched for all I was worth, and said—quite clearly and adultly—"No, baby-kins isn't hungry. She just wants to go home, thank you."

I got spanked.

"Did you bring us something fun?" Nathan asks after slugging Philip in the arm.

"Don't clobber your brother even when he deserves it," I tell him. "And I brought Rob."

"Rob? Is he a dog?"

"No. He's an alien. A filthy-rich alien who owns a lot of sailboats."

Philip and Nathan look at Rob. He's petting the two Lab mixes and fending off Rusty. And he's rolling his eyes because I called him an "alien." Or maybe it's because I described him as filthy rich.

Philip heaves a deep sigh. "He's not an ali'n. He's just a guy."

"But his eyes are kind of funny," Nathan adds. "Like Dad's when Mom says something dumb."

Ouch. If Matt wants to keep all his parts in working order, he'd better not be doing that where Kristie can see.

"You might be right about the alien part," I say, looking at Rob and frowning. "The green glow might just be radiation poisoning."

"Ha, ha," Rob says.

"Nicci!" Kristie runs out and grabs me in a hug. She smells like lily of the valley and has that "touch me, I'm pregnant" look that invites everyone to rub her belly. With her arm still around me, she turns to look at Rob. "Wow! Who's this? You didn't tell me you were bringing someone home."

Yeah. Right. Remembering what Nathan just said, I force

my eyes to stay straight and steady in their sockets while doing the introduction thing.

Nathan steps in between us. "In a couple of months, my mom is going to pop. *Bang! Pow!* And then Philip and I'll have a brother."

Rob blinks.

"Yuck," I say to Kristie. "Are you really going to explode? That could get messy."

Kristie slugs me in the arm.

"Mom," Nathan says, "Aunt Nicci says you shouldn't do that even when the other person deserves it."

"Yeah, Kristie," I say, grinning at her. "Aunt Nicci said so."

Kristie glances down to make sure Nathan isn't watching before mouthing a distinct "fuck you" in my direction.

Then Mom, Dad, and Matt are all there. I hug them, introduce them to Rob, and escape the crowd to find Grandpa. He's standing just inside the front door, waiting for me.

"Hi, Grandpa." I hug him and he awkwardly pats me on the back.

"Nicci."

We step back and look at each other. The clock on the china cupboard ticks once, twice, and chimes the quarter-hour.

"I got a box of westerns at Vernon Weeks' sale the day before yesterday," he says.

I nod. "Show me."

Grandpa Bradford is a tiny man with a neat mustache and a polished head. When I first met him—I was born overseas in a time when Bible Belt people simply didn't hop a 747 to be present at the birth of another grandchild, so I didn't meet him until I was five or six—I asked him why he didn't have any hair. He told me it had migrated to his ears, and bent over to show me. We've been best friends ever since. For seventy-nine of his eighty-nine years, Grandpa worked in and owned the family shoe store started by his father, who moved west of the Rust Belt as soon as he was able to get away from *his* father, who was the cobbler version of a tyrant. Grandpa is obsessed with shoes. He claims anything you want to know can be found out by looking at a person's shoes. Unfortunately for his ego, he's almost always right.

I think he knew his family's shoe-selling days were over the day my dad left for seminary. When Wal-Mart moved to town and set up shop, Grandpa sold the last of his stock, closed the store, and became obsessed with Max Brand, Zane Gray, Louis L'Amour, Luke Short, and the other purveyors of old west fantasy.

"It's over here." Grandpa sits down in his easy chair and slides a behemoth of a box filled with paperback westerns my way. I've read most of his wall-to-wall collection. Not just because it gives us something to talk about, but because in many ways, the dime-novel western is the U.S. version of a Kung Fu movie. Some bad guy kills a good guy who happens to be an important somebody to the hero, so the hero learns how to shoot a gun, and it all ends with a big showdown on Main. The hero gets revenge, the girl, and a spread with some cows.

"Five dollars for the whole box," he says, pride in his voice. "It works out to about five cents a book, I reckon." That's the penny-pinching Scot talking.

"Good deal," I say, sitting cross-legged beside the box. We're surrounded by stacks of books when everyone else finally comes into the house. The dogs snuffle us, the nephews whine for juice, the cat drops into my lap, and Mom throws up her hands.

"They're already at it. What did I tell you?" But she's laughing. She's still sizing up Rob, but I can see the possibilities swimming behind her eyes. Tonight, in bed, she'll say to Dad, *"He seems like a nice young man."* Dad will shake his head. *"Let's hope* so," he'll reply. *"You never know these days."* As if *these days* were any different from *those days* or any other days in Homo sapiens' history.

I introduce Rob to Grandpa, and cringe a little when he calls Grandpa "sir." Grandpa's eyes are stiff and still in his sockets, but I can feel him rolling them toward the plaster ceiling. Grandpa has working-class activism in his blood. Anyone who calls him "sir" must be trying to sell him something he doesn't want. I should have warned Rob, but it's such a part of my life that it got lost when I was trying to remember all the Parental Commandments he needed warning about—don't swear, don't mention drinking, lie about going to church, and never, under pain of death, say the word "sex." He took all the last-minute stone-tablet instructions with a shrug and a "sounds like my parents," so I quit before I reached the Grandpa Commandments.

Rob spies a model sailing ship my dad is building, and they drift off to talk about rigging, glue, and squares of canvas. Grandpa hands me a Luke Short book I haven't seen, and I'm reading the back cover when Kristie drops into the chair behind me.

"Where'd you find him?" she asks, leaning over my shoulder and whispering. "He's gorgeous! Nice, too."

"The elevator."

Grandpa gives a little snort. I look up at him, but he's looking at my shoes. I'm wearing the soft, scuffed Redwing boots I found for six dollars at the Salvation Army. At first, I think he's snorting at my boots, but then he looks over at Rob.

"Italian," he says. He pronounces it *Eye-tahl-i-uhn.* Then he goes back to sorting through the box of books.

Despite my heritage, I don't spend a lot of time looking at people's shoes. I grew up where most people didn't even *have* shoes, so shoes have never been a big part of my life, unless I was in the States and forced to wear them. Rob is wearing dark brown, loafer-looking things. And if Grandpa says they're Italian, they're Italian from lace to sole.

"So?" Kristie asks Grandpa, but Nathan or Philip chooses that moment to test his broadcast warning system, and she has to leave.

I blindly stack a number of Max Brand's finest together, not bothering to repeat her question. I already know the answer.

My parents actually live in Grandpa Bradford's house. When they retired, they started looking at houses nearby, wanting to be within shouting distance of the last surviving parent. But Grandpa argued that buying another house when he was living all by himself in a twelve-room, two-story monster was the dumbest idea he'd ever heard. He kept a couple of rooms and a bathroom for himself, and sold them the rest. That way, when Grandpa is—as he puts it—"feeling ornery," he can lock himself away with a bag of potato chips and some westerns. It runs in the family.

After a day filled with screaming great-grandchildren and four extra adult bodies in the house, Grandpa disappears into his sanctum. I envy him, but Mom has me making a Jell-O salad for tomorrow—obligatory Thanksgiving fare, along with green beans and little french-fried onions, candied yams, that sort of thing. Matt is boring Rob with the details of the hardware business—Matt manages one of those chain hardware stores. He and Kristie live about a hundred miles back into the Rust Belt, where hardware stores care about things like "Made in the USA" and what kind of steel went into that box of nails. I fill up the Jell-O mold and put it into the fridge to set.

"How about taking a look at the sunset?" I ask Rob. He's so eager to escape it's almost pathetic. Matt starts to follow us, still talking about hammers, but Philip grabs his leg and begs for a story.

"Remind me to thank that kid," Rob says as we slip out the door, three boisterous dogs at our heels.

"A bit much, huh?"

"No. Everyone's great," he says, forcefully eager.

I bend down for a stick and to remind Rusty that a leg is just a leg. "Matt's a little boring," I say as I throw the stick for the two Labs.

"Well, yeah, okay. Matt's a little . . ." he trails off.

"*Boring*," I finish for him.

He laughs. "I like everyone else. But I don't think your grandpa likes *me*."

I shrug. "He doesn't like a lot of people. You're in good company." But I don't tell him about the shoes.

That night, Mom gives me a number of sideways looks as she helps me make up the fold-away bed for Rob. She's curious, but not sure how I'll respond to her questions. It's funny how things change. Mom and Dad traveled half a planet away when they were missionaries. They met every conceivable type of human being, and successfully dealt with pickpockets, mosquitoes, and peeing in sugar cane fields. But now that they're back here in Dad's hometown, they've reverted to the forty begats and brown landscape. I'm only a few hundred miles away and in a city where the nationally accepted language is still English (with a few accompanying hand gestures), but Mom acts as if I were a different species of animal simply because I live in another state. As if Rob were more likely to be a serial killer than Johnny next door simply because he's not . . . from next door.

"Rob seems nice," Mom says. Meaning: *Let's talk about you and Rob.*

I lift the fold-away out of the couch and open it up. "He is."

"Did you meet him at work?" Meaning: *Do you have anything in common?*

"Sort of. He's a client of Graphics and Design. I edited his brochure."

"Oh." She lifts the mattress and hooks the fitted sheet over the corner. "What does he do?" Meaning: *Is he respectable? Will he be able to support you?*

"He owns a sailboat rental," I say as I snap out the flat sheet.

"How nice." *What in the world is a sailboat rental?* "Have you been dating long?" *Is it serious?*

I tuck in the bottom of the flat sheet before I answer. "Three, four weeks. Not long."

"Oh." She sounds surprised. When my mother was in college, a girl didn't bring a boy home to meet her parents until they were practically engaged.

"He seems nice," she says again when she can't think of anything else to say.

Sitting down on the bed, I smooth my hand over the blankets. "It's okay, Mom. We're not at the marriage and a mortgage stage. We're just having fun doing stuff together." As soon as the words are out in the open, I'm hoping she doesn't ask what kind of stuff we have fun doing together. Because the only example I can come up with is the motel bed this morning.

Oops.

Me and my big mouth.

"Well, that's good." She smiles, but her forehead is puckered in a little frown. "It's good for people to get to know each other first and not rush things." Meaning: *I wasn't trying to push you toward the altar, I just wanted to know how things stand.*

"Yeah." I get up and step around the foot of the bed in order to give her a hug. "It's really good to see you, Mom. I've missed you guys."

She smiles at me through wet eyes. "We've missed you, too. Especially Grandpa."

Later, after fighting for bed space with the cat and one of the Labs, I double my pillow and stare out the window at Orion's Belt and the rest of the stars. Nothing in this world is more ambiguous than home and family. "You can't go home again" directly contradicts the notion that "There's no place like home" or "Home is where the heart is." But here I am, surrounded by living proof—as exhibited by my parents—that not only *can* you go home again, but you can outwardly transform yourself *back* into the person you were before you left.

On the other hand, there's Kristie. Despite years of swinging herself up onto the prickly back of a water buffalo or hunting tadpoles in typhoon-swollen ditches, she's perfectly content to live in the Rust Belt, drive a minivan, and worry about the possibility of embedded razor blades in Halloween candy apples. Unlike Mom and Dad, she has rejected everything about the home where she and I grew up—some of the junk in my apartment comes from the time when Kristie sent "that Philippine crap" out to the curb with the garbage—and settled happily into the U.S. suburban lifestyle. Did her heart change because her home is with Matt?

Why is it that everywhere *I* go, nowhere feels right?

Orion's Belt has moved past the upper frame of my window. The Lab is snoring at the foot of the bed. I'm fighting tears when I hear a tap on the door.

It's Rob.

"Do you have my toothbrush?" he asks in a whisper.

"Maybe." I'm blindly digging through the junk on my dresser when he tugs me into his arms and kisses me. The kiss paralyzes me. With the fear that someone is going to walk down the hall and find him here, in my room, like this. On top of the almost tears, it's too much.

I push back. "Don't!" The whisper comes out in a hiss, more

violent than I meant it to be. I hand him his toothbrush. "I'm sorry, but—"

"I know. But I miss you." Whispered, the words sound sulky rather than sexy.

"Three nights." I hold up three fingers. "You can deal with it."

He grins. "On the way home, we're going to make up for lost time." With a last, quick kiss, he leaves, pulling the door shut behind him.

I frown. Right now, sex has all the appeal of a Jell-O salad.

Chapter
9

*T*hroughout most of the world, food is more than mere coal shoveled into the human steam engine. "Fast food" is a disgusting concept for cultures where cooking and eating are part of the joy of being alive. The daily meals are the place to relax and enjoy the company of others at the table. Festive banquets are the time to celebrate holidays, family, and friendship by means of a ten-course, four-meat, food-as-far-as-the-eye-can-see meal. Why have taste buds and appetite if food is only coal?

From what I can tell, Americans view food in three ways: coal, health, and time. The body runs on caloric energy, so that's a given. But obesity, heart disease, and diabetes are rampant, so it's not good enough to simply grab the densest caloric coal around. And time? Lord, who's got time? Especially for something as basic as mammalian gasoline. At any bookstore, the cooking shelves are lined with books that claim to help "cook healthy meals in fifteen minutes" or "make it fast and healthy at home." And for those people not cooking at home? Well, there's a reason why the Golden Arches can claim billions served. So far, the drive-through window is the closest thing to pay-at-the-pump.

Thanksgiving is the only banquet meal still clinging to the ancient, traditional foods. Christmas and the Fourth of July have sunk beneath the waves of time, leaving greasy stuffed geese, fried chicken, baked beans, and sweet corn floating on the water. But Thanksgiving is still about turkey, preserves, and family—despite the NFL.

I hear Mom tiptoe down the stairs at about four-thirty. The sun won't be up until the day has doubled its age, but around here, Thanksgiving dinner is a noon meal and the turkey has to go from raw to golden brown before then. I pull on a pair of sweats and follow her into the kitchen.

Without coffee, even the healthiest turkey inspires nausea. I avoid looking at the bare, white bird Mom is settling into the roasting pan, and set up the coffeemaker. Waiting for the stomach-saving caffeine, I start tearing bread for the stuffing. Mom and I work in silence, two people who have danced around each other in crowded kitchens a thousand times. When the stuffing is done and liberally stuffed into the bird, which is then stuffed into the oven, we sit down with our third cup of coffee.

"Thank you for helping," Mom says. "It went so much faster with two people."

I shrug. "Sure. I heard you go down."

"I was trying to not wake anybody up."

"You didn't. I was already awake." It's true. Maybe it was a result of sleeping in a bed I rarely sleep in. Or maybe it was Rob coming in for his toothbrush. Or maybe it has something to do with Italian loafers. I set my coffee mug down.

"Which do you think is more important?" I ask Mom. "Similar likes and dislikes or being able to talk?"

Mom purses her lips. "With what?"

"Men and women."

"Oh." She adds more cream to her coffee and thinks. "Both?"

"You're evading the question," I say, teasing her.

"Well, it depends," she says after a bit. "Why are you asking?"

I open my mouth to deny any specific reason, but Grandpa walks in and interrupts me.

"Shoes," he says. Then he picks a mug out of the drainer and heads for the coffee pot. This answer is so close to what I was thinking, I can feel my palms sweat. "It depends on shoes," he continues, sitting down at the table with us. My shoulders sag. Thank God. He's not talking about Italian loafers and Redwings, but shoes in general.

"Oh, Dad," Mom says, giving a mock sigh. "You're not going to start in about shoes again, are you?"

"Shoes can tell you all you need to know," Grandpa says. His eyes are sparkling. This is a shared joke between him and Mom. She pretends to not be convinced, and he pretends to convince her. He salutes me with the mug. "Take Nicci, here. If she's not barefoot, she's wearing whatever old thing she can find that don't pinch her toes. She probably doesn't even own a pair of lady's shoes."

"I do too," I say. "I can't wear boots to work."

"Ex-*act*-ly." He draws the word out and waves the mug for emphasis. "You can't tell a thing by what people are *forced* to wear. It's what they *choose* to wear that counts."

"I'd just as soon go barefoot," I mumble into my mug.

"See?"

I'm not sure what I'm supposed to see, but Grandpa thinks it's significant. I start to open my mouth to ask if he's suggesting I'm into being barefoot and pregnant when Kristie walks into the room and saves the day.

"Happy Thanksgiving," she says, her voice way too chipper for six in the morning.

"Happy Thanksgiving," says everyone else except me. I open my stupid mouth and say, "Happy kill an Indian and steal his land because God told you to Day."

Grandpa frowns.

Mom says, "Oh, Nicci."

Kristie slaps me across the top of the head.

I take my coffee mug and escape to the porch.

At ten minutes after noon, we've endured the long, traditional, premeal prayer and are passing our plates for turkey when the phone rings.

"That's probably Dick," my dad says, referring to Mom's younger brother who teaches Junior High in Oregon. Uncle Dick has a knack for calling when a person's mouth is full. Mom pushes her chair away from the table and goes into the kitchen to answer the phone.

Within seconds she's back, a puzzled look on her face. "It's for you, Nicci."

I'm in the process of ladling candied yams onto an overfilled plate. "For me? Who is it?"

"I don't know. A woman, but she didn't say who she was."

As I go to the phone, I'm picturing Carol, but that can't be right. She doesn't have this number.

"Hi, Nickle," says the woman on the other end of the crackling, overcrowded line. It's Ginger. The Ginger famous for teaching me chopstick etiquette.

Ginger and I were roommates during four long years of boarding school hell in Manila. I was there because it was the only option. Ginger was there because her parents had gone to the same boarding school when they were MKs and they wanted her to have the "same wonderful experience," even though Hong Kong boasted any number of perfectly good schools. Ginger was furious. I was filled with teenage angst. We spent countless nights lying in the same bed after lights out, holding whispered conferences about the unfairness of life. We endured psychotic dorm mothers, boyfriends, and punishments as if we were the same person. After graduation, we called a few times, sent a few goofy Hallmark cards, and eventually drifted apart. She invited me to her wedding three years ago, but didn't ask me to be a bridesmaid. There was a host of blond, beaming new friends for that.

"Hi, Ginantonic," I reply. "What's wrong?" There's no need to fall back on the "how've you been" platitudes with Ginger. Even though we haven't said a word in three years, I can hear *wrong* in her voice.

"I need to talk to you," she says, all choppy and broken sounding. "I had this number. I figured you'd be home. And I need to talk to you."

"Okay, talk."

"Not on the phone. I need to see you. Where are you? I'm in New Jersey."

"Ugh."

"Yeah, I know." She starts to laugh, but it sounds wrong, too.

"At least you won't have far to drive." I give her an address, a phone number, and we decide to meet after work on Monday.

I hang up the phone and stare at it.

Is there anything worse than having the past come out of the past and bite you on the ass? I'm supposed to be having a Thanksgiving dinner in my new life, but I'm giggling in bed with my old life thinking up vile tortures for the latest dorm mother.

Rob walks into the kitchen and gives me a hug. "Everything okay? Who was that?"

"An old friend."

"An old boyfriend?" He laughs and tugs on my ear.

"Worse. Much worse." I try to smile, but end up going back to the dinner table instead.

Saturday comes sooner than I expect, and Rob and I and some leftover pumpkin pie and turkey sandwiches are bundled into the SUV and sent off with all the fanfare of a wagon train headed west. Only we're heading east. Rob wants to stop at a motel for the night, but I'm thinking about Ginger and being fifteen again, not bouncing the bedsprings. We compromise, drive straight through, and I spend the night in his waterbed watching a disembodied warning light flash on and off as Rob pumps himself to an orgasm.

"Are you okay?" he asks afterward as he spoons up behind me. "You're so quiet."

"Uh-huh." I don't want to talk.

"You didn't seem to be into it. Did I do something wrong?"

I'm not sure what to say. It's not Rob's fault, but I feel like it is. I want him to understand me without my having to say a word. This isn't fair, and I know it. "No," I say. "Don't worry about it. I'm just tired."

"Get some sleep then," he says, pulling me closer, not realizing that I want to move farther away.

Within seconds, he's puffing little snores in my ear, and it's just me and the warning signal. On. Off. On. Off. I'm in desperate need of Pringles, a blanket, jasmine tea, and some quality time with Jackie Chan. Rob's arm is heavy on the side of my rib cage.

Ah, hell, Ginger. What's going on?

Like most Kung Fu movies, *To Kill with Intrigue* is about friendship. Jackie trusts a friend who betrays him—a traditional theme. As he sets out to avenge the murder of his family, he meets true friends along the way who teach him the real meaning of loyalty—again, a traditional theme. Lying here, looking out over the top of the city, I realize that these themes aren't just in Kung Fu movies. They're universal. Part of the human condition.

I've made a lot of friends since I came back to the States eight years ago, but no one like Ginger. Like two streams of lava, we bonded after being belched out of our old lives and pushed down the steep hill of adulthood. We were pulled apart after coming to the U.S., and we made new friends who were important to the time and place. But when life belches you out of another volcano . . . well, loyalty that springs up during the nastier episodes of life is the loyalty we return to again and again.

Ginger didn't say anything on the phone. But she called me. That's enough. I know it's bad.

I want to get out of this squishy, wet-sounding bed and walk around, sit in front of the window, *do* something. I feel suffocated with Rob behind and around me. But I don't know my way in the dark in this foreign apartment. The city winks at me. Cold. Indifferent.

On. Off. On. Off.

If Saturday came sooner than I expected, Monday comes two days too late. Sunday afternoon, I call Carol at the hospital, but she's gone home. I assume with her parents, but I don't have a number and I don't know the last name. I can't ask Kevyn because he isn't at work on Monday. Maybe he's decided to "be there" for Carol, even if he isn't sure he has the right. The fact that Bill wasn't at the hospital is a good sign in my book. I doubt a "hard-assed" Catholic like Carol's mom would appreciate marital infidelity in her own bathroom. Even from her son-in-law. Maybe everything has turned out for the best.

I sound like my mother.

At five minutes after five, I'm pacing the lobby, waiting for

Ginger. The security guard's eyes move back and forth with me. It's annoying. Worse than annoying. And to pass the time, I dream up a little fantasy as I'm pacing under his stern gaze. In it, I look like Melissa. I walk over to the reception counter, pull my shirt tight over heaving breasts, lick ruby-red Cover Girl lips, and whisper in his stunned ear, "Tonight I'm going to do lewd and lascivious things to the copy machines *before* making photocopies of my bare, naked breasts and stapling the results on every cubicle. But I can only do that if you take your eyes off me for one, teensy-weensy, little second."

He'd probably ask to see my building pass.

Someone knocks on the glass behind me. I turn around and Ginger has her open mouth pressed against the window. The security guard stands up. "Hey," he yells.

"Give it a rest," I say, and go out to hug my past.

Ginger holds me hard. "Your window tastes like shit," she says in my ear.

"Yeah, well. Three out of four people chose the windows across the street in a blind taste test, so I'm not surprised."

She laughs. I catch her face between my gloved hands and look at her. Her eyes are wild, but not like Carol's when she slapped me in front of the Coke machine. Ginger's eyes are wild with joy.

"Something's happened since you called me," I say, letting go of her face.

"Let's go somewhere." She looks up and down the street.

"There's a coffee shop—" I start to say, and at the same instant I remember . . . Ethan . . . but Ginger shakes her head.

"No. Somewhere outside."

"Up this way." We turn and walk in the opposite direction from the coffee shop and Ethan. Walk toward a park tucked away between buildings. I think it's private green space for the crumbling apartment building that survived the commercial boom, but the lock on the gate is broken. Fifteen minutes later, we're shivering in the near-dark, sitting among dead chrysanthemum and sedum stalks. Except for her chattering teeth, Ginger is quiet. Then she grabs my hand and squeezes it until the bones grind together.

"I'm so *happy,*" she says. She's practically bouncing on the wooden bench. I can't think of a single thing to say, so I wait. She drops my hand and stuffs her wool-covered fingers into her mouth, stemming a too-loud sound of joy.

Then she crushes her hands together in her lap. "I left John," she says.

"Whoa!" Thank you, Keanu Reeves, for supplying me with that witty word of surprise. And I am surprised. Three years ago, Ginger was all smiles and baby's breath as she stood in front of the conjugal altar. She had just finished a five-year teaching degree at one of those colleges where you sign a pledge to not smoke, drink, dance, or take the Lord's name in vain, and then swear on the Bible that you are one of the chosen few, amen. Back in our hot, little Philippine dorm room, we had argued for hours over which colleges to attend. The fact that Ginger hauled off and went to her parents' alma mater was a mystery along the line of the Shroud of Turin. She tried to explain it to me, but nothing added up.

John Larson, the guy who was all smiles and carnation boutonniere in front of the conjugal altar, worked for a local construction company building houses for all the coast people who wanted to get back to the center of the country and experience family values for themselves.

They met while working on a Habitat for Humanity house. Ginger even bought a tool belt.

So many smiles, so many angelic flowers, and way too many Christian rock solos from the blond bridesmaids. I stood around in my little black dress and wobbly heels, sipped nonalcoholic champagne, and wondered where my friend had gone.

Now she's bouncing on a bench.

Life isn't just funny, it's downright neurotic.

"Why?" I say at last, asking the inevitable question.

Ginger breaks off a dead sedum stalk and begins snapping it into little pieces. The joy bleeds out of her with each snap.

"No one has been able to understand," she says when the stalk is in bits around us. "Promise me you'll understand."

"I'll do my best."

"No. Promise me. Like you did when I told you about Aaron Wilcox."

Her freshman love—from a long way off. Aaron was one of the Most Popular Boys. Ginger was a bug with dreams.

I draw an *X* over my heart. "Cross my heart, hope to die, stick a needle in my eye. Plus whatever blood is necessary. You got enough last time." I hold up the index finger which still has a tiny, white scar.

"Ee-yew." Ginger makes a face. "I'd forgotten that last part."

"Hey, you're the one who wanted the oath. I'm not going to pass up an opportunity to make you feel guilty about trying to chop my finger off." I try to laugh, but memories stick in my throat.

We're silent for long minutes. The wind rattles the stubborn dry leaves still clutching a nearby tree. Less stubborn brothers and sisters flop helplessly along the brick walk. Just beyond the broken-locked gate, rush hour is reaching its peak. Headlights flash over the glass eyes of the buildings around us.

Ginger picks another dead flower. "We didn't talk," she says. She pauses long enough to break this stem into bits, but I know she's not finished, so I wait. She throws the last bits out into the dark. "We spoke to each other. About church, about work, about vacations, money, time, food. But we didn't *talk*. You know, the kind without words." Breaking off another stem, she pitches the whole thing. The wind catches it and tosses it back. She's looking at me, and I realize that this is the point where everyone else has said something. She's frightened I'll say something, too. Say something about expecting too much, working it out, the sanctity of matrimony, crap like that. But I spent four years with her, analyzing life while lying in a bunk bed. I know her. She's already thought those thoughts and done what she can. Saying something now would be an insult.

She must see this in my face because she sags into the bench and laughs. The laugh is broken and hiccupy. "God, I was *lonely*. Right after the wedding we moved to New Jersey. And we lived in this house—a great, big, brand-new house. In one of John's developments. And every house was gray, blue, or beige. And every woman living there was just like me. And just like me, they taught other people's children. Until they had children of their own. And then every day they put the babies into their sexually color-coordinated strollers and walked around all the neat little cul-de-sacs that were all like our neat little cul-de-sac." She pauses to suck in a breath of air. "And then John comes home one day and says, 'Wouldn't you like a baby?' as if he could trot down to Home Depot and pick me up a baby complete with a pink or blue stroller, and . . . *Jesus*, Nicci. Who have I been the last eight years? Who have I been since we left?"

I put my arms around her and we rock back and forth while she sobs. I've never seen Ginger cry. Not on the day when the dorm mother sewed floral ruffles onto the hems of all her shorts while we were at school. Not even when her long-term boyfriend decided it had been long enough. But a life is different.

Even now the tears are furious and short. Ginger pulls away and digs in her pocket for some tissue. I hand her mine.

"Do you understand?" she asks, fumbling with the plastic packet.

"All of it." I'm not just saying this. I do understand. She's had *the moment.*

The moment isn't a piece of time, it's a question. A realization. A trauma. The moment comes when you look up and see your life stretching out for seventy more years. And there, in front of you, like a giant roadblock, is the question: *Is this life good enough for the next seventy years?* But maybe that's the easy question. The next logical question—*Can I live like this?*—is the killer. Because it isn't a yes or no kind of question. It's a do or die kind of question.

I avoid moments.

"I'm going home," Ginger says after she's blown her nose.

I don't have to ask what she means. "Are your parents still there?"

She shakes her head. "The mission transferred them to Kuala Lumpur in ninety-seven, then pulled them back here last year."

"Oh. I didn't know that." We sit in silence until I ask for the details. "What are you going to do?"

"After the baby thing, I applied to teach English as a second language." She laughs. "At least that ed degree will be good for something."

"Aren't there a lot of people who want to do that? I mean, this is Hong Kong we're talking about."

Ginger laughs so hard, she has to stand up and stretch to get her breath. "How many of those people can speak Cantonese and enough Mandarin to get by?"

"I don't know," I say. "I'd think a lot."

She digs into another coat pocket and hands me a piece of thick paper. It's a "we're so delighted" letter.

"I already have the job," Ginger says, just as I work it out for myself. "I'm going home, Nicci. Eight years is long enough. I'm going home."

G inger and I walk back toward my office building. The security guard is still standing by the lip-stained window,
so we keep going. We're halfway to the coffee shop when an
empty taxi shows up. She hails it, and the world grinds to a halt
as she opens the door and leans on it, looking at me.

"Here." She hands me a piece of paper. "It's my number at
the hotel. I'll only be there until my plane leaves tomorrow
night."

"Quick flight." I stare at the paper.

"Cheap flight. One of those forty-eight hours in advance
deals."

"Oh." I look up from the paper to her face. Her eyes aren't
wild anymore. They're radiant. Like Christmas lights behind
glass. It's only the reflection from a streetlight, but I swear the
glow is coming from inside of her. "What about—" I wave the
hand with the paper. I'm asking, *What about all the loose ends here?*
Loose ends like John, the gray house on the cul-de-sac, parents,
legalities.

She laughs. "I told John to do what he likes. File for aban-
donment. Whatever. It's better this way. I'm the bad guy, he's

the poor, sympathetic victim who needs a shoulder to cry on. Preferably female." She laughs again. "John always wished I were blond. In twelve months, there'll be a blond Mrs. John Larson pushing a pink or blue baby carriage. Wait and see."

I'm not sure I want to wait and see. I'm feeling the surge of power as the 747 leaves the ground, the cabin air tasting of freedom as it roars to cruising altitude.

But I avoid moments.

"No," Ginger says. "Fuck waiting and seeing. Come visit me in Hong Kong."

She's always been able to read my mind.

From the other side of the car, the taxi driver gives a disgruntled bellow. Ginger slides in and shuts the door. I have my mouth open to say something—anything but goodbye—when she rolls down the window. "Fuck visiting. Come and *live* with me in Hong Kong."

The taxi's taillights are gone before I can close my mouth. The paper with her number written on it is a wad in my fist. If I want to avoid this moment, I'm going to have to put on a blindfold *and* close my eyes.

A hand grabs my arm, and I scream. But it's not the hand of fate. It belongs to a man-sized bundle of coats and rags, topped by a red scarf. When I scream, the bundle releases me immediately.

"Please, fair maiden," says a voice from behind the scarf. "I didn't mean to alarm you, but please. It's Galahad. He's suffered injury."

Always looking for Camelot.

"Art?" I ask. "Arthur?"

Jimmy's friend is shuffling back into the alley and doesn't answer me. I follow him, hoping Galahad is a garbage-fat cat or stray dog.

It's Jimmy.

He's lying on his back, blue eyes staring up at the sky without seeing it. I drop to my knees in the trash-littered alley. "Jimmy?" I shake his arm, but there's no response. Yanking off my glove, I press two fingers into his throat, hoping for a pulse. Nothing. "What happened?" I ask Art as I tug off the other glove and loosen Jimmy's clothing.

"One moment we were battling the black knight, then Galahad fell."

This doesn't help me much. I can't see any blood, but the light is bad and the alley floor is splashed with oil and leaking garbage. I pump Jimmy's chest once, twice, five times, then check for breathing and a pulse. I can't be sure. I puff air into his lungs, then pump again. He needs an ambulance, but there's no way Art could call for one.

Ethan.

"Arthur? I need help," I say, the words coming out funny as I work on Jimmy's chest.

"Help?"

"I need Ethan. Do you know who I mean? The man who lets you into the coffee shop."

"Merlin."

"Right. Merlin. Go and get Merlin. Tell him to call for an ambulance."

Art pushes to his feet. "Get Merlin."

"And an ambulance," I add as he reaches the mouth of the alley. "Run, Arthur."

I'm shaking and scared. I haven't done CPR since it was required in PE class. Maybe I'm doing it wrong. Maybe I'm hurting Jimmy, not helping him.

Oh, God.

Hurry. Please, hurry.

As if he's heard me, a gasping Ethan lands on his knees on the other side of Jimmy's body. He feels for a pulse, then takes over the heart manipulation without saying a word. Every five beats, I breathe into Jimmy's mouth. I know when Art comes back because I hear his quiet sobs. Somewhere in the distance, a siren is coming closer.

"Arthur, would you go flag down the ambulance," Ethan says. "Please." His voice is calm, but I know what he's really feeling. It's there in the way he moves as he tries to make Jimmy's heart beat.

Blue and red revolve around the alley walls. Blue and red. Celestial and earth. Heaven and hell. I'm dizzy from breathing for Jimmy. The paramedics push me aside. They work frantically for a little while, but soon their movements become less frenzied.

I'm standing between Art and Ethan. Art is yelling at Galahad to wake up. Ethan is silent. He's watching the paramedics, but he knows. We both know. Next to a paramedic's knee, Jimmy's hand is lying on the alley floor. He's wearing yellow-and-red plaid gloves with fake shearling lining. The left glove has a burn mark.

One of the paramedics sits back on his heels. "He's gone." The other is already packing up the equipment. Pushing up from a squat, the first paramedic comes over to us. "You found him?" he asks Ethan and me. Ethan shakes his head.

"The maid aided us," Art says.

The paramedic glances at him, dismisses him.

"Art found me," I say, and he looks at me. "I couldn't feel Jimmy's heartbeat so I started CPR while Art went for help."

He raises his eyebrows. Not because I did CPR, but because I'm on a first-name basis with human bundles of rags. "He was probably already dead," he says. "Looks like a heart attack."

"Oh." But I don't think the paramedic's right. I felt Jimmy. He was still there. Still there when Ethan came. Maybe he was waiting for Ethan. Waiting with all the dignity of the man who accepted my gloves. There's something cold and wet on my chin, and I realize I'm crying.

"You knew him?" the paramedic asks.

I nod. "But Ethan and Art were his friends."

"He had a lot of friends," Ethan says. His voice is rusty, creaking in the cold wind that whips around the buildings. "A lot of people . . ." He takes a breath and loses some of the rust. "A lot of people are going to miss him."

It's amazing how a human being can go from worthless trash to worth something—even a little something—just because someone says they care. The paramedic loses the indifferent attitude.

"Any family?" he asks.

Ethan starts to shake his head, but I remember Jimmy reaching out to touch my face. Something about his—

"He may have a daughter," I say.

"He does. He does," Art says. "She lives in the Valley of the Stones."

"Where?" the paramedic asks.

I look at Ethan and he shrugs. "Do you know where the Valley is, Art?" he asks.

Art thinks, then shakes his head.

I touch his shoulder. "What does it look like?"

"Big stones, little stones, most about this high." He holds a hand at knee level. "Some big. Like houses. Some tall with wings."

"The cemetery," Ethan and I say together.

The paramedic sighs. "Maybe something will come up when we run the fingerprints." He turns away to help his companion.

I can't watch them put Jimmy in a body bag, so I walk up the street a little ways. Somewhere, far away, a clock chimes the hour. My brain skitters away from black body bags, red taillights, and jumbo jets, and fastens on the little details of life.

The last bus left fifteen minutes ago. Walking alone, at night, from the closest subway stop to Watertown? Out of the question. I'll have to take a taxi. Do I have enough money to take a taxi? No.

I'm solving the knotty problem of where to find an ATM when Ethan touches my shoulder.

"You okay?" he asks.

"No. You?"

"No."

I look around. The ambulance is turning the corner, following the same path as Ginger's taxi. "Where's Art?"

"He went with the ambulance. The guys offered to drop him off at a shelter near the hospital."

"They can do that?"

He shrugs.

The movement causes me to really look at him for the first time tonight. He's not wearing a coat, just a flannel shirt, jeans, and the green apron. His arms are crossed over his body, and he's shivering, rocking from foot to foot as he tries to stay warm.

I pull off my scarf and wind it around his neck. He jerks back a little, then goes still when I look up into his face. There's a vertical frown line between his eyebrows, just over his nose.

"I'm okay—" he starts to say.

"Shut up." My gloves are oversized. I tug them off and hand them to him.

"I—"

"Just until the coffee shop."

He almost smiles, then puts on the gloves.

We walk back to the shop, our steps lining up. No one is leading, no one is following. We're just together. Thinking similar and different thoughts.

"You gave him those gloves?" Ethan asks as we reach the painted glass door. "The ones he was wearing?"

I nod, then realize he isn't looking at me. "Yes."

The bell rings as he pulls the door open. I follow him into the shop, and life's little details assault me. Inside, it's warm. Too warm. And it smells brown, like coffee beans.

"He talked about you," Ethan says. He's looking out the glass door, his head and shoulders silhouetted by the orange glow of the streetlight. "Asked me what I did to drive you off."

I blink. "What?"

He laughs a little. "I think he was joking."

I open my mouth to say something, but nothing comes out. He turns away from the door. Unwinding the scarf from his neck, he drapes it over my shoulders, then hands me back my gloves. I'm not sure what to do. I still need to find an ATM. But I'm just standing here.

Ethan goes behind the counter. The partition is still up and the door to the shop was unlocked. He didn't even stop to lock things up when he ran out to help Jimmy, but now he comes back with the key and locks the door. "Fuck my uncle," he says, and he flips the red and white sign by the door, closing the shop to the world. He doesn't say anything else, just walks past me and through the swinging doors to the back of the store.

I'm not sure what to do, so I follow him.

The back room is filled with boxes and a big sink. The brown smell is stronger here—coffee beans concentrated in one place, stacked together from floor to ceiling. Colombian, Arabica, Jamaican, French Roast, Espresso—my brain grabs helplessly at the words printed on the boxes, scrabbling at the ice, trying not to remember blue eyes looking at nothing. Through a tunnel of boxes, I see another door. This one opens onto stairs. A dim glow from above turns the stairs into a biblical woodcut. I almost expect angels to appear, walking up and down Jacob's Ladder. But it's just some dark steps. I climb up to the glow.

More boxes. Filters, parts, new grinders, new coffeemakers, old coffeemakers. Just past the boxes is a fold-away couch.

Ethan is sitting on the couch, elbows on his knees, head in his hands. I should feel embarrassed. Awkward. This is someone else's grief. Instead, I look around for something to do. Somewhere to put the thoughts in my head.

Across from the couch is a homemade kitchen. A hot plate, two pans, a skillet, and a sink. Above the sink, on wood shelves held up by metal brackets, are the necessities of life—Ramen noodles, crackers, soup, canned veggies, bread, and a bag of rice. It's the lowest shelf that grabs my attention. A teapot. I recognize it immediately. At least I recognize its origins. I fasten onto that familiarity and loosen the detail-oriented leash. The mess in my head leaps forward—a dog released into a wide-open field—and clutches the teapot.

The Yi-Xing region of China is famous for its pottery. Particularly for its teapots that glow with the distinctive purple and reddish hues of the clay found in the area. And unlike their British cousins, which hold a whopping forty-eight ounces on average, these teapots are delicate and personal, some holding as little as a half a cup. Unglazed, a Yi-Xing teapot must be cured—the best pot using only one type of tea throughout its life—the flavor and color of the tea soaking into the clay, harmonizing with it. A well-cared-for teapot is passed down from generation to generation, gaining in value with each brewing.

This particular pot holds about two cups. Its round, simple redness contrasts with the woven rattan and bamboo tray where it sits together with two matching drinking cups. Beside the cups is a gold tin of jasmine tea. The ride-three-colors-of-T-and-walk-four-blocks kind of tin.

I know what to do now. After putting a pan of water on the hot plate, I take off my coat. The water is almost boiling by the time I kick off my shoes and spoon some of the tea into the pot.

Ethan doesn't move until I set the tray onto the upturned milk crate that serves as a coffee table. Sitting beside him on the sagging couch, I pour tea into the two cups, then hand him one. The skin around his eyes and mouth is gray, but he smiles, takes the cup and leans back. I tuck my feet under me and sit sideways on the couch. Jasmine curls around us. Fragrant memory smoke.

"It was my grandmother's," Ethan says. "A present from a friend. Nothing but jasmine tea. Ever. A week before she died, she gave it to me. I think she knew."

"That she was going to die?"

"That my mother would leave."

I'm not sure what to say to the last bit—it's too ambiguous. But I can feel the moment when his grandmother handed him the teapot. Frail hands, young hands. The awe, the wonder, the sudden uneasiness as he begins to understand why this is happening, and the inevitable pain. I know that much. For now, it's enough.

We drink the tea in silence, lost in memories. Separate. Together. Stealing a piece of time from the world and making it ours here in this coffee-encrusted room.

At some point, I fall asleep. I wake up on the couch. I'm warmed by sunlight and a blanket Ethan must have laid over me. And there's an angry voice buzzing in my ears.

"What the hell do you think this is?" The voice isn't buzzing, it's hissing. Then I hear Ethan. Low, soothing, unapologetic. He's trying to explain something.

"I don't give a damn what happened. I took you in because you're Susan's kid. And goddamn if you don't end up just like your dad. My shop isn't a fucking whorehouse. Get her out of here. Then get yourself out of here."

I'm the problem. Ethan's getting his ass kicked because I'm here. I push the blanket aside and sit up. The hissing stops, and

I can feel eyes following me. Standing up, I put my shoes and my dignity on.

"Fuck my uncle."

Just a few words from last night, but it doesn't take a genius to figure out who Hissing Man is. "You must be Ethan's uncle," I say, stepping forward, holding out my hand, my best copy editor voice in place.

Hissing Man is short, red-faced, and his eyes and mouth are opening and closing rhythmically. He's got a good dance beat going before he thinks to shake my hand. "Uh . . . yes. I'm his uncle."

The fine art of bullshit. A moment to learn, a lifetime to master. Just like Kung Fu. And—in Jackie Chan movies, anyway—bullshit is all part of the game. Apply a little bullshit and trick the master into thinking you're hard at work, taking your punishment, filled with respect, injured, weak, exhausted, and even, as a last resort, trick him into thinking you have to take a piss if that will get you off the hook.

I won't have to go that far.

"You have a nice shop," I say. "I work at Graphics and Design. Up the street?" I add helpfully when the dance beat gets faster, an eyebrow tick now keeping time. It would be funnier if I wasn't so pissed off. This is the guy who wouldn't let Jimmy and Art into his shop on a day when the temp didn't hit freezing. He would probably step over their frozen bodies before he'd let them in. But that makes me think about Jimmy's blue eyes going cold. . . .

I shove the image down and give the uncle a winning smile. "Ethan and I were talking . . . you should come up to the office sometime. We could set you up with a new marketing design for the shop here. . . ." I trail off deliberately, leaving the idea hanging in the air. A nice line of bullshit.

He goes for it. A little, fat fish on a hook. The dance

rhythm gives way to stars and he's practically bobbing with conciliation. *Ethan, I had no idea. Marketing. Brilliant. I knew I was doing the right thing when I let you stay here.* Blah, blah, blah. Over the bobbing head, Ethan raises an eyebrow at me. I smile and bat my eyelashes a time or two.

The uncle is still bobbing when he backs down the stairs. Ethan shuts the door on the horrid little man and the sickening smell of doughnuts.

"I'm sorry," he says.

My coat is neatly laid across a chair. I'm pretty sure I didn't leave it that way. "Because I got you in trouble?" I ask as I put it on.

"No. Because my uncle assumed we were . . . Because my uncle is . . ." *a piece of shit.* We both hear the words even though he doesn't say them out loud.

I slip the coat's buttons through the loops. "Why do you keep working here?"

"Why do you keep working at Graphics and Design?"

"Good point." I laugh, but it isn't funny.

We stand looking at each other, one of us happily barefoot, the other in toe-pinching heels. I don't want to go. But I can't stay here.

"Thank you," I say when something has to be said.

He nods. "Thank you for the tea."

Pretty soon we're going to be bowing and curtsying.

"I have to go to work now," I say, gesturing toward the door. "Okay."

"I hope I didn't ruin your night." At his puzzled look, I stumble on down this railroad track of thought, wishing the train would run me over. "By taking up the couch. I hope you got some sleep."

He smiles. "I don't sleep on the couch."

"Oh. Okay then." I turn to leave, but his hand is on my arm.

"Nicci . . ." Then nothing. The clock on the wall ticks. Something is there, just beyond my reach. I can feel it. I want it. I think it's in the lower notes of his voice as he says my name again. In the darkness of his eyes. But it's so nebulous I don't even know what I'm looking for.

I swallow.

He lets go of my arm. "Take care."

"You too."

There's nothing more to say. I open the door and walk down the stairs, one careful step at a time.

Chapter
11

Since the majority of Kung Fu movies are about the human journey from childhood to adulthood, it isn't surprising that somewhere along the line, the hero is going to get his ass kicked by the villain. In *Fearless Hyena*, Jackie has an unexpected meeting with his grandfather's murderer. So angry he can't even speak, Jackie charges the man. Over and over, like a maniac. Of course, he gets his ass kicked. The difference between Jackie and me is that at the end of the movie, Jackie kicks some murderer ass. I'm just asleep at my desk.

Sort of asleep. I can smell my own unwashed body still encased in yesterday's clothes. The hem of my skirt is dirty from the alley floor—despite a pathetic attempt to wipe the yucky stuff away with damp paper towels—and both stockings are ready for the trash can.

I don't have any money for lunch. And I'm too embarrassed to walk around begging until a good Samaritan shows up and lends me seventy-five cents for a candy bar. Someone down the hall is popping popcorn in the lunchroom microwave, and my stomach growls. For the first time in twenty-four hours. I pick up my coffee mug and follow the scent. Maybe I can absorb a few popcorn calories through my skin while hunting down some more caffeine for my body.

The coffee pot is empty. Kevyn is sitting at his usual table, eating popcorn straight from the bag. I start another pot of coffee—it's free—and sit down across from him.

"Hi," I say, managing to sneak a few kernels in the process.

He doesn't look up. "I'm sorry about the other day," he says. "At your apartment. All that blubbering."

"Forget it." The popcorn is salty and loaded with toxic, fake butter. It's marvelous. I sneak some more.

"I wanted to call Carol—" I begin, when it looks like Kevyn isn't going to say anything more.

"She's home," he says.

"Home?" Dear God. "Not with . . ." *Bill?*

"With her parents." Kevyn shoves the popcorn bag my way. His shoulders slump.

"Can you give me her phone—"

"I love her," he says, interrupting me. It's a miserable-sounding confession. As if he thinks I might beat him with some sort of chastity whip because he's thinking adulterous thoughts.

"Yeah, I sorta figured that," I say. The popcorn is all gone, and I'm drinking coffee heavily laced with sugar and creamer before he responds.

"You knew?" Like he didn't all but tell me the other day.

I nod.

"I'm pathetically obvious, aren't I?"

I shake my head. I'm too tired to offer consolation on the unhappiness of life. And after last night . . . Jimmy . . . it just seems like life should be there for the grabbing rather than the sobbing.

Maybe.

Kevyn writes Carol's number on a napkin while I make another oversugared cup of coffee. Back at my cubicle, I try to call her, but the phone is busy. I put the phone down and pick up one of the bendy toys that litter my desk. This one is a tiger. I twist it into a growling, crouched shape, tail lashing . . .

. . . and I think about Hong Kong. And I think about Ginger packing a suitcase in a motel room, getting ready to grab life with both hands. After a minute of rummaging through my coat pockets, I find the paper ball with Ginger's phone number written on it and smooth out the wrinkles. I want to call her, but I'm afraid. And too damn tired to overcome my fear of . . . something. Maybe that she'll convince me I'm not grabbing life, just sobbing.

I turn away from the phone and go back to work.

There's a new guy in development. If the crappy copy he sent me this morning is an accurate indicator of education, I don't think he made it past kindergarten. After struggling with his grammar for an hour, I'm so tired I turn away from the computer and put my head on the desk. Just fifteen minutes.

Someone knocks on the cubicle wall. Maybe if I stay very, very still, they'll think I'm dead and go bother somebody else.

Fat chance.

"Nicci?"

I lift my cheek and get my chin onto the desktop. It's Melissa. "Hi," I say, but the word comes out funny because I can't move my chin.

"Are you all right?" She comes in and bends down, peering at me. I don't have the energy to remember why I'm upset with her.

"Uh-huh. Just tired."

"Did you sleep in your clothes?" she asks, picking at the suit jacket I tossed over the chair this morning.

That's what I'm trying to do, I almost say, but it would require too much effort. "Yuh-huh," I mumble instead.

Melissa pushes my jacket to one side and sits down. There's something different about her, but everything's kind of blurry and I can't tell what it is. Oh, yeah. I reach for my glasses and put them on. Before I can get a good look at her, she's talking again.

"I'm sorry," she says. "About the other day. At the copier. I don't know what got into me, but I shouldn't have said that stuff . . . about sailing and all."

Everyone must be in an apologetic mood today.

When I figure out what she's talking about, it seems ridiculous that she should even have to apologize. In one week, everything has gone from complicated to worse. Last week, my biggest fear was being a fool. Now I don't care if Rob is making a fool of me. I don't care if I'm the biggest fool in the world. Last night I breathed into a dying man's mouth. And being the latest in a string of girl toys is hardly something to get excited about compared to that. But I'm not sure how to explain this to Melissa.

"Don't worry about it," I say, getting my chin off the desk at last.

She has her hands folded in her lap—clasped together like a prayer. A sort of white-knuckled kind of prayer. Her fingers are bloodless with the pressure. Through blear-clearing glasses, I can see the ridges of glue on each short, unpainted nail. My first thought is something like, *Oh, that's how she grows the perfect nails.* My second thought isn't really a thought, it's a realization. Melissa isn't wearing any makeup, there's a nasty run in one of her cream-silk Victoria's Secret stockings, and she's a lot smaller than usual.

"I am sorry," she says again. Then she stands up.

I'm tired. So tired I ache in places that don't even exist. But I remember Melissa walking to the Coke machine, putting herself between me and Carol's hurt. She may have done it for the attention, but I still owe her. "What about you?" I ask. "Are you all right? You seem a little strung out."

This is what she's been waiting for. She sits down, relief in every line of her body. "I don't have anyone to talk to," she says. She's leaning forward in the chair, a hungry dog's eagerness in her eyes. "I'm pregnant."

I must have a neon sign over me that blinks LAY YOUR BURDENS HERE with a big arrow pointing down to my head.

"Congratulations," I say.

Melissa shakes her head. "No. I didn't mean to."

And what do I say to this? I close my open mouth. "Uh . . . wow." Shakespeare isn't getting any competition from *me*. "What are you going to do?"

"That's just it. I don't know *what* to do!"

Exhausted brains still work. I know, because this is the precise moment when mine kicks in and reminds me that Melissa has been . . . well, as Philip would put it, "humping" the boss.

"It's *his*, isn't it," I say, not bothering to make it much of a question.

She nods.

"He's married, too."

She nods again, her hands twisting even harder.

"Ah, fuck," I say, because that's the only thing there is to say.

"We've been so careful," she says. "I just don't know how . . ."

Careful? That's what she calls making it on the boss's desk?

I'm very judgmental when I'm tired. Fortunately, it's also hard to think and talk at the same time.

"Are you going to tell him?" I ask. It's a better thing to say than, "*Yeah, guess it's hard to find a condom in the paperclip drawer.*"

Her eyes cloud over. And I'm glad I didn't let the bitchy judge out to play. The complete . . . *anguish* on her face hits me and drags me into her pain, forcing me to understand why telling the guy is such a big deal. I mean, who are we kidding? The boss isn't going to leave his wife. And he sure as hell isn't going to admit to the affair. Assuming she wants to keep the baby, Melissa could drag him through a paternity suit and get child support, but that would be unpleasant all around if the boss wants to get nasty and take a whirl at the wheel of the blame game. And if she doesn't want to keep the baby? Even more questions. Should she tell him? Give him a reason to fire her? Because he's not going to want an assistant with that kind of power. Sex is bad enough. There are laws against sexual harassment, after all. But a baby? An aborted baby? Ouch. I can name at least two clients who would yank their accounts if they found out.

Lots of questions here.

"Do you want the baby?" I ask. That seems like the most important question right now.

"I don't know," she whispers, looking down at her lap. "With my salary"—a grimace—"if I say something . . . with *no* salary. But it seems so wrong to just . . . it's not the baby's fault."

"No," I say. "But it's not your fault that the father is willing to play but not pay."

She nods, or at least I think she does. She's still looking down at her lap. I can see tears dripping onto her skirt. Reaching across my desk, I hand her my box of tissues. She blows her nose. We sit in silence.

"Will you go with me?" she asks after a moment has turned into five. "If I decide to . . . you know?"

It's an easy answer. "Yes."

She smiles at me. One of those angels around the baby Jesus kind of smiles. Happy, sad, relieved, and filled with future pain—all trapped in the upward turn of two lips. And I realize she's not who I thought she was, not who she pretended to be.

I try to stay out of the judge's bench. I figure it's not my place—except when I'm too tired to know what's good for me. But I took one look at Melissa's augmented boobs, blond hair, and stiletto heels, and passed an instant sentence. No jury, no defense, no attempt to dig for the truth, no picking up fairness on the way to first impressions. Her snobby, tough girl, so much better than the rest of you attitude cemented the judgment. But now she turns out to be just another frightened and lonely human being. So alone she has to take her problems to a near stranger—me. I always assumed her relationship with the boss was mutual user-friendliness. Now I want to go punch him in the nose for taking advantage of a lonely kid all alone in a lonely city.

Okay, Melissa's only a year or two younger than me, but I'm feeling all protective now. As if the boss had been banging my little sister. It has something to do with those bare nails and the rinds of adhesive. It's as if she's been stripped naked in front of the entire building. And it pisses me off.

Pulling a Post-it note from my cube, I write down my address and phone number. "Here," I say, handing it to her. "Call me anytime, drop by anytime. I'll be there, okay? Whatever you decide, I'll be there." I know she can look me up, but it seems right to give the numbers to her.

She takes the note. "Thanks, Nicci. I'm sorry . . . about this. It's just . . . there isn't anybody—"

"It's okay," I say, before she can drag the humiliating loneliness out of her chest. "Just call me or come on down here whenever you need to talk, okay?"

Her smile is stronger this time, and looks a lot more like the Mona Lisa's than a long-suffering seraph's.

Drinking too much coffee in the afternoon makes me jittery. Not the shaking hands, hyperactive kind of jittery. Worse. My stomach ties itself into a granny-knot of dissatisfaction. Nothing is right. My life as I know it is unworthy. And perfect is just beyond my reach. Forever. And that puts me on the edge of tantrum tears because perfect is so beautiful, so . . . perfect. But here I am, and there it is, and as Kipling would put it, "never the twain shall meet."

I drank too much coffee this afternoon.

And I spent the last twenty minutes of my day thinking about calling Ginger.

I didn't. And I feel like a coward. More frustration.

By the time I get onto the bus, I'm deep into cranky mode.

The bus is a drab collection of drab people driving down a drab street in a drab city covered with drab holiday glitter, and dear *God*, couldn't this fucking place have just the tiniest bit of color?

As if in answer to my thoughts, the bus stops in front of a shop window filled with colored Christmas lights. Trains wheel around a tinsel-covered spruce, dolls nod, rocking horses rock. Color? No, fake. The old-fashioned Christmas no one ever had growing up. The good old days squeezed into counterfeit collective memory thanks to thousands of *Ideals* images.

I lean my head against the frosty window and close my eyes. Jimmy touches my face and tells me he can see the soul of God.

"Hey! Hey, you! Don't you want to get out?" The bus driver's angry voice jerks me awake. I pull my battered self out of the bus and walk the remaining blocks to my apartment, leaning into an icy headwind the whole way.

Never the twain shall meet.

Rob's SUV is parked in the spot where angels fear to tread. He's waiting for me in the hallway outside my door. A mixture of irritation and worry twists his face.

"Where were you?" he asks. "Are you all right? What happened last night?"

His hands are sunk deep into the pockets of his cashmere coat. Broad shoulders, leather shoes. I have the sudden image of him tripping on the second-to-last step and landing on an outdoorsy-looking blonde. Somewhere nearby, there's a pink stroller.

"Is your friend okay?" he asks, and the blonde and the stroller disappear.

"She's moving to Hong Kong," I say as I fit the key into the lock. Rob steps closer to me. I can smell his scent over the smell of the mold lining the hallway.

"Did you move with her?" he asks, teasing me. "You were gone all night. I kept calling, but you weren't here. I couldn't even get you at your office."

He hasn't come any closer, but I'm feeling crowded. I open the door to the apartment. "Someone I knew had a heart attack," I say.

Rob follows me in and shuts the door behind him. "Christ! Is he . . . she all right?"

"He's dead." I get a certain pleasure in making the words as bald as possible. I'm trying to get him to do what I want without my having to tell him, without my having to even know what the right thing is. It's a sick, nauseating game. My stomach screams. But the caffeine jitters are turning the longing into a gnashing sort of need that's chewing its way out. Just one perfect thing.

Just one.

Please.

Never the twain shall meet.

"I'm so sorry," Rob is saying. "Were you close?" He's taking my coat, trying to put an arm around me. I evade it.

"No. I only saw him twice."

Rob's holding my coat and he looks confused. "Then why . . . ? You're so upset."

People only care about people they know, right?

"Yeah." I start stripping off my clothes. There's nowhere to go, after all. This is a no-room apartment and damned if I'm going to try and maneuver around my clothes in that microchip of a bathroom. Naked, I walk into the shower and shut the door.

Five minutes later, just when the water is starting to warm up, Rob pulls the curtain aside and steps in behind me. He lathers his hands and rubs them over my back, my breasts, my hips, my thighs.

If you can't soothe her with words and concern, soothe her with sex.

Never the twain shall meet.

Sex is a brain thing. Just because it involves the body, everyone assumes it's a body thing. But the brain rules. Rob's trying for gentle, but the black, jittery, coffee-and-grief-induced demon comes screaming out of my brain at warp speed. I turn in his arms and what started out as comfort turns into teeth and tongues and fingernails on skin. He picks me up, and with my feet dangling a foot off the floor, we stumble out of the bathroom and into the bed. Rob remembers the condom, and then I'm taking out all the anger and emptiness and disappearing taillights by taking him in between my legs. Memories flash faster than heartbeats. Ginger's face as she says, *"Fuck visiting. Move to Hong Kong."* Carol's eyes as she slaps me. Jimmy's empty ones as he looks at the winter sky. Melissa's small, defeated shoulders. A red-clay teapot.

And somewhere—*somewhere*—perfection.

I reach for it. Wrap both hands around the wooden arm of the futon and strain forward. It's not fair. It's too far. I buck up against Rob, screaming frustration into my pillow as my body explodes. He comes harder than ever before, but I can taste a faint tang of fear in the sweat from his pores. Even neighbors can be psychos. What about lovers?

The caffeine monster retreats, and it's just me and Rob and my tears. These he understands. His fear disappears as he tucks me close into his body. "Sh, sh. It's okay. Don't cry."

I want to tell him to stop using the high, squeaky voice people use with children, but I'm shaking too badly. Not because Jimmy's dead. Not because of grief. Not because Ginger's plane took off five minutes ago. I'm shaking because in that last screaming moment, I saw Ethan's face.

Just out of reach.

Chapter 12

My mom has this saying, "Tears cleanse the soul." And maybe it's true, because the next morning I feel more like myself and less like a wet newspaper flapping in the gutter. I'm not sure what happened to me yesterday, but it probably had something to do with exhaustion and eating nothing but a half a bag of popcorn for two days.

Rob is still asleep when I leave to catch the bus. I'm a little relieved. He likes breakfast and a chat. I like coffee and a grunt. I'm not much good for anything else before ten. And I'm not exactly sure how to face him after last night. I'm embarrassed. Ashamed at the nasty way I treated him. But I don't want to apologize, I just want to forget the whole thing.

Work is insane. The usual Wednesday—the day everyone remembers it's two days until Friday and they're already two days behind getting started on the week. During lunch, Melissa sits at my table, elegant red nails in place, silk perfection on the legs. Not even a hint of dark shadows under her eyes, but she's wearing makeup and a high-voltage smile. We don't talk about babies or bosses, and everything feels normal.

Normal. It's a beautiful way to be.

I love homogeneity.

And everything stays normal until Friday morning when Ginger sends me an e-mail with an attached pic of Hong Kong's neon Nathan Road. "I'm here!" she writes. "It's even more wild than I remembered. Alive, messy, crazy. You have to come, Nicci. Love, Gin." I stare at the tumbling jumble of colored lights and wait for the hot fire in my chest to die down. Ginger knows me way too well. She knows I can ignore the written word, but I've never been able to resist a picture. Words call up memories, but images create desperate yearnings.

I take a deep breath and I can smell, taste, and hear every nuance of the damn picture. Ginger and I spent one summer together in Hong Kong—the last summer before we came back to the States for college. She dragged me to every well-known and little-known spot she could think of. And the smells and tastes and sounds must be burned into my memory, because the sensory gaps are too easy to fill. I'm trying not to smell the steaming rice, charred meat, smoke, cement, exhaust, and human bodies massed together in one place. I'm trying to stop my mouth from watering at the memory of blackened, marinated chicken roasted on sticks over an open fire and sold by the vendor on the corner. I'm trying not to hear millions of voices rising and falling in glorious Cantonese tones, the horns, shouts, barking dogs, diesel engines, and crying children.

But I can smell everything.

I can taste everything.

I can hear everything.

My finger itches as it hovers over the delete key—I don't need this right now. I've just found the normal setting on life's cruise control. Eating out with Rob and having nice, normal sex for dessert. Carol getting better. Normal-sounding on the phone. Melissa in limbo. Acting normal. Christmas on the way. Shopping for presents. Normal excitement and anticipation.

Even the strange, post-shower incident thingie is something I can shove to the back of my mind.

But I can't hit the delete key.

The phone rings.

My hand stops doing the helicopter imitation over the keyboard and reaches out to pick up the phone.

It's Carol.

"I thought you might like to come over for dinner," she says. "To my parents, I mean."

I exit my mailbox and Hong Kong's streets disappear. "Sure," I say to Carol. Dinner sounds good. No questions to threaten the status quo. No moments. Very normal.

"Kevyn can bring you and take you home. Unless you'd like to bring Rob."

"He's out of town this weekend." As I say the words, I realize I'm feeling pathetically grateful for Carol's invitation. I hope it's just because I want to see a friend.

And not that I'm avoiding anything.

I'd laugh, but it isn't funny.

"I'll call Kevyn, then," Carol says. She sounds happy.

Happiness is a virus. When one person has it, everyone else gets it, like it or not.

I like it.

By Friday, normal is standard procedure, and I'm ready to be happy.

Carol has put on a few pounds since I saw her at the hospital. But they look good on her—filling out the haggard flesh of her face, giving her an apple-cheeked vitality she probably hasn't worn since she married Bill. She hugs me, then hugs Kevyn as he comes through the door after me.

His hug is a teensy bit longer than mine.

It's not my imagination.

The house is one of those three-story, stands cheek-to-cheek with its neighbors, kind of houses. The kind only old, old residents of this city can afford. And then only because it's been handed down from dear old granddad, who passed away in the summer of fifty-six. It's a homey kind of house. A lived-in kind of house where the same walls have watched the same family sit down to pot roast for seventy-five years' worth of Sundays. Looking around, I begin to understand why Carol knows the names of everyone at Graphics and Design, why she cares for the whole world as if it were one more layer of her extended family. Change its exterior, and this house is prime real estate in a Bible Belt town with forty begats to every family.

After dinner—pot roast—Carol's dad and Kevyn don aprons and settle in to do the dishes. I'm enjoying the sight of manly muscles in pink and yellow frills, but Carol tugs my elbow.

"Come on," she says as she pulls me away from the kitchen entertainment and past the family room where her mother has *The Tonight Show* cranked to full volume. I follow her to a door leading off from the front hallway. She opens the door and chilly, lemon-oil air curls around our feet.

Carol turns on the light and smiles at me. "I love this room."

It's an old-fashioned parlor. Complete with piano, fireplace, threadbare oriental rugs, a giant Christmas tree, and furniture that looks as if it belonged to distant ancestors. I sit the edge of my butt down on a horsehair-covered chair. "It's nice," I say, then I laugh as I realize how unenthusiastic I sound. "It's overwhelming, actually."

Carol laughs, too. "I know. That's why I like it. I always feel like I'm trespassing." She leans back on a velvet daybed. "I used to sneak in here with my tea set and play lady of the house."

It doesn't take a lot of imagination to picture Carol—dark curls falling on her cheeks—pouring tea into a porcelain cup covered in pink roses. Maybe for a doll or a stuffed rabbit.

"Poor Kevyn," Carol laughs. "He put up with more doughy cookies. They probably made him sick."

A doll or a stuffed rabbit or Kevyn.

"Did you play doctor?" I ask.

"Oh, shut up." But her face is pink, like long-forgotten china roses.

I've got my mouth open to tease her some more, but she changes topics on me.

"How are you?"

"Fine."

"Don't do that," she says. I raise my eyebrows. She rolls her eyes. "You're seeing somebody."

This is such an old-fashioned way of putting it, I start to deny doing any such thing before I realize what she's asking.

"You mean Rob?"

She nods. "Tell me about him."

Still interested in other people's happiness. Even after Bill. How does she do it? I'd be thinking homicidal thoughts about the male half of the population. Or at least the Bill part of the male half of the population.

"He's nice," I say, then trail off. I'm struggling for something to say. Some way to tell her about Rob without falling back on the usual occupation and physical description kind of answers. Or sex. "Fun. We go out a lot. He took me on a carriage ride once." But that makes me think about the lunchroom, Melissa, Carol slapping me in the face.

"Thanks for all the details," Carol says, her eyes rolling again. "What about . . . ?" She waves her hand meaningfully. "You know . . ."

I grin. "Not telling."

"Do you love him?"

The white lights on the Christmas tree begin to spin.

"What?"

"Oh, come on, Nicci. Is it serious? Do you love him?"

In my stomach, the pot roast is getting ready for an encore. I'm back in the post-shower thingie moment, that grasping, clawing moment when I screamed because perfect was just out of reach. Just beyond Rob and me on the futon . . .

"Nicci?"

I gasp out something. Probably unintelligible because Carol's forehead screws up into a frown. Tonight was supposed to be normal, for Chrissake. Normal. No moments.

The doorbell rings.

I paste a smile onto my face. "Someone's here."

It's Bill.

He staggers into the hallway before Carol can shut the door in his face. A perfect advertisement for why people should install peepholes or beside-the-door windows.

"I need to talk tcha you," Bill begins. "Carol," he adds, after swaying back and forth for a moment. As if he couldn't remember her name right off the top of his head. Needed to think about it first.

Ten years of marriage and it boils down to this. A whiskey-soaked confrontation in a hallway smelling of onions and pot roast. All the Julie and Rich movies in the world can't make up for the fact that Bill likes other women and Carol doesn't like that.

Carol crosses her arms across her body. "I don't think so," she says in that tone of voice that says she doesn't need to think about it all.

Bill swallows, closes and opens his eyes slowly, and tries to find a level spot on the hallway floor. "Carol, I need to talk to you," he says carefully. "It's not right."

"What isn't?" Carol asks. "The fact that I won't talk to you or the fact that you had your dick in someone else's mouth?"

Oh, boy. I'm thinking serious thoughts about becoming one with the paneling when Bill makes it personal.

"She wanted it," he says. "Just like *her*." He jabs a hand in my direction. "She wanted it, too. Begged me even though I tried to get away."

Big mistake. I step forward, but Carol's already there. "You lying, no-good, filthy, son of a *bitch*," she says, her voice nearly knocking a few family portraits off the wall. "You fucking piece of—" And she slaps him. Hard enough to drown out the final, appropriate comment.

Then Bill makes a bigger mistake. He shoves Carol back into the wall. I catch her before she falls to the floor. We're both down, and Bill is heading our way when Kevyn slams into the hallway. And Kevyn's fist slams into Bill's nose, all of Newton's law chiming in to help.

Bill goes down. The house shudders, and half the family pictures follow him to the floor. Shaking the sting out of his knuckles, Kevyn stands over the fallen enemy. A knight in a frilly, pink apron.

Carol pushes to her feet. I reach out to catch her hand, to stop her from going to Bill, but she's cradling Kevyn's clenched fist next to her cheek.

"Are you all right? Did he hurt you? Your poor hand," she says while rubbing his fingers. Kevyn's face turns red.

"I'm all right," he says.

Carol's dad steps into the hallway, his pipe still caught between his teeth. He's taken the time to get rid of his apron before coming to see what all the ruckus is about. "Go put some ice on that, son," he says to Kevyn.

"Ice. Of course." Carol leads the bruised knight away to his ice pack.

"What's going on?" Carol's mother asks from the family

room where the television is still blaring. "I thought I heard a noise." She looks through the door.

"Bit of a commotion," her husband says around his pipe. "Might take some cleaning up." I'm not sure if he means the pictures or his prostrate son-in-law. Probably both.

"Oh, my." She walks over to Bill and peers down at his face. "Drunk, too." A slippered foot prods Bill's ribs. "Get up!" she says to his unconscious body. "Get up and stop bleeding all over my rugs."

Bill groans.

Carol comes back in with a plastic bag of ice. She hands it to me. "Nicci . . . would you mind?"

I'm still staring at Carol's mother. She's digging her toe in Bill's ribs again. "Mind what?"

Carol waves the bag of ice. "For Bill."

"Oh." I take the ice, and Carol goes back into the kitchen and—presumably—Kevyn. I stand up and walk over to Bill, rescuing him from an actual kick in the side. "Someone should probably call the police," I say to no one in particular. "Even if you don't want to press charges, he would have a place to sleep it off."

"Humph!" Carol's mother snorts.

"She's right, dear," her husband says. He picks up the phone.

Bill's moaning a little. The moaning gets worse when I lay the plastic bag full of hard ice cubes onto his nose. I can't deny a certain degree of pleasure in the task. Especially when the moaning takes on the sound of a grown man blubbering.

"Serves you right," Carol's mother says.

My thoughts exactly.

Kevyn is quiet as he drives me home. He has to double park in order to let me out. I have the door open when he finally breaks the vow of silence.

"I've never hit anyone before," he says.

I laugh. "It was a good way to start."

"I'm not planning on making a habit of it." The tone of his voice says he didn't get the joke.

"I didn't mean you would. Just that Bill deserved it."

"Yeah. I guess." He smiles. "Carol kissed my hand."

He sounds like God leaned down out of the sky and smacked him over the head. This guy is from a different century. Judging by the look on Carol's face when she had Kevyn's bruised hand against her cheek, she probably wanted a kiss with tongues while pressed up against the wall, and settled for planting one on Kevyn's black-and-blue knuckles. Then I remember the house, the family pictures, the pipe and the toe. Maybe not.

I say good night and climb the stairs to my apartment. After having Rob in constant attendance since Thanksgiving, I'm surprised that I don't feel lonely. I may even feel relieved. Tossing my coat over a chair, I sit on the futon and spread my arms out. The night is mine. Tomorrow, too. Sighing with pleasure, I let my head fall back.

And Carol's question hits me full in the chest. A bad case of heartburn. *Do you love him?*

What's a girl to say? Especially after watching ten years of love bleed out of a broken nose and onto a Turkish rug.

Love hasn't entered the Rob plus Nicci equation up to this point. I like him, he's fun, my parents like him, the sex is great . . . all the things I said or didn't say to Carol. But love? As far as I know, Rob hasn't said the "L" word. And I know I haven't.

Isn't love something out of another century?

Kung Fu movies aren't known for romance. A lot of them should be. They are epics. The witch in *To Kill with Intrigue* loves Jackie. She even tries to force him to remain with her. But his love for another woman causes the witch so much pain, she makes a bargain with him: defeat her and she will allow him to leave, but every time he tries to defeat her and does not, he must do whatever she wants. In grand operatic style, Jackie attempts to fight the witch three times and is forced to swallow a burning coal, have his face disfigured by a brand, and finally to drink wine he believes is poisoned—thus telling the witch that he would rather lose his voice, his status, and die than live without his love and without revenge on the man who has stolen her. Realizing that he will never be hers, the witch gives Jackie her blood to drink—the means of transferring her power—and sends him after his true love.

And Carol wants to know if I love Rob.

Would I be willing to swallow a hot coal, be branded, and drink poison just to be with Rob?

I dig my can of Pringles out from behind the platter, pop *Dragon Fist* into the VCR, and leave my thoughts to themselves. Some things are better left alone.

Not that Carol could ever leave anything alone. She calls me Sunday afternoon. She wants to go Christmas shopping. She wants me to go with her.

"Just shopping?" I ask.

"What do you mean?" Her voice is too innocent.

I try to think of a polite way to put it, then give up and go for the gusto. "I don't want to talk about Rob and me."

"Oh. I promise not to ask. Now will you come?"

This is flimsy. At best. Carol is the kind of woman who crosses her fingers and negates a promise. It's that easy. On the other hand, I have new ammunition these days. For every question about Rob, there's an equally nasty question I can ask about a certain knight in a pink apron.

Carol wants to shop at the mall. We walk in one direction looking at decorated store windows for agonizing hours—at least it seems like hours—before she claims to have forgotten something "back there."

"Why don't you wait for me?" she says, pointing to a bench near the mall's center. Then she heads back the way we just came.

I'm not sure why I'm here if we're going to split up. Malls give me claustrophobia. Sitting on the bench, looking up at the glittering, white Christmas tree ringed with screaming children waiting to see Santa, I find my catalogue-shopping beliefs validated once again. The joy of an impersonal phone call or Internet visit takes on a rosy hue as Santa yelps dramatically for the thousandth time as the thousandth sticky hand tugs his fake beard.

Carol appears beside me, carrying a pink-and-white-striped bag. She sits down with a triumphant sigh. "They still had it," she says. I peer into the bag. Something black lace peers back.

"But what is it?" I ask.

Carol blushes and drags the bag closer to her feet. "Nothing."

I tug the bag back toward me and take a better look. "*Almost* nothing," I say. It's a black thong and some kind of uncomfortable-looking bra thingie with low-cut mesh cups. "Kevyn's going to need a doctor if he sees you in that."

Carol's cheeks turn as pink as the bag's stripes. "Who said anything about Kevyn? I'm just buying it for me."

"Uh-huh. Should be real comfy under your gym clothes." So I was right about Carol wanting tongues up against the wall. "Why don't you just tell him?" I ask.

"Tell him what?"

It's my turn to roll my eyes.

"I can't," she says. "It's too soon."

"But not too soon to buy see-through bras and undies?"

Carol sighs and slouches back against the back of the

bench. "Cucumbers, zucchini, peaches, even carrots," she says. "I mean, yesterday at the grocery store I just stood there and I thought . . ." she trails off. "You know. It's been a while."

Sex has always been an . . . optional sort of thing with me. I mean, it's fun and all, but not a valued part of my existence. Until Rob, sex was the thin chocolate drizzle on the bundt cake of life. With Rob, sex is the cake, because that's all there is.

Leather is the only thing Italian loafers and Redwing boots have in common.

Hit me in the head with a two-by-four.

My ears are buzzing. I can't get any air.

"Even before I caught Bill," Carol is saying, "we didn't, you know, do *it* all that often."

"Hmm-mm," I manage to mumble through the buzz.

"Are you all right?" Carol asks. Then she turns pink again. "I'm sorry. You probably don't want to hear this."

I swallow the buzz. It tastes like a hot coal. "No," I say out loud. I clear my throat of the coal and the rasp it left behind. "That's not it. I just . . ." Carol's looking at me. Expectant. "Nothing," I say. "It's nothing."

Chapter

13

*H*ere's the question: Does a personal revelation require action? Is it bad to have a relationship where the general purpose is sex? Okay, that's two questions. But sex for sex alone is pure, simple, uncomplicated. And it takes care of that basic loneliness problem. And if everything is going along all right, why mess it up just because you saw the light under the Christmas tree at the mall? Rob. Nicci. No strings. Perfect. Right?

So what was all that screaming about the other night? A caffeinated nightmare?

Rob is waiting in his SUV when Carol drops me off outside my apartment building. She sees him and gives him a thumbs up. It reminds me of the scene in *Dragon Fist* where the defeated master falls back into his student's arms, gives the bad guy a thumbs up, and says, "Good Kung Fu!"

The bad guy kills him.

"Maybe I should give *you* the undies," Carol says.

I try to laugh. "He'd die of shock."

"White cotton kind of girl, huh?"

Not quite, but almost. Blue, black, heather gray, and the occasional flowered variety. And the thong and push-up bra I wear once every three years. If that even counts.

I tell Carol I'll see her tomorrow and walk over to Rob, visions of cucumbers, squash, and peaches dancing in my head. Not the most romantic sort of vision, by the way.

"Hi," he says.

"Hi." I haven't felt this unsure and ridiculous since the episode of the little black dress. I have to stop thinking so much. "Come on up."

His Italian loafers squeak as he follows me up the stairs to my apartment. I've got my key out when he turns me around, and catches me between his body and the unopened door.

"I missed you," he says. Then his tongue is in my mouth and he's warming his hands under my clothes, on my breasts.

My semiconscious brain hears someone coming up the stairs. "Inside," I say. We laugh as I fumble the key, dropping it to the floor.

We're only half undressed when Rob rolls on a condom and leans me over the back of the couch.

Maybe cake is good enough.

Rob doesn't spend the night. He says it's because he has an early meeting. I think it's because futons are a lot harder than waterbeds. But I'm not complaining.

I've always been a little bit misanthropic. During my sophomore year of high school, the school counselor's office decided to torture everyone under eighteen by administering personality tests. They said it would help us "identify the strong and weak areas of our lives." As if we should all strive diligently toward the goal of a red-ink, toothy line that never strays very far from the (supposedly) happy medium. Class by class, we took the test. The questions were pathetically obvious and irritatingly black and white. "Which would you prefer," one question read, "to stay home and read a book or go out with friends?" What kind of question is that? What about the details? Is the book good? Or is it something by Flannery O'Connor? What are your friends doing tonight? Going to a Julie and Rich movie? Going out for pizza? Playing kick the can?

After agonizing moments, I chose to stay home and read a book. The counselor called me in three weeks later. *"You are an off-the-chart introvert,"* she said. *"And you're a melancholy-choleric."* I didn't even know I had cholera. Wasn't that what the shots were for? No, no. Apparently, I was good in emergencies, but a lousy conversationalist and a too-deep thinker—no fun to be with, but capable of lifting the car off the accident victim and successfully dialing 911. Oh. What a relief. The counselor visit ended with an admonition to try and be more friendly. Nicer. Less withdrawn. Get that red spike back down to the middle.

Two years later, they gave us the test again. My results would have made a jack-o'-lantern proud to smile. Perfect jagged line. The counselor gushed at my improvement and gave me a sucker. Just another of life's little rewards for being dishonest. After all, the questions *were* pathetically obvious.

It's easy to be dishonest when that's what everyone wants you to be.

But what about when the only other person in the room is you? Can you even tell when you're being dishonest with yourself?

I pull Grandma Bradford's quilt over my head and go to sleep.

On Monday, I realize it's been a week since Jimmy died. It feels like a hundred years. The bus is late, and some conscientious soul turned off the coffeepot in the lunchroom. The office won't burn down, but I'm left with bitter, cold dregs.

Seven days without Jimmy's blue eyes looking on the world.

Technically, I'm supposed to be working, but I'm doodling a Christmas list instead of looking over the latest set of promotional materials.

"Nicci?"

I crumple the list in my fist and drop my hands into my lap. "Yes?" I say, friendly, noncholeric smile in place.

But it's only Carol. She's back at work this week. My smile slips into normal, then freezes when I see who's standing behind her.

"Security almost kicked him out," she says, jerking her thumb over her shoulder at Ethan. "He was wandering around looking for you."

"Hi," I say, but I'm thinking about Yi-Xing teapots and silent conversations.

"Hi."

I don't know what he's thinking about.

Carol gives a little wave and a wink and goes her merry way. Of all the people I know, Carol is the only person who might receive a jack-o'-lantern's mouth on a personality test.

Honestly, that is.

Ethan points to my paper-covered chair. "Can I move these?"

"Sure. Go ahead." I hold out my hand for the papers. He makes them into a neat stack before giving them to me.

He's wearing a suit. I realize I've never seen him in anything but jeans and a flannel shirt. And a green apron. The suit doesn't fit right. It makes him look smaller, older, tireder.

"I didn't realize security was so tight here," he says after he sits down.

"Yeah."

"My uncle sent me over. He's all excited about a marketing package."

I get the feeling he isn't thanking me for picking up the fumble with his uncle last Tuesday morning above the coffee shop. He's looking into my eyes. A hard look. Sharp. Aimed across the desk. I think he might have been looking for a reason—an excuse—to leave the room with the broken-down couch and instant kitchen. Why?

He looks down and shifts his shoulders inside the jacket. His shoulders move, the jacket stays put. Toy soldier clothes. I wonder if I look as out of place in my sales-rack designer label. Probably.

I take a deep breath and keep the conversation at face value. "If you're here about marketing, you need to talk to somebody else. Because I'm just a copy—"

"No," he interrupts. "I met with someone a couple of aisles over."

"Oh."

"I just wanted to see you."

Honesty this time. Just like the night he said he was lonely. I don't understand everything he's thinking and feeling right now, but I know this is honest. And it makes me feel like I've just had a cup of hot chocolate on a cold day.

I'm warm and happy.

His honesty makes me reckless and daring. There's something else he said on Halloween night that I want to ask him about. And the choleric part of me isn't afraid to bring up a socially unacceptable topic.

"Remember that night?" I ask Ethan. "When you said I could tell Carol about Bill or not, but either way she wouldn't thank me?"

The flow of words hits him. I can see his hands tighten, see the tendons and veins on his wrists become more visible.

He nods once. "How did it turn out?"

This isn't the direction I want to go. "Fine," I say before taking a breath and plunging in. "What did you mean?"

A vertical frown line appears between his eyebrows. "Exactly what I said."

"No, what did it mean for you?"

For a minute, I expect him to deny everything. Or tell me to mind my own business. Which I should be doing. But there's something about him that keeps me from being a normal, well-adjusted adult. Or maybe it makes me more well-adjusted than I've been ever since I took that personality test.

Ethan lets out a long breath.

"My dad was . . ." He trails off. His hands close into fists and then relax. "When I was eighteen, I walked in on him and a woman I thought was Mom. I shut the door, went down the stairs, and saw Mom pull into the driveway." He starts to laugh a little. "She surprised me. How did she get there when she was upstairs? And I sort of blabbed it all out."

"What happened?" I ask when he doesn't continue.

"She slapped me a few times, then went out to bring in the groceries."

"Oh." This is—as my grandpa would say—beyond the pale. I don't get it. "Why?"

Ethan shrugs inside the suit jacket. The skin around his eyes and mouth looks pinched, painful. I'm sorry I ever asked. I'm not embarrassed, just sorry that I made him hurt like this.

"I didn't mean to dredge all this—" I start to say, but his smile stops me.

"That was the night my grandmother gave me the teapot. A few days later, Mom packed a bag, emptied the bank account, and took a world tour." His smile gets warmer. "Maybe she already knew about Dad. Maybe catching him was the excuse she was looking for. I don't know."

In all this, he hasn't said a word about himself. I'm waiting. Hoping.

"Do you think children repeat the mistakes of their parents?" he asks instead.

I pick up a pen and slide it through my fingers. End to end. I'm not sure my parents are even capable of making mistakes. At least not mistakes like this. Their mistakes are things like not returning a defective item to the store, paying too much on their income taxes, stuff like that. I remember Grandpa's grandpa—the tyrant cobbler. There's nothing like that in my grandpa. Or in my dad.

"No," I say.

"You're so sure of it."

"You're not?"

He starts to smile, but my next words wipe it away.

"What did you do after your mom left?"

"Moved in with my grandmother for a week."

The week before she died. I started digging this hole. Now I have to dig myself and my dignity out of it.

"I'm sorry," I say. He starts to shrug it off, but I stop him. "No. I'm really sorry. This wasn't any of my business. I shouldn't have asked you—"

"If I hadn't wanted to answer you, I wouldn't have," he says, stopping me cold in the middle of a sentence. Then he smiles. His eyes smile, too. Sunshine on a flooded, muddy river. "This is the first time I've bothered."

Bothered to what? He's not just talking about my questions. If he were, I would ask more. Because I have a lot more. Like, what did he do after his grandmother died?

"I took a job on a fishing boat in Alaska," he says. "Stayed up there until last year."

Great. He's just proven once again that anyone who feels

like knowing Nicci Bradford's innermost thoughts can read the headlines on her face. This is a problem only select personality tests are capable of pointing out. I know this because . . .

. . . because I took every conceivable kind of personality test in high school. Maybe it was the thing to do. Maybe the counselor's office declared it a raging success. But the test craze leaked into every facet of our lives. Some tests were more professional than others. My dorm mother—the psychotic one— gave us peer personality evaluations. Her test was vicious. Every girl in the dorm rated the personality of every other girl in the dorm. Friends gushed over friends and dissed enemies. Except for Ginger's gushing evaluation, I got lots of comments like, *"shows all of her emotions"* and *"too sarcastic"* and *"needs to learn to control her expressions."* Then there was that one comment—at odds with all the others: *"Laughs a lot but is really hard to get to know. I can't tell what she's thinking."* I think that evaluator had me mixed up with someone else. Especially when she said I spent too much time in front of the mirror doing my hair.

I'm not sure what purpose those peer evaluations had, but I *started* spending a lot of time in front of the mirror. Not to do my hair, but to twist my face into what I hoped was a pleasant, bland, neutral expression. Hey, I might be a sarcastic, angry person, but darned if I was going to look like one. It didn't work. I got the same evaluations the next year.

It's nice to know some things never change.

"Alaska, huh?" I say, trying to paste a pleasant, bland, neutral expression onto my face, as if I haven't just been fishing for details about the man sitting on the other side of my desk.

It doesn't work.

He laughs. Actually laughs.

I swear to God, a rainbow slides down that laugh and lands in my cubicle. I can feel the last drops of the tropical rain and hear the Maya birds fluttering in the dwarf palms. The wind sighs through the trees, and I can smell the earth sucking up the water . . . and a great, fat rainbow spreads itself over my desk.

I'm just getting used to the colored lights when Ethan's laugh disappears and he turns serious.

"The night at the coffee shop? Halloween? Mom had just called to tell me she was getting married. To a chef. In France. Five minutes after that, Dad called to tell me what a worthless whore my mother is." He starts to laugh again, but this time there's no rainbow.

"That might have been just a little bit hypocritical," I say, holding up a closely aligned thumb and forefinger. The red spike for sarcastic choleric jumps a bit.

"Yeah." He lets out a long breath.

Something about the sighing sound he makes catches me and slumps my shoulders. Isn't anything real anymore? Ethan's mom and dad, the boss and Melissa, Kristie and Matt, Ginger and John, Bill and Carol . . . what are these relationships made of anyway? Did they start at the movie theater? Over coffee? On a scaffold? On top of a desk? Just as important, why did most of them end? Because of loneliness? Or was it just a need for power and a new taste thrill? Knowing what I know about human nature, maybe I should try and figure out why some people actually stay together. Because it doesn't seem to be the happy medium.

"What are you doing for lunch?" Ethan asks.

Given my recent thoughts, that gets my attention.

"Bologna and wheat in the lunchroom," I say.

"Sounds awful."

"Pretty much."

He's giving me that sharp look again. He wants to know about lunch. Lunch together. It sounds simple, but it's not.

"It's just lunch," he says, effectively reading my facial head-lines.

"I only get a half hour."

He shrugs as if to say anyone who bothers to let fascist rules about lunch-hour behavior dictate their actions is either stupid or brainwashed.

I'm neither.

I take an hour.

Chapter 14

*I*n my family, Christmas is all about decorating the tree, singing carols, eating, eating some more, and talking a lot. Presents aren't a big part of it—there's something too . . . *unnatural* about getting up at four in the morning to make sure you're the first in line to get the latest video-game player or talking doll for junior. When I say presents aren't a big part of things, I mean they aren't the main focus. We still open presents on Christmas morning—assuming, please God, that Christmas doesn't fall on Sunday. If that happens, Christmas is postponed for several boring hours as some guy behind a pulpit talks about peace, love, and goodwill while everyone out in the pews dreams of huddling around their trees, drinking coffee, and laughing.

Yes, laughing. Christmas morning with my family is all about laughter. It's everyone's goal to find the looniest presents out there. Not tacky stuff like a talking dead fish, but something that is exactly what the recipient would want and yet . . . not. It's harder than it sounds. And for some reason, it's incomprehensible to outsiders.

Matt's mother happened to stay with us one Christmas. She's a walking medical book, so it wasn't a surprise that Kristie gave her the Operation game. The one where the patient's nose lights up if you make a mistake taking out his organs. Kristie's mother-in-law threw the game onto the floor. The poor plastic man's nose lit up. Matt spent the rest of the day scuttling back and forth between the two women in his life, trying his hardware best to nail things back together. And Kristie kept sniffing and having to blow her nose. *"My darn allergies."* Everyone knew she was trying not to cry. Even her mother-in-law, who sometimes managed to hide the smug smile.

Just another one of those happy, Kodak moments.

It's the week before Christmas, and all through Nicci's apartment not a bare space can be seen. Wrapping paper, colored lights, candles, paper snowflakes hanging from the ceiling, and a tree, of course. I love Christmas. I suppose it's possible I might go a little overboard with the decorating. It's obvious Rob thinks so. He grumbled about having to help carry the five-foot spruce up to the third floor, but I tuned it out by singing "The First Noël" at the top of my lungs. By the last flight of steps, no one would have been able to tell if I were singing a Christmas carol or just yodeling. But Rob stopped complaining. And the tree is fabulous. Five feet of fragrant evergreen, covered with lights, glass ornaments, and tinsel.

I tweak the velvet bow on Grandpa's gift—a pair of pearl-handled cap guns complete with leather holsters. It took me forever to think up this gift, and I can't wait to see his face when he opens it.

Rob is lying on the couch, watching the news. I'm so absorbed in wrapping presents, I actually jump when he turns off the TV.

"It's going to be great having Christmas together," he says. "My parents usually go to midnight mass on Christmas Eve. I thought we could go with them and, if the weather's nice, go sailing on Christmas. What do you think?"

I think I'm frozen.

Conversations are a funny thing. They inspire laughter, tears, boredom, comradeship—all depending on the time, place, and participants. Rob's words have filled me up with wet cement. It's hardening. I can feel my throat begin to close, and my stomach is a slag heap in the middle of my body.

Rob hasn't said a word about Christmas. Until now. I already have a bus ticket for a night-before-Christmas-Eve Greyhound race across the Rust Belt. I leave the day after tomorrow. It never even occurred to me that Rob was assuming we would spend Christmas together. Here . . .

But Rob went with me for Thanksgiving. So—as Mom would say—tit for tat. He must have assumed I would go with him to his parents for Christmas, but he never said anything and—

—and it's not fair.

Guilt swamps me for even daring to think the words.

Ever since the night after Jimmy died—the night I reached for perfection and found empty air—I've been keeping Rob at a distance. Not physically, we *are* still going at it like crazed weasels, but just at a distance. I can't say at a distance emotionally, because I never let him get close in the first place.

So I feel guilty.

"I—" I begin.

"What do you want for Christmas?" Rob interrupts.

Looking up from the velvet bow, I blink at him. "Huh?"

"I was thinking of getting you something special." He's hinting at something.

I'm feeling dense, because I don't get it.

"Marriage is the next place to go, isn't it?" he asks. His smile is teasing, indulgent. And he's waiting for something.

Is he waiting for me to squeal and throw my arms around him? I've got the window wide open, and the apartment isn't hot. But I'm sweating. Big, fat drops of fear sweat oozing down the gap between my shoulder blades. In sophomore biology class, I learned about the fight or flight adrenaline rush. Maybe that's what's wrong. I'm feeling cornered. Which explains why I want to lash out, bite, kick, and run for my life—all at the same time.

I don't think this is the proper response to a marriage proposal, but it's never happened to me before so I'm not sure.

"Marry you?" I choke out.

He leans back into the futon and links his hands behind his head. "Sure. Why not? Let's get married."

Just like that.

"You must know I love you," he says, his tone matter-of-fact. "I was planning on flowers and a ring and down-on-my-knees beside the Christmas tree, but I don't think you'd really like that." He laughs. "I could take you to my parents' house and trip on the stairs."

He's confident. As confident about this as he was about making me come in my clothes below the deck of his boat.

Only this time I'm not sure I want to come along for the ride.

I swallow. "Um . . . it's a big step."

He nods, graciousness and benevolence personified. "You want some time to think about it?"

I'm not sure. I'm not sure time will help. I don't know what will help.

"Yeah," I say. "I think I . . . need some time."

"Okay." He laughs. "But I want your answer by Christmas morning. Or else I might retract the offer."

He's teasing, but he's making it sound like a business deal, and that doesn't help me chip the cement out of my stomach.

It doesn't help at all.

And thoughts of Christmas morning remind me of the

other bomb he dropped. The one he dropped right before his marriage proposal turned my happy, pre-Christmas anticipation into a nuclear wasteland.

"I'm not sure about Christmas," I say.

Silence.

Rob sits up and leans his elbows on his knees. "You think you might need a little more time? That's not a problem, I guess." He sounds puzzled. As if he can't figure out why I would reject him.

Guilt isn't mental. Guilt is physical. I know, because I want to throw up.

"Um . . . no," I say. "I mean about spending Christmas to-gether. I . . . I had already planned to go to my parents. I already have a ticket—"

He stands up and I stumble to a halt. Lines bracket his mouth. I'm not sure if he's hurt or angry. A little of both, maybe.

"I think I'd better go," he says.

Please. Yes. Go.

But those aren't the words I can say out loud. Those are the relieved thoughts in my head. And this is one of those rare times when honesty is definitely *not* the best policy.

The apartment door shuts before I can find the right words to say.

I don't believe in prophetic dreams. My brain has to dump its garbage sometime, and it likes to take out the trash while I'm asleep. Although some people might disagree with me, I see trash and prophecy as mutually exclusive. But this dream is different.

I'm walking through deep snow. My legs drag and pull and won't cooperate. I keep falling. It's not cold, but it's annoying. Suddenly, I hear hoofbeats. The logical part of my brain points out that it's impossible to hear hoofbeats in the snow, but the dream brain turns around and sees a big, black horse. The kind I always wanted when I was a kid. Grandpa is high above me on the horse's back, and he's got the pearl-handled cap guns strapped around his waist. He tips his black cowboy hat in my direction. "Nicci, darlin'," he says in a TV-style western accent. "It's been a pleasure knowin' ya." The black horse rears. Grandpa waves his hat and rides away. I try to run after him, but before I can force my legs to move, he's nothing but a black speck. Then he's gone. And he's left me behind. The loneliness is unbearable. Tears freeze on my face. The snow is so deep, I'm falling—

And I wake up. Safe, warm, and in my own hard, little bed. Best of all, Grandpa hasn't ridden away. The thudding in my chest eases along with the fear and loneliness.

But the dream won't go away. At work, I'm a nervous wreck. Fear slips up on me at the oddest times. Just as I'm about to get up for coffee. Just as I press the start button on the copier. Just as I delete a worthless office memo about turning off the coffee-maker.

Last night, in the hour or so between Rob's stomping out and bedtime, my conscience and I had a talk. It said I was being selfish. Rob wants me to spend Christmas with him. Most people would think that was sweet, not a pain in the butt. And maybe I owe it to him. After all, he drove me across the Rust Belt and paid for a motel. As my eyes closed, I decided to call Mom and explain the whole thing. But now . . . now all I want is to go home and see Grandpa. Make sure he's all right. Because even though I don't believe in prophetic dreams, I can't help worrying that my subconscious brain might have picked up on something.

There's only one problem.

If I spend Christmas in the Bible Belt, I'm not going to

spend it with Rob. Which means tension, stress, explanations, anger—all those things introverted melancholics like me hate.

And I still feel like throwing up.

I've been focusing on the Christmas problem and have pretty much convinced myself that the marriage proposal was a joke. I mean, people don't toss proposals across the room as if they were a Nerf ball. I've never been one of those girls who fantasizes about having some poor swain kneel in the mud and beg for my hand. Rob's right about that much. I've never given marriage much thought at all. But somewhere in the back of my head was this idea that a proposal—getting married—would be something that came naturally. Not something that reached out and choked me to death.

Rob calls me. He's sitting in traffic.

"Will you be home on time tonight?" he asks. No hello. No how are you doing. No nothing. Just a blunt question.

The hairs on my arms bristle. "Yes," I say. Equally blunt.

"Good." A horn blares close beside him. I have to hold the phone away from my ear for a second. When I put it back, he's talking.

"—about yesterday."

"What?" I say.

There's a pause. "You want me to say it twice?" I can't tell if he's frustrated with me or with the traffic.

"I didn't hear you," I say, working a note of calm into my voice. "The traffic."

"Hunh. I said I'm sorry about yesterday."

I want to ask him what he's sorry *for*. For getting angry? For leaving? For tossing the foam rubber proposal at me?

"Uh . . . okay," I mumble, nice and generic.

Conversations are more than just a funny thing, I realize. They're exhausting. One time when Rob and I were at a Greek restaurant, I saw an obviously married couple at a nearby table.

They were conspicuous in their silence, which began as soon as the waitress took their orders. After five minutes or so, the wife said something. The husband grunted. The wife said a few more things—probably about her dreadful day at the office. In the middle of this absolute fountain of words, the husband stopped the waitress and asked if she would turn on the TV. "There's a game on," he said. The waitress turned on the TV, and the man watched football over his wife's shoulder for the rest of the meal. She ate dinner and read the wine list.

Maybe talking had become too exhausting.

"Did you hear me?" Rob asks over the noise of a semi.

"Yes."

"You're angry, aren't you?" His laugh is tired and sarcastic. But I'm not angry, I just don't know how to respond to his vague apology.

"Look," he says, "I'll come over tonight and we can work it out, okay?"

"Okay."

He hangs up.

Disconnection. It means a break in communication, a separation, a completion of a task. I hang up the phone.

I'm exhausted.

Rob is waiting by my stop when I step off the bus. Catching my shoulders in his hands, he leans over and kisses me. A few lewd cheers erupt from the commuters around us.

"I'm sorry for being such a grouch yesterday," Rob says next to my lips.

I nod. "Me too."

He lays an arm across my shoulders, and we walk down the street to my apartment building.

"Where do you want to eat tonight?" he asks.

I shrug. "Anywhere. I'm not really hungry, so you decide."

He's silent until we reach the door of my apartment. "You're still angry, aren't you?" he asks.

I open the door. "I was never angry."

"Then you're staying here for Christmas." He sounds satisfied, happy. His tone says it's all settled now, and that's a good thing.

Exhausted to my very bones, I hang my coat on the hook by the door. "I can't, Rob," I tell him. "There's something . . ." I trail off. How am I supposed to explain a dream, a feeling, a fear with no shape? "I'm worried about Grandpa," I say instead.

Rob drops down onto the couch. "He seemed all right to me. Why would you worry?"

Yes, why worry? I shrug. "Just a feeling."

Deep lines appear along either side of Rob's mouth. "Fine. I understand if you want to go home. You don't have to make stuff up to convince me."

This snaps me out of my exhaustion. "I'm not making up anything. I'm worried—"

"Okay. I'm sorry. I shouldn't have put it like that."

He's not sorry, and his face has settled into grooves and creases. I don't know what to do. I don't want him to be angry. I want to make peace. I want us to be happy and laugh.

I want him to understand me without my having to say a word.

Instead, we're north and south, east and west, up and down, dark and light . . . never meeting.

Sitting down next to him on the couch, I touch his arm. "Rob. I'm sorry. Last night . . . last night I had decided to stay here for Christmas, but I . . ."

There's no way I can tell him about the dream. He's too practical for that. I thought *I* was too practical for that.

"I have a bad feeling about Grandpa," I finish.

Rob crosses his arms, digging his shoulders into the couch.

"Woman's intuition, huh?" He looks and sounds like a little boy who's been told to come out of the pool because of a thunderstorm. Disbelieving, hurt, angry, frustrated.

Guilt swims around in my stomach. I almost open my mouth to say, *You're right. It's stupid. I'll stay.* But I can't.

"I'm sorry," I say instead. "Believe me, I'm sorry. If—" I start to say, *If you'd told me sooner,* but I catch myself just in time. I don't want to sound like I'm blaming him.

He shrugs his shoulders, digging them further into the couch. "I guess," he says.

I'm not sure if he means he guesses I'm sorry or if he guesses he's accepting my apology. It takes all my barely existent people skills to keep from sighing. Loudly. Not only am I exhausted, I'm frustrated. Why can't Rob be as easy to talk to as Ethan?

What kind of thought is that? Closing my eyes, I lean back into the couch. But when I close my eyes, I see rainbow laughter. My reflection in Ethan's eyes. Eating lunch on a pier with our feet hanging over the water. And I hear my own muffled scream for perfection.

My eyes fly open as Rob's mouth closes over mine. He's kissing me. A little harder than usual, but with the same skill. I don't feel like going here. Not while we're poles apart. But it would take too much effort to stand up against this, too.

"Come here," he says, and he lifts me onto his lap. I can feel his erection hard against my left thigh. One hand cups the back of my head and pulls me down for another kiss, the other untucks my shirt and rubs circles on the bare skin above my waistband. There's tension in his movements, but he's unhooking the front clasp on my bra, and I'm starting to slip into the nympho fog, so I ignore it. When he rolls my nipple between his fingers, the slight pain makes me wet, and I'm happy to help pull my sweater and shirt over my head and free my arms from the bra straps.

"Here." Rob brings my hands to my breasts. "Touch yourself."

This is awkward. I've never done this before and I feel shy, embarrassed.

"Do it," he urges. I do, and he watches while he unzips the side zipper of my skirt. I'm still feeling awkward and shy, so I'm relieved when I have to take my hands away from my breasts to help him slide my skirt, hose, and underwear over my hips.

I reach for the knot in his tie, but he catches my hands. "No. Like this." And turning me around, he pulls my bare back up against his chest so I'm sitting on his lap, facing away from him. His arms come around me and he pushes my knees apart. "Like this," he says again, as he brings my hands up to my breasts. I can feel the heat from my face bleed down to my chest. I feel open, exposed, sitting back against him—nearly lying back against him—in the harsh light from the bare ceiling bulb. It's too much, so I shut my eyes and shut out the image of myself. Rob's hands are hot on my inner thighs. Hot on my stomach. Hot on my hands where they squeeze my breasts. His lips and the edge of his teeth graze the point where my neck meets my shoulder.

"Touch yourself," he says again.

I stop in confusion. I'm not sure what he means. My eyes are still squeezed shut. Then his hand pulls mine down between my legs, and I understand. Swallowing, I do what he asks. I'm embarrassed, but I'm restless, too. I want him to be happy. I want me to be happy. And if this is what it takes . . .

Rob's hands close over my breasts, pinching the nipples, kneading. His erection presses into my back as my hips begin to move in time with the strokes of my own fingers. Then his lips close over the tender spot on my neck, and he sucks hard, teeth nipping the skin.

It drives me over, and I'm arching up into his hands, gasping, collapsing back against his chest.

We sit for long minutes. My breathing is almost normal again. I try to sit up, but he holds me still.

"No."

I'm confused.

His mouth is close to my ear. "Just something for the road," he says. "So you'll remember what it feels like. And so you'll have something to think about when you're trying to decide what your answer is going to be."

Then he slides me off his lap, kisses me hard, and walks out the door.

Chapter 15

*B*y stretching out my oversized T-shirt, I can see the blue and purple mark Rob made on my neck and shoulder. An old-fashioned hickey, like the kind I never wanted. Standing here in my parents' bathroom, using the mirror three generations of Bradfords have used for shaving and preening, the mark looks obscene. Only it's not the hickey that's the problem. It's how and why it came to be there that bothers me.

Sighing, I turn out the bathroom light and find my way by memory to the night-dark bedroom. I should be tired. The bus trip was a comedy of errors. First, barely grabbing the Greyhound's tail after work yesterday. Preholiday traffic. Then the bus broke down in the middle of somewhere. I didn't get home until this afternoon. And I'll be leaving again tomorrow. Less than twenty-four hours. Less time than I've been awake. But being a junior copy editor means I have to be in my cubicle— ready, if not willing, to work—on the day after Christmas.

All the same, I'm glad I'm here.

But I can't sleep.

It's Christmas Eve. All over the country, children aren't

sleeping. They're thinking about tomorrow morning and presents and trees and stockings. I wish I were dreaming about toys and sugar plums—although that wouldn't be possible since I've never figured out exactly what a sugar plum is. (I have a hard time believing that kids would dream about candied fruit, even in a poem.) Instead, I'm lying here thinking about Rob and Grandpa and Carol and Melissa and . . . me.

My brain isn't going to let me sleep, so I might as well put something in my mouth. Pulling on a pair of sweats, I tiptoe into the kitchen, fill the teakettle, and put it on to boil. In the nursery rhyme, the poor dog didn't get a bone because the cupboard was bare. But I'd prefer a bare cupboard to Mom and Dad's tea selection. Fruit teas, herbal teas, one empty box that held a decent black tea—all in those little premeasured baggies with strings. No green tea in sight. Not even packaged cocoa mix. I finally close my eyes and pick a tea, hoping the choice won't be too offensive.

I'm just sitting down to have a cup when Kristie appears like some ancestral ghost and scares the crap out of me.

"Hey there," she says, still standing in the doorway. The only light in the kitchen is the one over the stove, so she's in the almost-dark. She's wearing something long and white, and looks like the special effects from a bad TV movie about a family living in a house with things emitting ectoplasm.

I realize I've been pouring honey into my tea for a good fifteen seconds. "Shit," I mutter.

Kristie hesitates. "Should I—?"

"Not you. The honey," I say. "Too much honey. You scared me."

She laughs a little. "It's this robe. Nathan says it makes me look dead."

"That's one way to put it."

"What kind of tea is that?" she asks, leaning over to sniff.

"Chamomile and peppermint, I think."

Kristie wrinkles her nose.

She's doing the close-your-eyes-and-grab method on Mom and Dad's tea cupboard when she asks, "Why didn't you call yesterday? When the bus broke down?"

"I tried. The pay phone at the station was out."

"Couldn't you have used the station's office phone?"

"There were eighty people on the bus," I tell her. "Eighty people who were going to be late for Christmas and who wanted to use the phone. What do you think?"

She shakes the water in the teakettle.

"It's hot enough," I tell her. "It just finished boiling." I'm being rude. About the phone. About the water. But Mom said the same thing. As if it were my fault the bus broke down and the only phone for ten miles was an antique from the last century that someone had hung on the wall for looks.

"You should get a cell phone," Kristie says. "For emergencies like this."

I want to tell her the facts of living in a big city on a salary that isn't enough to keep a gnat going, but her next sentence swipes the words out of my mouth.

"Grandpa was so worried. He stayed up most of last night waiting for you to call."

"Great," I mumble into my tea. So that's why Grandpa looked subdued and tired tonight. I come out here because of an idiotic dream and, in the process, end up being Grandpa's worst enemy by making him worry and not get any sleep.

"Where's Rob?" Kristie asks. "I sort of thought he was coming."

I've just taken a sip of scalding tea, but I manage to get it down without having it lodge in my sinuses. This topic is worse than my irresponsible behavior with fiber optics. "He's having Christmas with his parents."

"You didn't go with him?"

I don't bother to say anything. After all, the answer is obvious.

Kristie sits down across the table from me. She frowns a little, then leans over and pulls the neck of my T-shirt to one side. "Wow," she says, letting the jersey snap back into place. "You'd better hide that tomorrow morning."

"Thanks." I tug the neck of the T-shirt up and over the purple bruise.

"I guess you guys have been a little busy."

"Yeah."

She's teasing, but her words throw me back into that last humiliating moment after Rob stood up to leave.

I think that's the exact moment. The moment when he slid me off his lap, and I realized he was using sex to punish me. Maybe there were other moments that led up to that moment, but the other day, in my apartment, naked on my couch . . . that's the minute—the second—where I can stretch out my hand, put my finger down, and say, *"Here's where it ended."*

Because Rob and I are finished.

He doesn't know it yet, but he will.

Kristie is looking at me cross-eyed—she always does that when she's working something out in her head—so I paste a smile on my face and take another sip of honey and herb water. Her eyes uncross.

"Did you and Rob have a fight?"

This is nastily close to the truth. But I owe it to Rob to tell him first. Maybe not exactly *owe*. It's just one of the principles in Nicci's code of ethics, and it doesn't matter whether I *owe* it to Rob or not. So I smile harder.

"I'm tired," I tell Kristie. It's not a lie, but it counts as a diversionary tactic.

"Oh." She stirs her tea. I haven't seen her put anything in it.

"What about you?" I ask. The aimless stirring is a dead give-away.

"Nothing. Just tired." More obvious diversionary tactics. "I couldn't get the kids to sleep. I even tried reading them *The Night Before Christmas*."

"It's the sugar plums," I say.

Kristie gives me a funny look.

"They're worried about getting candied prunes tomorrow," I explain. "What adults don't realize is that the author of that poem hated little kids, so he stuck in that bit to give children nightmares about getting nothing but prunes for Christmas."

Kristie rolls her eyes. "You are *such* an idiot. Sugar plums are candy."

"Oh, well. Blows that theory, I guess." We erupt into giggles.

"Don't you ever wish we were kids again?" Kristie asks when the giggling stops.

"No."

"Just no? That's it?"

I roll the stiffness out of my shoulders and try to explain. "Being a kid means someone is always telling you what to wear, where to go, what to do . . . yucky."

Kristie's laugh is sad this time. "And you don't think that happens now?"

I start to say, *Of course not*, but I stop before the words are out. "It shouldn't," I say instead. Warm neon lights flash in my head and I hear Ginger yell, *"Come and live in Hong Kong,"* as her taxi pulls away. I take another sip of tea and realize what's missing. And it's not childhood.

"Guts," I say. "If we had courage, it wouldn't happen now."

Kristie is silent for a few minutes, then she pastes the pregnant-lady-needs-her-rest smile on her face. "I'd better try and get a few hours of sleep," she says.

I nod. "Good night."

She's almost to the door when she turns around. "I wish I were a kid again," she says.

Then she's gone.

After she leaves, I go into the living room and turn on the Christmas-tree lights. Lying on the couch, I let the colors take me to crowded, narrow streets half a world away.

I wonder what I would do if I were braver.

At some point I fall into a dreamless sleep.

Christmas morning dawns several hours before the sun comes up. The dawn consists of two nephews jumping up and down on my stomach, and screaming, "Merry Christmas, Aunt Nicci!"

Fortunately, only three hours of sleep out of forty-eight leaves me euphoric rather than grumpy. I maneuver the nephews past the full stockings and into the kitchen.

"Why was you on the couch?" Philip asks.

"'Why *were* you on the couch,'" I say absently. I'm hunting for the bread in the breadbox. Then I remember Mom keeps it in the freezer.

"I wasn't," Philip says.

"No, stupid," Nathan tells his brother. "Aunt Nicci was correcting you. You talk like a baby."

Philip screws up his face.

Holding a frozen loaf of bread in one hand, I point a finger at him before he can let out a scream. "Don't *act* like a baby. The next time Nathan says you talk like a baby, just tell him he wets the bed."

"Do *not!*" Nathan says.

"Do *to!*" Philip responds.

It may not be peace and goodwill toward men, but at least they're not screaming.

I've put on a turtleneck and I'm guarding the brainless wonder of a toaster when Grandpa comes in. "What are they fighting about?" he asks, looking for coffee.

But I can't answer. The problem isn't just a sleepless night worrying about my being stranded while waiting for me to call. Not unless he's having lots of sleepless nights. He's thinner. And his shoulders hunch just a little more sharply than they did at Thanksgiving.

"Merry Christmas, Grandpa," I tell him. "How are you feeling?" I'm hoping I sound cheerful and innocent rather than worried.

"Tired," Grandpa says. "I must not be sleeping very well." Then he smiles. "Merry Christmas to you, too, Nicci."

I try to smile back, but I'm watching him gallop his horse over the horizon, leaving me behind in the snow.

Fear should make a person edgy and alert. It has the opposite effect on me this morning. I'm fighting to stay awake by the time the rest of the clan straggles in for Christmas breakfast. The nephews have finished their toast, and I'm trying to figure out how to take caffeine intravenously when Mom shoos us into the living room for stockings.

Grandpa Bradford has always had a bit of the patriarch in him. On Christmas morning, he likes to sit back in his easy chair and watch. He usually rummages through his stocking and laughs at his presents, but his greatest joy is watching his family. His pride in leaving a mark on the world in the form of progeny is obvious. Except for today. Today he pulls things out of the bright, red stocking in an almost mechanical way. After smiles and thank-yous, he leans back in the chair and closes his eyes. At first I think I'm the only one who notices, then I see Mom watching Grandpa. Across the room, our gazes meet. She smiles, but a thread of communication passes between us.

She's worried, too.

After stockings, the kids and Matt settle down to play with the toys from Santa while Dad fiddles with the stereo. Mom and Kristie are laughing in the kitchen, but I'm still sitting on the couch and watching Grandpa napping in his chair. We both jump when he opens his eyes and looks at me.

"You didn't bring that young man," he says, as if we had been having a conversation that was momentarily interrupted.

"No."

"Humph."

I'm not sure what that means, so I stay silent.

"Are you happy working up there?" he asks. By "up there" he means anywhere east of here.

"It's okay. Pays the rent." I slide along the couch until I'm close to his chair and we're only sitting a few feet apart.

"Lots of jobs pay the rent. What's important is liking what you do."

This is eerily similar to the conversation Kristie and I had last night. To the one Ginger and I had weeks ago. And if I'm not just making stuff up out of nothing, it's similar to what Ethan *didn't* say when he sat in my cubicle and laughed his rainbow laugh. . . .

"Yeah," I say. "I know."

"So are you happy doing what you do?" Grandpa asks again.

I try to ignore his all-seeing eyes and concentrate on the Christmas tree. If I squint, all the colored lights turn into stars.

"No," I say.

And the word surprises even me. I hadn't planned on *really* answering, but sometimes what we plan is lost in the truth.

"Don't waste your time," Grandpa says. But he means, *Don't waste your life.*

I don't like where this conversation is going. And it's full of undertones I don't understand. Or don't *want* to understand.

We sit in silence for a minute, listening to the Christmas carols playing on the stereo. Nathan and Philip are arguing, and Philip has just told Nathan he wets the bed. Matt is confused.

I can't stand it anymore. "Are you okay, Grandpa?" I ask. "You seem tired."

He frowns a little—he doesn't like personal questions—then he smiles. "I'm *old*, Nicci. Old people get tired. It's nothing to worry about."

Too late.

I force a smile and change the subject. "Have you read all those books yet?"

Grandpa relaxes. But after telling me about a few of his latest favorites, he escapes to his room "for a nap." I think about helping Matt referee, then decide one of the benefits of not helping populate the earth is being able to walk away. Or at least walk into the kitchen where the brown-sugar-and-salt smell of ham is leaking from the oven. Mom and Kristie are finishing up the latest pot of coffee and relaxing at the table.

"I wish you didn't have to go so soon," Mom says.

"Me, too," I say, milking the near-empty carafe for the last, precious drops of caffeine. "Maybe next year I can take off an extra day." But the idea of sitting in my cubicle for another twelve months is starting to nauseate me.

After Christmas dinner, Grandpa seems his old self. Worrying turns to sleep-deprived depression as the hands of the clock spin madly toward the time when I have to leave.

Matt brings it up first—he's not a Bradford, so he didn't grow up learning the fine skill of denial. "You'd better get ready to go, Nicci. You wouldn't want to miss the bus. Or maybe you do." And he laughs.

I shoved everything into my backpack after dinner, but I still have to find my shoes. It seems so horribly pointless—leaving my family on Christmas so I can go back to work.

Work for what?

Just find your shoes, Nicci.

When I stand up, Nathan and Philip wrap themselves around my legs and scream, "Don't go, Aunt Nicci," in feigned anguish. Under the best of circumstances, having two small boys hang on my legs would be annoying. Three hours of sleep in three days while worrying about Grandpa is not the best of circumstances. I know they don't really care if I leave or stay, but this is the sort of thing kids do in order to get the entire room to look at them.

It works.

"Oh, how sweet," my mom says.

Grandpa chuckles.

Matt and Dad run for the cameras.

I roll my eyes. "Yeah, sweet. C'mon you guys, let go." I start to walk toward my room. Tears turn to giggles as the nephews hang on. Leg weights aren't what I need right now. I shoot a look of appeal toward Kristie, but she's already on her way.

"Let her go," she says.

And I realize Kristie looks exhausted, too.

Everyone piles into Matt and Kristie's minivan to drive into town and see me off. Everyone hugs me and the nephews try the leg-weights trick again. This time everyone tells them to get up so they won't get dirty. Watching Nathan's and Philip's confusion, I mentally offer incense and gratitude for the twenty years I've lived since I was six. The bus driver yells out the door at the last stragglers, so I climb in and find a window seat. As the bus pulls away, I wave through the glass and try hard to keep from crying.

And I answer the question I asked myself last Thanksgiving. The question about whether or not a person can go back home. The answer is: You never really leave. I know, because it hurts every time I wave goodbye.

"Is that your family?" a voice asks in my ear.

I turn to find an elderly woman sitting in the seat next to me. "Yes," I say. "I have to be back at work tomorrow."

"What a shame. When I was young, workers got a little more time off for the holidays. Of course, no one but the big shots had paid vacations back then."

"I don't have paid vacation time *now*," I tell her. We both laugh, even though it isn't funny.

"It sounds like you need to get a new job," she says. "Of course, that's what I told my girl and look what happened to her."

I have no idea. I wait, but the woman is shaking her head and muttering. Leave it to me to pick the one seat next to the lunatic. I glance around, hoping to find a nice, safe ex-con who's just been paroled, when the woman leans over and looks at me.

"She went off and married the bum. Just like that!" She snaps her fingers six inches too close to my nose. "And then they hightailed it off to the heartland. No living in a run-down steel town for them. Unh-huh. Then what happens when I go to see them for Christmas? She says, 'Mom, you'll have to stay in a motel.' And you know why?"

I shake my head.

"Because *his* family was there. All settled in. They can afford to *fly* where they want. But there's not even a couch for her mother because I had to take the damn bus." Pulling out a tissue, she blows her nose. "So I just turned around and got back on the bus. I think I'd rather spend Christmas alone in my own house than alone in a motel room."

She sniffs, then reaches into her bag and pulls out a little travel pillow. After fluffing it, she tucks it under her chin and goes to sleep. I'm still staring at her when she begins to snore.

Is there anyone in this world who isn't crazy with loneliness?

Chapter 16

he bus pulls in just as the sun is coming up. I don't have time to go back to my apartment. I can't afford the extra hours it will take. As it is, I push through the glass doors of the office building fifteen minutes late. No one seems to notice. The security guard looks like he went to bed smashed and woke up the same way.

I wash my face in the office restroom and apply a liberal amount of deodorant to my underarms. I don't think I'll be raising my hands with a great deal of confidence today. And jeans and a sweater don't exactly fit the guidelines for office apparel. I twitch the sweater into place. It will have to do. From the bleary, post-holiday faces around me, I don't think anyone will bother to bust me.

I'm on my way back to my cubicle when I bump into Melissa.

"I was just coming to see you," she says, not looking up from her shoes. "Would this evening be okay?"

For a minute, I'm confused. Then I realize what she's asking. *Will you come to the clinic with me?*

"You're doing it tonight?" The day after Christmas? It

doesn't fit in with my idea of post-holiday bliss. Or any day, for that matter. But Melissa doesn't look like she was doing a whole lot of celebrating yesterday, so maybe it doesn't make any difference to her.

"Yes," she whispers, still fascinated by her shoes.

Looking at the part in her blond hair, I wonder how the boss celebrated Christmas. If he ever thought about the assistant from the office.

"Did you tell him?" I ask. "About the baby?"

"No," she whispers. I think she's crying. She looks up, and I know she is. I'm wondering if the boss is the stupidest human being on the planet or if he's deliberately ignoring the watery change in his assistant. Maybe he thinks having sex with him is such a religious experience it brings tears to her eyes. Maybe I'm feeling a little sour on the male half of the population lately.

Not true. There's Kevyn. He seems okay in an old-fashioned, chivalric sort of way.

Then I remember the rainbow on my desk.

Ethan.

I'm not going to think about that . . . about him.

"When do you want to go?" I ask, trying to keep my blurry, bleary brain headed in the right direction.

"I . . . I have to be there by six." She swallows back a hiccup. "I'm sorry it's so late in the day. I tried to get an earlier time, but—"

"It's okay," I tell her, and I mean it. She smiles a rainbow smile through the rain of tears.

By six p.m., it's been dark for nearly two hours. And the weather has turned cold. Nasty cold. The tall buildings create a giant wind tunnel, and the generated force takes my breath away as Melissa and I step out of the taxi. She pays, and I huddle into my scarf, waiting. In one way, the cold and darkness are a bless-

ing. Only one tightly bundled protestor has braved the pavement. He or she stays in the shelter of a nearby building, but
manages to shake a sign in our direction.

MURDERER! it reads, and blood red paint drips from the
words.

Melissa's breath catches. I can hear it, even over the wind.
But maybe she's just struggling to breathe in the arctic blast.

The clinic is warm. Warm furnace, warm colors. Yellow
walls, green-blue furniture, golden wood, and old magazines.
It's a general ob/gyn clinic. And it's crowded. The post-
Christmas kind of crowd. Exhausted and frowning as the magi-
cal buildup to Christmas drops them into the anticlimax of the
day after.

"We'll take you in for prepping in a minute," the powdered
matron behind the desk says to Melissa. "Just have a seat." She
starts to turn away, then as an afterthought says, "You can hang
up your coats over there." I do, but Melissa shakes her head.

"I'm cold," she says as she sits down. Her mittened hands
are shaking in her lap. I sit next to her, take her hands between
mine and rub them. She doesn't seem to notice.

"It's going to be okay," I tell her. I'm not sure if it's true or
not, but I know that physically she's going to be all right. Mentally? I haven't the faintest idea. This isn't something I've ever
experienced. It's something I'm fanatically paranoid about expe-
riencing. So fanatical that I'm on the pill, but I've never told
Rob, just so he'll take part of the responsibility for making sure
we always use a condom.

Used a condom.

Past tense.

Melissa snaps into the present. Her eyes focus on her
hands, which I'm still rubbing. She gives me a tiny smile. "I hate
doctors." She pauses. "I hate this."

"I can imagine. It's not fair."

Pulling her hands away, she takes off her mittens and fumbles in her coat pocket. I reach for the clinic's box of tissues and hand it to her.

After blowing her nose, she wads her hands together in her lap and stares across the room for long minutes. I wish I knew what to say. I don't, so I keep my mouth shut. Sometimes people say the stupidest things when they desperately want to wrap the other person in a soothing blanket of sympathy and compassion. Instead they end up infuriating the very person they want to help. Sometimes, silence really *is* golden.

Suddenly, Melissa takes a breath. And I watch her weave the ballsy, gutsy, slightly snobbish assistant out of thin air and put her on. Standing up, she hangs her coat on the rack and stops to check her makeup in the wall mirror before sitting down again and turning to me.

"I never thought he loved me," she says. Her voice is quiet and practical. "I was lonely. And it felt good to have someone want me—want to hold me and touch me." She smiles. It's a rueful, self-deprecating, adult kind of smile. "And it was fun—almost a fantasy. One of those out-in-the-open kind, you know?"

I think about Rob and the sailboat, and I nod. "I know."

"Now I'm paying."

"That's crap," I say. "No one should have to pay for being lonely."

"I am," she says, just as the powdered matron calls her name.

And I'm left in a warm room, surrounded by women. How many of them are Carol or Kristie or Ginger or Ethan's mom? How many of them are paying for being lonely?

What about me?

From the moment the doctor (or nurse) slapped me on the ass and forced me to take that first breath, I've been making decisions. And each decision pulls up a new set of variables and starts me down the path to more decisions, which in turn create additional new variables requiring even more decisions. . . .

If it were possible to stretch back in time and make a tree-diagram of all the decisions in my life . . . it would be a big fucking tree. And sitting here in this room full of women, I realize that it's impossible to avoid *the moment*—that moment when you have to answer the question, "Is this life good enough for the next seventy years?" It's impossible to avoid something affected by a decision made on Tuesday of last week in between getting coffee and going to the bathroom. Avoiding *the moment* might mean what looks like an insignificant decision today ends up stealing ten years of your life tomorrow.

Like deciding on cake or frosting.

I shiver.

"It's a little chilly in here, isn't it?" the powdered matron asks. She's straightening the assortment of children's books and old magazines in the rack next to me.

"Yes."

She pats me on the shoulder. "Your friend will be all right," she says. Then she's gone.

Her words are like a light. Through the fog in my brain, I stumble toward them, leaving my selfish thoughts behind. Stumble toward a prayer to whatever gods are out there that Melissa will be okay.

After what feels like hours, she walks past me toward the coatrack. She's shaking and tiny—but steady enough to make it out the door and into the taxi the matron called for us. We sit in silence as the taxi takes us back to her apartment. I'm worried, but every time I think of something to say, it sounds stupid.

"It's snowing," Melissa says.

And looking out the taxi's window, I see white cotton balls floating down onto the street. "Yes."

The taxi pulls up to her building. I send him off into the snowy night, and we take the elevator to her floor.

"Do you want me to stay with you?" I ask after we're inside her apartment.

"No. Thank you. I'll be okay." She doesn't look okay. And I'm not sure it's such a great idea to leave her alone.

"I'll be fine," she says in response to my frown. "I just need . . . some time. Alone."

I take the T back downtown and just catch the final outbound bus for Watertown. Sitting on the cold seat, I feel the last four days catch me and shake me like an old sock. I lean my forehead against the frosted window and watch the snow drown the city.

Sometime during the night, the storm turns icy. I don't find out until I wake up two hours too late with no electricity and a dead alarm clock. One look out my window, and I can see the city is buried in nearly thirty-six inches of snow and ice. And snow still falling. Thirty-six Christmas-card inches. Other than some kids building a snowman on the sidewalk, the world is wonderfully silent.

I hug myself with the forbidden joy of a snow day. No buses. No work. I want to run down and help the kids with their snowman.

After coffee.

I'm one of the lucky people who has steam heat and a gas stove. While the water boils, I dig out some batteries for my portable CD player. The radio tells me what I already know. The city isn't moving except for emergency personnel. And the poor DJ. Maybe he got caught at the station. If so, I hope they're paying him big bucks in overtime.

I gulp a cup of coffee, then grab a carrot and go outside to help the kids finish their snowman. Most of them are from my street. Some of them I've actually met, and these feel no shame about throwing snowballs at my head. After an hour-long snow-ball fight, I cry peace, and go back inside to warm up in the shower. Hot water. Two days on the road without a bath. I can't get enough of the stuff.

Pink and warm, I concentrate on the sensations of terry cloth on my skin, cotton underwear, sweats, and the soft flannel of an old shirt. Flopping down on my bed, I stare at the ceiling and try to decide how to spend the day.

Because I'm not going to think about anything important. Not one damn thing. Not Rob. Not Melissa. Not Grandpa . . . And I'm worrying about how tired Grandpa looked the day be-fore yesterday.

No, no, no, no. I need some free time from all this. I need a break from my own melancholy morbidity. There's that fantasy jigsaw puzzle Kristie gave me. The perfect cubicle or the city being swamped in jungle or something like that.

I turn up the radio. I don't know the song, but I try to sing it, try to dance to the arcane beat of five years ago. Don't these songs ever die? The neighbor beneath me beats on his ceiling with a broom handle.

So much for the holiday spirit.

I twirl around and thump my heel on the floor one last time. A mild expression of defiance.

The neighbor thumps back.

But I'm frozen.

My twirling has landed me in front of the snow globe Rob gave me right after the day we went sailing. It's a sailboat on a mirrored sea. If you turn the globe upside down and shake it, the boat rocks while glitter flakes swirl and fall. And if you want music, there's a windup music box in the wooden base that plays one of those familiar tunes no one can name.

Just something for the road. So you'll remember what it feels like. And so you'll have something to think about when you're trying to decide what your answer is going to be.

It's no use. I can play in the snow, take a shower, daydream, do a puzzle, read all the books in the goddamn library, but nothing is going to change. I'm still going to have to deal with the decisions sitting in my path. Only then will I be able to get on with it.

Whatever "it" is.

The computer is dead without electricity, so I pull out a notebook and three pens. A red one for cons. A blue one for pros. And a green one for doodling. I'm ready to decide how and when to tell Rob. What to do about Grandpa. And do I start looking for another job? What if I can't find one? How will I pay the rent? Do I want to stay here? And then there's Hong Kong and Ginger, but that's so far away and the money isn't there and oh, my God—

—I can't do this.

I shove the notebook and pens across the table, and drop my head onto my arms.

The phone rings.

Obviously, the telephone lines are made of sturdier stuff than the electrical ones.

"Hi, beautiful," Rob says. "Enjoying your day off?"

"Of course." The coffee in my stomach begins to churn. I need more time. More time to figure out what to say.

"Want me to come over?" he asks.

I hedge. "Aren't you supposed to stay off the road?"

"That's for wimps," he teases, "not men like me. How about it?"

Like nothing happened last week. Like he didn't strip me naked and make me touch myself just to punish me for needing more time.

"You'd better not," I say out loud.

He's quiet for a moment, then says, "I want to talk to you."

I'm picking at one of the pages in the notebook. Ripping off the corners, wadding the pieces into little balls, ripping off more paper.

"What about?" I ask.

He's silent, then he laughs. "Playing hard to get? I just want to be there when you say 'yes.'"

My hand crumples the entire sheet. Then the next. I have to tell him now. Here. On the phone. Because he's expecting me to walk down his path for the next seventy years.

"Rob—"

"Yes, Mrs. Cole?" he asks, the teasing note back.

I take a deep breath. It's hard—so hard—to get the words out.

"I-I'm sorry. I can't," I say.

Something dark breaks free from my chest, like an ice sheet slipping away from Antarctica.

"Please understand," I continue into the silence. "I don't think . . . it's right. We're not right."

"That's crap, Nicci," he says. His voice sounds all stretched and thin. I desperately wish this weren't happening over the phone, but there wasn't any way to avoid it. And I wish I could explain.

"You wear Italian shoes," I say at last, falling back on what Grandpa tried to tell me at Thanksgiving. "I wear work boots."

"What do shoes have to do with anything? That's the stupidest damn thing . . ." He trails off. "Why shoes?"

I'm not sure how to answer his question. I can be nice—and vague—or I can be honest. I go with honest.

"Other than sex," I say, "what have we got in common?"

He's quiet. Digesting. "What else do we need?" he asks. He doesn't mean he thinks we don't need anything more than sex, he's asking what I think we need.

This is easy.

"Talking," I say immediately.

"What?"

"We don't talk."

"Bullshit. We talk all the time." He's starting to get angry.

"No. We talk like two strangers who've just met."

I want him to understand. But how can I put words—labels—onto something that is so nebulous, so intangible? How can I describe the instant connection, the ability to reach each other, the meshing of two minds even when the bodies have been apart? How can I describe what I have with Ginger and my grandpa?

What I have with Ethan.

An entirely inappropriate thought, given the circumstances.

Rob is quietly breathing into the phone. "You're not making any sense," he says after three breaths. "I think you're just scared of changing things. You shouldn't be. We'll talk about this later."

"It won't make any difference," I start to say, but he's already hung up.

I drop down onto the futon and stare at the phone.

I feel like crying. Not because I'm essentially breaking up with Rob, but because I hurt him.

But marriage?

I'm not even sure I love the guy. And I can hardly count the offhand *"You must know I love you"* that he tossed out when he proposed. He's never said the words for real.

Maybe I'm the one who's screwed up. I don't even know what I'm looking for. Just some nebulous bullshit about communication skills. And yet . . .

It's important bullshit.

Hauling myself up out of the futon, I put some water on to boil for tea. As I sip the jasmine brew, I try and figure out what

I'm going to do now. Maybe I should try and call Rob back, but I don't have anything to add to what I've already said. And I don't know how to say it differently. I don't know how to make him stop hurting.

If he's hurting. He sounded more angry than hurt on the phone, but maybe that's just his defense against rejection.

I'm starting to sound like my high school counselor.

Outside the window, snow is still falling. When I look down, I can't see any of the tracks the kids and I made this morning. The snow angels and piles of reserve snowball ammunition are buried. Even the snowman is shorter than he was a few hours ago. The magic of the day is buried as well. I can't get it back.

But, strange as it sounds, I feel freer, lighter, happier than I've felt in months. All the questions about my relationship with Rob have disappeared along with the relationship. The agony I'm going through right now has nothing to do with me.

It's guilt. (*And excuses.*)

Guilt because I didn't say anything sooner. (*But how was I to know he'd want something more than bundt cake?*)

Guilt because of the way I handled things on the phone. (*Oh, that's rich. What was I supposed to do? Wait for him to come and pull my undies down again?*)

Guilt because I was knowingly involved in a sex-for-sex's-sake affair. (*That's just the old-time religion talking.*)

Guilt because I might just have been using Rob—Rob, who obviously had something deeper and more spiritual in mind than simple fondling. (*Oh, yeah. Right. And he was just falling over himself talking about his feelings.*)

Guilt because in my heart of hearts I know that I might have said yes to Rob's proposal if it wasn't for Ginger. And Melissa. Not to mention Carol and Bill. And even Kristie. (*No excuse.*)

I don't want to end up married just because I'm scared of being alone. I shouldn't have to pay with my life.

I'm descending into melodrama. I don't actually think it will help, but I pick up the phone to call Carol or Kristie or someone. Just to talk. But the phone lines have gone the way of their electrical brethren. The phone is dead. As Dickens would have put it, "Dead as a doornail."

I half expect Rob to try and drive over, so when someone knocks on my door just as I'm about to go to bed, I steel myself for a long night of hashing it out. But it's not Rob.

It's Melissa.

Her nose is red, and melting snow drips from the ends of her hair. "Ooo. It's so *warm* in here," she says, holding her hands in front of the radiator.

"Are you crazy?" I ask her. "Did you walk all the way over here?"

"From the end of the green line—" she begins.

"And after last night," I interrupt. "What were you thinking?"

She turns around. Her smile is angelic. "I had to talk to him," she says, as if this explains what she's doing in my apartment.

"You mean . . ." I wave a hand in the general direction of her belly.

"Yeah. It took me *forever* to walk to his place, but I couldn't sit in my apartment a minute more knowing . . ." She stops to blow her nose. I hope it's from the cold and not from crying over the no-good bastard. "I couldn't stand it that I went through all that . . . last night," she says while wadding the tissue. "And that he would get off. Totally. Be smiling at me the next time I'm at work. Touching me. No way."

"So you froze your butt off—"

"—to go and tell him." Taking off her coat, she sits down on the couch.

I shake off the worries and decisions that have been hovering over me like a plague of locusts all afternoon, and sit down beside her.

"Last night I decided I would tell him," she says. "First thing this morning. Then this." She waves a hand toward the window, toward the snow. "I was just . . ."

"Fuming?" I ask, supplying a word from Grandpa's vocabulary.

Melissa thinks for a moment. "Yeah. Fuming. So I walked to his house—do you know he lives in a mansion thing? With a yard?"

I shake my head.

"It makes you wonder," she continues. "I mean, I do all the work in that office and I'm lucky to pay my rent. What's he got that I haven't . . . ?" She trails off. We both look down into our laps, then grin at each other. "Oh, yeah," she says. "I forgot what got me into this mess in the first place."

We giggle. It's almost like being in the bunk bed with Ginger, crucifying dorm mothers and the nasty physics teacher.

Melissa points to my drinking cup, which is still sitting on the coffee table. "What's that?"

"Jasmine tea."

"What an odd cup."

"A friend from Hong Kong gave it to me for Christmas a long time ago." I pour some fresh tea from the pot and hand the cup to her. "Try it."

She sips and I watch peace settle over her face. If I didn't know better, I'd say jasmine tea has healing properties. Of the mental kind.

"So what happened?" I ask, after she's downed the tea.

"He answered the door and his face got all red. Like this." She puffs out her cheeks and holds her breath until her face turns pink. Letting the air out, she laughs. "And when I told him, he went purple. 'Don't bother coming back to work,' he says."

I can feel my jaw hit my chest. "Just like that?"

"Uh-huh. Oh, there was some other stuff. Threats. 'Don't you even *think* I'll pay you anything.' Stuff like that."

"Wow!" I stare at her. "What a—"

"—no-good, stinking, son of a bitch. I know." She starts to laugh. "But you know what? I'm happy. Jobless, but happy."

Powerless. That's the word that comes to my mind. I understand the happy part. She's happy because she's been honest with herself. Ended the lie she's been living for the last few weeks. I know exactly how she feels. It's how I felt when I hung up the phone this afternoon. But a nagging sense of justice makes *me* unhappy that the boss is "getting away with it." The only suffering he'll feel is the suffering of interviewing applicants for Melissa's job.

In *Drunken Master*, Jackie gets even with—count 'em—four all-around worthless human beings. A rich brat who beats up a poor man. A local rip-off artist. A nasty individual who carries a big stick and uses it on Jackie's master. And finally, the assassin who humiliates Jackie partway through the movie, then makes the mistake of trying to murder Jackie's father, resulting in the famous drunken-style match at the end of the movie. So all the bad guys get thumped. Much to the great satisfaction of the audience, which is made up of people who wish all the bad guys got thumped in real life. Why is it that people get even only in movies?

"What are you going to do?" I ask because I don't know what else to say.

"Get a new job, I guess." She grins at the understatement. "I did tell him that he'd better give me a good reference. Or else I'd fuck him in a different way."

I stare at her. "You did? You did not."

"Did to." She laughs. "He went all red and purple at once. Even a hint of a scandal and *poof!* his reputation is shot. I don't even *have* a reputation, so I've got nothing to lose. And he knows it."

Maybe people really do get even in real life. Sometimes.

I fall back on life's petty details. "You'd better stay here to-night. I have some peanut butter and jelly if you're hungry. The milk might even be good." Frozen, maybe. I put all my refriger-ated stuff on the fire escape this morning. Why let food rot in a warm fridge?

Melissa wolfs two sandwiches while she waits for the milk to thaw. She helps me set up the futon, then promptly falls asleep. Lying in bed, listening to her snore, I go back to won-dering about my own life.

Sometime during the night, the electricity comes back on.

Melissa shakes me awake long before I'm ready to wake up. "Nicci! The plows have been through."

Which means the buses will get through.

Which means I have to go to work today.

Groaning, I drag myself up into a sitting position.

"Thank you," Melissa is saying. She's already wearing her coat and she's pulling on her mittens.

"You're going?" I ask. A stupid question, but I haven't had any coffee yet and I'm not exactly a debate-team star even with a full pot under my belt.

"Yes. I've got a new life to figure out," she says. She's smiling, but she's scared, too. It's in her eyes and in the way her lips tremble. "Thank you for being there last night. And the night before that."

I nod. There's not much to say. "Call me," I finally tell her. "Let me know what happens."

"Okay."

And she's gone.

I've seen a lot of people walk out of my life the last few weeks. Some more permanently than others. I'm not sure I like it. But I don't think I have a choice.

The glittering snow of yesterday has been replaced with brown plow slush. The sidewalks are a mess, since half the store owners and building managers haven't bothered to clean their respective bits and pieces of the public domain. Everyone is grouchy. And cold. And going to work when they'd rather be tucked up warm in bed. But then, maybe I'm projecting.

Another concept well loved by my high school counselor.

The security guard at my office building cheerfully wishes me a Happy New Year when I sign in. I look at him, trying to figure out if he's the real guard, an escapee from an asylum, an alien, or just plain sarcastic.

He smiles.

I smile.

"Yeah. Happy New Year to you, too," I say. And maybe just saying the word "happy" makes a person feel better, because things are looking . . . "merry and bright," as the song puts it. I have a lot of things happening right now, but I'm doing okay, right? So why should I complain?

Well, for one, someone in personnel must have hired a Kindergarten Dropout to write copy. And KD has written all the copy in my in-box.

For seconds, the ever-helpful Carol brings Rob to my cubicle before I've had my ten o' clock cup of coffee.

"He was wandering the hall looking for you," she says. "The security guard almost threw him out." She raises her eyebrows in a waggle. *You've been a busy girl!* the waggle says.

I ignore her and her waggle, and look at Rob.

"We need to figure out what your problem is," he says.

This isn't a good beginning.

Carol looks up at him, then over at me. She leaves without saying a word. Smart woman. I want to leave without saying a word, too.

And on the way out, I want to hit Rob.

Sometimes, confidence is sexy and appealing. Sometimes it's annoying. And sometimes it's just plain rude. Because confidence—supreme confidence—can lead a person down the garden path of believing that he (or she) has all the answers. All that's left is for the rest of us ordinary mortals to fall in and march to the beat of Mr. Supremely Confident's drum. This only works if Mr. SC is a drill sergeant.

Rob is not a drill sergeant.

"I have a problem?" I ask in a sticky voice that hints that my problem is a little over six feet and blocking the door to my cubicle.

He shoves the papers and dictionary off my chair and sits down. Unfortunately, those papers were important. Now one of them is under his shoe.

"We need to talk," he says, trying again. "Why don't you want to get married?"

I agree that we need to talk. He deserves an answer given in person rather than on the phone. But being told I have a problem, and seeing that paper under his shoe . . . well, I'm pissed off. At him. So I'm not as delicate as I would be in normal circumstances. If this is anywhere close to normal.

"I don't love you," I say. I can't be more blunt than that.

"Love is just an emotion," he says. "We're good together. Lots of people don't have that much."

"So why did they get married?"

He shrugs. "How would I know? Besides, it's not a problem for us."

I'm not sure about that, but I drop it. "We don't talk," I say instead.

"You said that yesterday." He sounds exasperated. "I have no idea what that means. I don't think *you* even know what it means. We talk all the time. We're talking right now. What's your next objection?"

"What are you trying to do?" I ask, careful to keep my voice from going up an octave or two. "Rent me a sailboat?"

The look on Rob's face tells me something I should have figured out a long time ago. Something I probably *would* have figured out if it hadn't been for the nympho thing. Rob's a great guy. Kind, sexy, pleasant, outgoing . . . as long as he gets his way. When he doesn't get his way, he twists the situation until his way pops out or somebody feels guilty. All this time, I've let myself get pulled along because it felt good when he touched me.

When he touched me, I wasn't lonely anymore.

"Are you making fun of me?" Rob asks.

Now he's manipulating me. Or trying to.

"You're not taking me seriously," I tell him. "You can't just dismiss everything I say."

"I'm *disagreeing* with you, not dismissing you." His face is smug as he leans back in the chair.

To be fair, he may have a point. On the other hand, I don't want to marry him. That should count for something. So I do some manipulating of my own.

"What about dogs?" I ask. "I don't like dogs."

He blinks. "You'd like a Lab."

"Kids?" I did tell him I was allergic to kids.

"You'll come around," he says, smiling the confident smile.

"I want to live in the interior of China."

"Nobody wants to live in the interior of China."

"Kung Fu movies?" I ask.

He links his hands behind his head. "Just a phase."

I pounce. "Where am I?"

"What?"

"Think about what you just said. What I just said. In your mind, I don't exist. I'm just an extension of what you want."

His eyes narrow. "Don't pull that metaphysical crap with me."

"What's metaphysical about the fact that what I want in life can be thrown out like yesterday's trash?" I'm trying to keep my temper. And I'm trying to keep from being the office entertainment for the day by keeping my voice low.

Rob doesn't bother. He's standing up, leaning on my desk, towering over me. Intimidating me. Too bad for him, I don't intimidate easily.

"This has something to do with that friend of yours, doesn't it?" he asks, loud enough to be heard four cubicles down. "The one from high school. The one who went to Hong Kong." He spits out the words as if being in Hong Kong led to a life of coercing people into not knowing what's good for them.

As if I don't have a brain to think with.

I want to stand up and glare at him—an eye for an eye—but that would look like his intimidation techniques were working, so I stay in my chair.

The phone rings.

"Don't get that," Rob says.

"It's my office," I say, and I pick up the phone.

"Nicci," Mom says in my ear. "I'm sorry to call you at work, dear."

This is a bad sign. Mom never calls me at work. In her mind, my office is perched on the top of a lonely, ivory tower. The entrance is a pair of pearly gates, and the phone lines are solid gold—all guarded by Saint Peter himself.

"It's okay," I tell her. "What's up?"

"You can't live in the past," Rob says to me, continuing our conversation as if I weren't on the phone. "You need to make friends here. In the present."

"Is that Rob?" Mom asks.

"Yes," I say to her.

Rob smiles. "You know it's true," he says, assuming the "yes" was for him.

"That's good," Mom says. "You'll have someone there with you."

My heartbeat kicks up a notch, and a warning siren begins wailing in my head. Not only does Mom think my workplace is holy, she also believes people should stick together when bad things happen.

I ignore Rob's smile. "What's going on?" I ask her.

"It's Grandpa, honey. We took him to the hospital yesterday. I tried to reach you at home—"

"My phone is out," I interrupt. "What's wrong?"

"The doctor isn't sure, she thinks—"

"I'll introduce you to the wives of some of my friends," Rob says, loud enough to drown Mom's voice. "They're great people. You'll like them. It might make you more comfortable—"

"*Shut up!*" My shout rockets throughout the entire office floor.

The office noise around us grinds to a stop.

Rob's face goes white. His lips wad up into a mean knot.

"Honey?" Mom asks, her voice quivering.

I swivel my chair around, turning my back on Rob. "Not you, Mom. What did the doctor say?"

"He may not . . . Grandpa may not have . . . very long."

"Fuck me," I say. And I don't care if Mom hears me. My chest is collapsing. "Fuck me. I'll be right there, okay? As soon as I can find a bus or a car or something. I'll be there."

"The doctor thinks he may have—" Mom starts to say, but Rob is swinging my chair around.

"Don't turn away from me," he says, his gray eyes steel balls above the wadded-up mouth. "This is important."

The phone hums in my ear. I don't know if Mom hung up or if Rob disconnected me. I don't care. Pushing Rob away, I stand up and pull on my coat.

"You can't just walk away," he says.

"I'm not marrying you," I tell him as I pick up my bag. "Live with it."

He grabs my arm.

"Let go of me."

Something in my tone tells him this is for real. He lets go of my arm, but continues to block the way out. "We have to talk."

I'm trying to figure out the logistics of slipping around him versus simply kneeing him in the groin when the security guard shows up.

"Is everything all right?" he asks, looking from Rob's face to mine.

"I want to leave," I tell him. And I've never said anything more true in my entire life.

"Step aside, sir," the security guard says to Rob.

Rob gives me a long, hard look. Then he moves out of my way.

I walk past him.

Each foot to the elevators is agony. I don't know what to do. I'm supposed to be good in a crisis. Able to lift the car off the accident victim and dial 911. The explanatory notes on the personality test must have meant somebody else's crisis, because I can't even make myself breathe.

I finally reach the elevators. Standing in front of the panel, I push the red arrow button over and over until a pair of doors swish open.

Just behind the doors is the boss. He's leaning one shoulder against the polished, steel wall, but he straightens up when I step into the elevator.

"I hear you've been seeing one of our clients," he says before the doors close all the way.

Holding on to the railing for support, I mumble something.

"I've been meaning to talk to you about this," he continues. "If you terminate the relationship, I won't take it to the board. Dating a client is against company policy. I'm sure you understand."

The doors open onto the lobby.

"I understand that it's illegal to fuck your office assistant," I say. "That didn't stop you from doing it."

Stepping out of the elevator, I cross the lobby and leave forever through the giant glass doors.

Even though it's illogical, I go through life as if the people I love were planning on living forever. As if they had a choice. I skip along my merry way, confident that when I need them, they'll be there. Most people do this. Unless forced to by illness or necessity, the human being shies away from living with the constant reminder of death. Denial and religious fervor are the usual methods. Even people in war zones adjust. I'm not sure if it's naivete or self-delusion.

I stumble along the street. It takes a city block for me to realize that I should have called the rental car places and other possibilities from my office. But I wanted to get away from Rob. Now I'm cold and phoneless.

I smell coffee and realize I'm standing in front of Ethan's place. Okay, Ethan's uncle's shop. Pulling open the door, I'm surrounded by warmth and coffee scent. I look around. Ethan's uncle sees me, rubs his hands together and heads in my direction. Ignoring him, I push through the doors that lead to the stockroom.

The staircase is still at the back. I'm not sure why that's surprising. It takes the last of my energy to climb the steps and knock on Ethan's door. From below, I hear the uncle call my name. No one answers the door. Exhausted, I lean my back against it and slide down to sit on the steps.

"Ms. Bradford?" the uncle says from the stockroom downstairs. "Are you looking for something?" He thinks I'm still in the stockroom.

The lock above my head jiggles.

"Ms. Bradford?" Uncle calls again.

"Nicci?" This time, it's Ethan.

I try to stand up, but I can't make my legs work. Ethan reaches down and helps me. His uncle appears at the bottom of the stairs.

"Is everything all right?" he asks.

"Fine," Ethan says. "Just some detail work on the account."

"Oh, good, good." He gives me a curious glance, then leaves.

"Nicci!" Ethan gives me a shake. I try to focus on his face, but he's blurry.

Pulling me into his apartment, he kicks the door shut and helps me to the couch. "Sit here. I'll make some tea."

I'm hoping for jasmine, but it's black tea with lots of sugar.

"Drink this first," he says. "Then you can have the jasmine."

He thinks I'm in shock. Maybe I am. I take a sip of the sugar with tea and shudder.

"This is awful."

"Blame my grandmother," he says. Putting a finger under the mug, he nudges it up to my mouth, urging me to drink it down. "She thought sugar-tea cured everything."

His grandmother.

Ah, hell. Grandpa. I start to shake.

Ethan takes the cup away before I drop it and puts his arms around me.

I'm not a touchy-feely person. During emotional moments, I'm practically allergic to the feel of another person's skin. But this is different.

And surrounded by Ethan's arms, I realize I didn't come here for a phone. I came for a harbor.

Chapter **18**

I n *Fearless Hyena*, Jackie does everything he can to get out of work or training. He gambles. He pretends to train hard while goofing off. He disguises himself so he can make money fighting, which his grandfather has forbidden him to do. Then his grandfather is killed. Overnight, Jackie goes from shiftless to workaholic—training so hard, his new master has to slow him down to keep him from killing himself. When someone you love is in pain or dying or dead, all the things that seemed so important yesterday become insignificant.

The shaking has nearly stopped when Ethan gives me a cup of jasmine tea. I try to let the scent of *sambac* guide me to a calmer place, but I'm too raw inside to locate pleasant memories.

Ethan must understand, because he doesn't say anything. He just slides a phone book and an ancient, olive green phone in my direction.

"Here," he says. "A rental car is probably the fastest way. Unless you can afford airfare." He's focusing on the little details.

Helping *me* focus on the little details.

I nod and make a few calls. In movies, the hero or heroine

always says things like "money is no object." For the working stiff—especially the working stiff who's just told her boss some home truths in the elevator—the available credit limit on her card makes calling around for the best price the *only* option. A call to a travel agent tells me flying is out of the question. I finally find a Flintstones-style car for rent. I may have to put my feet down and run to help it get over the mountains, but it will do the job.

If I hurry, I can catch the bus and have enough time to go home and pack a bag before picking up the car. Now if I can just find my coat.

"You're still wearing it," Ethan says.

Looking down, I see he's right. "Thank you," I say.

I don't just mean for telling me where to find my clothing. But for being everything that he is and not being what he isn't. I want to stay here, but I have to go. Pushing up from the lumpy couch, I look down into his face. I can taste the worry he's feeling. It's a mixture of sweet concern and bitter memories. Like a leftover Halloween Sweet-Tart. I swallow the tears in my throat, and the frown line over his nose cuts deeper into his forehead.

"Don't take this the wrong way," he says, "but do you want me to go with you back to your place? Or to the rental?"

"I'll be all right," I say.

He's not offering to go across the Rust Belt with me, but I know he would if I asked. I'm tempted, but I'm not going to ask. I feel stupid enough already for coming here in the first place.

"Don't," he says. "Sometimes people need each other."

There's no point in explaining that he's not just a generic person, not just a fragment of the larger group "people." I came here because he's a magnet and I'm an iron filing. I can't seem to stay away.

"I'd better go," I say instead.

He nods, and walks me to the door. For a long time, we stand facing each other, not knowing what to say. He reaches out and wraps the dangling ends of my scarf around my neck.

"It's cold out there," he says.

"Yes."

Then he holds out his hand. A twenty-dollar bill sticks out between his fingers. "Take it," he says.

It's my turn to frown. "No."

Money is a complicated thing. We hand money to cashiers and think nothing of it, but giving money to each other is awkward and painful. Maybe it's pride, but I don't want money from him. Ever.

"It's for a taxi," he says. "The car rental is out by the airport. Just ditch the pride and get to your grandfather four hours sooner."

I ignore the money and concentrate on his face. The lines around his eyes are deeper. He's reliving his grandmother's death. In some way, he's making up for an event in the past. I'm not sure—

He flinches and his eyes close. "My grandmother died in the hospital. Alone. I was stuck in traffic. I left my car in the middle of the street and ran, but I was too late." He opens his eyes and looks at me. "Just fifteen lousy minutes. I wanted to tell her that I would miss her."

The sour-sweet worry is flavored with old despair. Eighteen, with his parents split up, and the last stable person in his life . . . This is his way of telling his grandmother that he misses her. Eight years too late.

Wrapping my fingers around his hand, I take the money. I know it's his last twenty. And he's giving it to me. It doesn't matter if I pay it back next week because he has to eat this week.

"Don't worry," he says. "I can always sneak downstairs and

eat packets of sugar and creamer." It's a joke. But I have to clear my throat before I can speak.

"Thank you."

I drive all night. Fear and familiar songs on the radio keep me awake. I drive too fast. Sometimes I slow down for the curves. Bits and patches of snow and ice ripple under the little car's tires. It's a good thing most of the road is clear.

The sun is coming up when I reach the brown fields. Blue-purple snow lines the dips between the contour farming waves, and here and there a cloud of birds rises up from feasting on the leftover corn. I pass the turnoff to my parents' house and go on into town and to the hospital. Just in case. Ethan has bet twenty dollars on my seeing Grandpa. I wouldn't want it to go to waste.

I'm clinging to the hope that my mother was exaggerating. Sometimes she says things are "horrible, awful," but life has merely tossed a mild curve ball—something like a cockroach infestation. On the other hand, sometimes she says things are only "bad," but this time life has thrown a hardball. Like a tornado picking up the house (and the cockroaches) and dropping it (and them) fifteen miles later.

I'm hoping that she was exaggerating, but I don't have much hope.

The hospital is white. They've tried to friendly it up with blue carpet and pastel watercolor paintings, but it's still white. All hospitals are white and smell like bleach. And fear. And death. The sleepy receptionist gives me the once-over.

"Visiting hours aren't until eight," he says. "You're welcome to wait—"

"I've just driven all night," I tell him. "I'm afraid my grandpa is dying. I have to see him."

His eyebrows pull together. "And your grandpa is . . . ?"

"Noah Bradford."

"Oh!" Suddenly the receptionist is all smiles. "You must be little Nicole."

"Yeah. Little Nicole." I'm trying my best to not be sarcastic, but I don't have time for the forty begats right now.

"Room four-oh-one," he says. "Take the elevator to the fourth floor and turn left."

The nurses at the station on the fourth floor give me funny looks, but they don't stop me. Grandpa has his own room. It's dim, but I can see Kristie asleep in the chair by his bed. Grandpa wakes up when I open the door.

His smile is worth the all-night drive and borrowing of Ethan's twenty dollars.

"Nicci," he says, so quiet it's not much more than a whisper.

"Hi, Grandpa." I sit on the edge of the bed. He reaches for my hand, and we hold on to each other.

Hospital beds distort space, mass, and proportion. Lying here on the white sheets, in the raised metal bed, my grandpa has become a short, flat, weightless man. Smaller than he's ever been in real life. The *plump* has gone out of him. As if he were a feather pillow that's lost most of its feathers.

We sit together, saying nothing, holding hands.

We both know he's dying.

"I want you to do something for me," Grandpa says. I'm not sure if he's whispering because he's weak or so he won't wake Kristie.

I nod.

"Beside my bed at home, there's a book." He smiles and pauses for a breath. "I want to know how things turn out. Can you get it for me? Read it to me?"

I don't know if Grandpa really wants to know the book's ending or if he just wants us to have something to do while we sit around waiting for him to die. It doesn't matter.

"I'll go right now," I say.

"Good girl." He squeezes my hand. Then he turns his head on the pillow and closes his eyes.

I tiptoe out of the room and shut the door. Leaning against it, I fight the pain in my chest. This isn't the time to collapse. There isn't anyone to hold the tiller. Just me. And I have to be able to hold Grandpa's tiller, too.

I'm almost back to the elevator when someone at the nurse's station calls to me.

"Are you related to Noah Bradford?"

Turning around, I see a woman who wears the mantle of doctoral authority. "I'm his granddaughter," I tell her.

"Then your family has updated you on his condition?"

"No. I've been driving all night. I just got here."

"Oh," she says, drawing out the sound. "You're the one who lives out east."

"I guess."

She starts to smile, then lets it drop. "I'm afraid it's cancer. The pancreas. Very advanced." Halting, she waits for me to draw my own conclusions. But I already know he's dying.

"How long?" I ask.

"I can't be certain, of course. Three, maybe four days."

Not that long. I can feel the short amount of time in Grandpa's fingers. "Thank you for telling me," I say out loud. And I am grateful. A lot of doctors keep information like this from the family, preferring to give them hope until the very end. Or worse, assume that because the patient is old, he or she is already half dead, so why not finish the job by telling everyone that the end is near?

Driving out to the house, I cry for the first time.

"So, how have you been?" Kristie asks. We're sitting in the hospital cafeteria. The food is better than the Vend-o-Crap machine at the office, but just barely. I have a mouthful of scrambled eggs, so I have to chew before I can answer.

"I've been gone three days," I say.

After driving out to the house, I only stayed long enough to dump my things and pick up Grandpa's book. Dad and Mom were pretending to eat breakfast. Dad's face was white and pinched with exhaustion as he leaned over his corn flakes. *Is* white and pinched. It's his father in the hospital bed. But at least Dad can put his trust in the afterlife, can look forward to seeing Grandpa in some nebulous place called Heaven. For me, Grandpa will simply cease to exist.

Mom and Dad drove with me back to the hospital. Grandpa was sleeping—the doctor is giving him medication for the pain—so I set the book where he would see it when he woke up, and followed Kristie down here to the cafeteria.

"I know it's only been three days," Kristie says. "I need something to talk about. How have you been?"

I force myself to swallow another bite of rubber eggs and answer her question. "A security guard had to rescue me from Rob, and I told my boss where to shove it in the elevator."

Kristie barely avoids having a mouthful of coffee go up her nose.

"You *what?*" she manages.

I explain the details. Her eyebrows pull together in a frown.

"Your boss deserved that," she says after thinking it over for a bit. "But Rob? You were such a cute couple. And he's so perfect. Money, his own business, a car he can actually drive. I really thought you might settle down with Rob."

"I don't *want* to settle," I say. I might as well have said *"I don't want to be like you."* Because Matt has his own business and could drive for NASCAR if he wanted.

Kristie turns a shade of pink and presses her lips together.

And I remember her exhausted face at Christmas, the sad question about a return to childish things.

"I'm sorry," I say. "I'm tired and I'm being rude."

"But you meant it." It's part statement, part question.

"We don't all have to want the same thing," I say instead of answering the part question. "You've always wanted marriage and kids and the house in the suburbs. I haven't. Big deal." But this isn't true. At one point, Kristie wanted to be a pop star with, as she put it, "gobs of cash and a new guy every week." I guess it appealed to her during the five minutes of rebellion she experienced at thirteen. Well, maybe longer than five minutes. The agony of pretending to be an audience while she danced around singing into a hairbrush seemed to go on for years.

"I was pregnant when I married Matt."

The family movie in my head has a meltdown. The reel spins out of control, 16 mm film flapping in the breeze.

I start counting months, hit a year, and Nathan's still unborn.

Kristie's watching me. She laughs, but it isn't a happy sound. "Not with Nathan. I lost the baby. Just a few months after we got married."

My mouth opens and closes several times. "You never said—"

"I didn't tell anyone."

"But Mom—?" If anyone could guess it would be Mom.

"If she figured it out, she didn't say anything," Kristie answers before my question is all the way out.

Okay. These aren't the sorts of confessions I expect from my family. Someone else's family, maybe. But not from Kristie the saint. She and Matt *did* decide to get married after an obscenely short time, but she was all smiles and joy, so I figured it was love at first sight. Except for the day she moved her things into Matt's apartment and threw out all her stuff from the Philippines. Stuff now sitting in my apartment. At the time, I thought it was disgust with anything from her old—or as she called it, *"crappier"*—life. Now I'm not so sure.

"Is this what you wanted?" I ask her. Did she want the house, the two-point-four, the minivan, that hardware store man? It's not an appropriate question. I realize this when her eyebrows hit the ceiling. I duck down and get busy buttering my toast.

I keep forgetting about my mouth.

Kristie has always been the model of angelic goodness and perfection—despite the little slip into . . . how did that Sunday School teacher put it? *"Fornication. Without God's blessing in the form of marriage, relations between a man and a woman are nothing but fornication."* And she spit out the word "fornication," turning four syllables into two.

I'm different from Kristie because I always blurt out the obvious question. I was six when I heard the Sunday School teacher's lesson on fornication. We were visiting a church that gave money to "help support mission work overseas." After absorbing the lesson, I raised my hand and said my dad and I were fornicating. It took three other teachers and the Sunday School superintendent to calm the teacher down and ask me what I meant. I carefully explained that I was related to my dad, but since we weren't married, we must be fornicating. Things got sorted out eventually, but the church stopped sending my parents money. And despite Kristie's stern, semi-adult lecture on keeping my mouth shut, the best I've managed to do is keep a foot in it. When it comes to conversational quagmires, sometimes I keep on the tufts of grass, sometimes I sink up to my knees. This time, I'm over my head.

"I'm sorry," I tell her. "You don't have to answer that."

"You surprised me, that's all," Kristie says. She pushes her cafeteria tray to one side.

"Having someone you love die . . . it really changes your perspective, doesn't it?" she says just as I finish my toast.

"He's not dead yet."

"I know, but we both know—"

"Yeah." I know it, but I'm not ready to talk about it.

"I love Matt," Kristie says out of the blue. "He's a good man. And a good friend. I'm glad we're together."

I'm waiting for the rest of her thought. When she doesn't continue, I ask the obvious question. "But?"

She looks up from the table and smiles. "I had big dreams. I'm not unhappy," she adds quickly. "Not that. But to have this life, I gave up the other lives I was dreaming about."

"Like being a pop star?"

This surprises a laugh out of her. "You remember that?"

"How could I forget?" I hold my fork in front of my mouth, roll my eyes to the ceiling, and in a fake falsetto sing, "Ooo, baby, you make me—"

Kristie smacks me, ending the impromptu concert.

"I gave that up when I was thirteen," she says while I rub my shoulder in mock agony. "Did you know I was taking archaeology?"

"You said something about it once or twice." A hundred times, actually.

"Egypt. Tel Aviv. I wanted to see everything, do everything."

I start buttering her leftover toast to give my hands something to do. "So, go now."

"The kids—"

"—will love it."

"It won't be the same," she says.

"As what?"

"As being an archaeologist."

I shrug. "Hire a nanny and join a dig, then. They're always looking for volunteers."

When she doesn't answer, I look up from the stubborn grape jelly packet I'm trying to open. She's frowning. In a puzzled sort of way.

"Why didn't I think of that?" she says at last.

I raise my eyebrows and take a big bite of toast and jelly. It tastes better than my foot.

People are in and out of Grandpa's room all day. He's a pillar of small-town community life, and everyone is paying their respects. Sometimes Grandpa is awake and he'll nod and smile. More often he's asleep. But the visitors keep us busy answering hushed questions in the hallway. The flow of people ends when a hospital volunteer brings in a dinner of rancid peas, cold chicken, and gelatin stuff. This is still a farming town and visiting ends with the evening meal. I'm not sure why the hospital is sending Grandpa dinner. He's in no shape to eat. The meal leaves the room untouched, but will probably turn up again on a claim to Medicare.

Mom and Dad look exhausted. I've dozed on and off throughout the day, so I tell them to go home with Kristie and get a good night's sleep. This is a euphemism for tossing and turning and worrying while lying in bed. We all know it. We all pretend it isn't true.

As soon as the last person leaves the room, Grandpa looks at me and says, "Shut the door, Nicci. Read to me."

I shut the door, locking out the hospital sounds, then open the book and start reading. For nearly an hour we follow the adventures of a young cowboy caught up in a border war. Grandpa stares up at the ceiling, but I know he's awake and listening. I hope he's out on the range, away from this hospital and death.

I'm about to start a new chapter when a nurse opens the door and walks over to Grandpa's side. She has an air of authority and a tray with a bottle and a syringe. "Time for your medication," she announces as she fills the syringe and reaches for the tube leading from the IV to Grandpa's arm.

Grandpa shakes his head. "No. Don't want it. Want to finish the story."

She ignores him. "You're in pain. This will make you feel better."

Grandpa rolls his head on the pillow. He looks for me, finds me, his eyes are pleading. "I don't want to sleep, Nicci. I want to finish . . ." He trails off, coughing.

"Do you have to give it to him?" I ask the nurse.

"Do you want him to be in pain?"

"Of course not. But I don't think I'd want to . . ." *sleep the last hours of my life away.* I can't say the rest out loud.

"If I don't give this to him, he'll be in so much pain it won't matter," she says, as if she's heard what I didn't say.

"Maybe—" I begin, but Grandpa interrupts me.

"Just do it. Do it."

The nurse is already compressing the syringe, squeezing the painkiller into his veins. "There," she says, all cough syrup and saccharine. "You'll feel better now."

"You've . . . done it. Go away," Grandpa says to her.

I blink. I've never seen him be rude before.

The nurse's mouth twists. She's from out of town. Doesn't know Grandpa. Doesn't know he's not like this in real life. Doesn't care beyond the fact that she's fulfilled the doctor's orders. The door clicks behind her.

"Read, Nicci," Grandpa says. "Read the book."

Two pages later, his eyes are closed. Thin blue eyelids in a sunken face. We only have a few chapters left. Why didn't I ask her to postpone the medication?

Why is hindsight always the best sight?

I sit in the puddle of gold made by the bedside lamp and watch Grandpa sleep. I'm grateful for each breath.

Chapter
19

Sometime after two or three in the morning, I fall asleep. I dream Grandpa is leaking feathers and down. I try to catch them and put them back in, but he keeps getting flatter and floppier until he's nothing but a sack made of dried-up skin and clothes. The wind tosses the empty Grandpa-sack around, whipping it up and away. I try to run after it, but my legs are so heavy.

I jerk awake. I'm curled up in the chair by Grandpa's bed and I can't feel my feet. My joints snap and pop as I lift my legs out of the chair so the blood can reach my numb toes. The pins and needles of pain bring me all the way awake.

If I sit quietly, I can hear Grandpa breathing. A shallow, rasping sound around the oxygen tube in his nose. His bald head gleams in the lamplight, and a memory sneaks up and grabs my chest in its claws. Me—about eleven or twelve—pretending to polish Grandpa's head with a dish towel. Mom and Kristie giggling. Dad trying to find the camera. Grandpa making threats about dropping "young hooligans" in the pond while his shoulders shake with laughter.

Setting the book down beside the lamp, I leave the room. I pretend I'm only stepping out for a drink of water, but it isn't true. I'm drifting in the wind, no one is at the helm. After aimlessly roaming the halls for a quarter of an hour, I take the elevator to the first floor and try to find a Coke machine. The receptionist is standing at the front door, staring out through the glass at the parking lot. He must hear me because he turns around.

"It's snowing," he says. And looking past him, I see about three inches of white stuff on the ground. "A little earlier and we would have had a white Christmas," he continues, smiling. "My kids would have liked that. Do you think it will stick around for New Year's?"

"What time is it?" I ask instead of replying.

He looks up at the clock on the wall. "Almost four."

I nod. This is a detail. I need details.

"Yep," he says. "Four in the morning. Won't be light until seven-thirty."

I nod again, but I'm looking outside. There's someone out there. Someone walking toward us, head down against the snow-filled wind. The automatic doors slide open. Cold rolls across the floor, pushed down by the overwarm, bleachy, hospital air. The someone from outside stomps his boots, leaving snow on the all-weather mat. Then he looks up.

"Can I help you?" the receptionist is asking.

Ethan opens his arms, and I'm in them.

"Oh," says the receptionist.

Ethan smells of snow and damp and bus exhaust. His cheek is cold against my nose. The second hand on the wall clock stops. Time stretches thin around us. I close my eyes and hand over the tiller, let everything go into the all-night stubble on his cold cheek and the warmth of his hands on my back.

Please don't let me go. Don't make me go. I want to stay here forever.

The second hand on the clock falls. The receptionist coughs, and time snaps fat and into place. I step back at the same time as Ethan's hands drop to his side.

Details.

"How—?" I begin.

"Miguel said I was sulking. The guys in the coffee shop took up a collection, and Miguel drove me to the bus station." He starts to smile, but the worry line between his eyes drowns it out.

He doesn't need to ask about my grandpa. I can tell by the sudden tightness around his lips and eyes that he knows.

"We were reading this book," I say. "He wanted to know how it ended. Then a nurse came in . . . painkiller. I didn't think to ask her to wait until the book . . . Now he's asleep, and I'm afraid . . . afraid we won't finish."

Ethan cradles my face in his hands. His thumbs sweep away the tears that I didn't know were there until his warm fingers push them cold across my cheeks. He doesn't say anything like *"It will be okay,"* or some other meaningless garbage. He just listens. Is just *with* me, holding on to the tiller while I desperately try to take in the sails of my out-of-control life.

A clock in the nearby gift shop chimes four times.

Ethan's warm hands leave my face. But I'm not alone anymore.

"I should go back upstairs," I say. He nods. As we take the elevator to the fourth floor, I wonder if I should be asking myself—asking him—why he bothered to come all the way across the Rust Belt for someone he barely knows. But before the elevator doors open, I realize that kind of question is irrelevant.

I don't believe in fate. The main reason I rejected religion was the lack of proof for the supernatural. And fate is nothing more than the supernatural. The human brain seeks patterns, logic. Where it can't explain something, it creates an explanation. So I don't believe in fate. And yet sometimes when I meet someone, I have the feeling that I've known them before. That I already know them as deeply and as intimately as I know myself.

Ethan is one of those people. Is it fate? Can certain people be destined to meet in life? Or is it just similar thought patterns traveling the same river?

He knew I needed him. And here he is.

Some people would say that makes him . . . I don't know. Overprotective. But this isn't about protection, it's about two sticks being harder to break than one. I have a brief image of Jackie Chan holding up a bundle of chopsticks in *New Fist of Fury*, trying to convince the people around him that they cannot fail when they stand together. Ethan's just adding his stick to mine, making me harder to break.

The door to Grandpa's room is still open. I only meant to leave for a minute or two. And like a little kid, I'm suddenly afraid that he's stopped breathing because I left him and wasn't there to help him. But everything is exactly the same. The lamp, the book, the rasp of Grandpa's breathing. Perhaps it's my imagination, but he's smaller and thinner, lighter than when I left. But he's still here. If I touch him, he'll still be here in the dwindling sack of skin and bones that keeps him in the bed.

Ignoring the blurry wetness in my eyes, I pick up his hand. His eyelids flutter, then open in panic.

"Nicci?" His voice is thin, high. I squeeze his hand and he relaxes. "You're . . . still here."

"We haven't finished the book yet," I tell him.

"Yes." Something catches his attention, and he turns his head.

"Who . . . ?" he asks.

He's looking at Ethan, who is standing near the room's

other bed, just beyond the circle of light. But even across the dark room, I can feel Ethan's strength. Feel him holding me up. Two chopsticks together.

"No!" Grandpa cries. "I don't . . . want—" He starts to cough. "No medicine," he gasps.

I squeeze his hand again. "No, Grandpa. This is my friend. Ethan . . ." And for the first time it occurs to me that I don't even know his last name.

Ethan steps up beside Grandpa's bed, finding the one place where the lamp will shine on his face and Grandpa can see him without twisting his head. "Mosley," he says. "Ethan Mosley." No "sir." No false but polite statements about it being "a pleasure." Just a strict adherence to the Grandpa Commandments.

"Noah . . . Bradford," Grandpa says. And a pleased smile tugs at one corner of his mouth. He tries to lift a hand, but in the twenty-four hours since I arrived, he's grown too weak to move. "Let me . . . see . . . your shoes," he says after giving up on his hand.

Ethan's eyes widen. I try not to laugh as he looks around for a way to show Grandpa his feet. Finally, still standing by the bed, he lifts one foot up into the air.

Leather work boots. A size too big. Hey, I grew up Grandpa's granddaughter. I can tell these things. But I've never noticed Ethan's shoes before now.

Grandpa begins to laugh, but the laugh turns into a cough. When he catches his breath, he looks up at Ethan, who has both feet firmly back on the floor. In a whisper so faint Ethan has to lean over to catch the words, Grandpa says to him, "I'm glad . . . glad I got the chance . . . to meet you."

But this isn't a polite inanity someone says after being introduced.

Something hot and burning catches in my throat, and I have a hard time swallowing it down.

Puzzled, Ethan looks over at me for an explanation.

Not a chance in hell.

"Good," Grandpa says as I close the book on the hero, the girl, and the new spread with some cows. He can barely work his face into a smile, but he tries. His face is loosening, drifting, falling into the bones. "Good. I like . . . that one."

Outside the window, the sky has gray highlights. The golden lamplight is dimmer. Details. I nod in response because my voice seems to have stopped working with the last page of the book.

Grandpa rolls his head and looks out on the new day. "I think . . . call . . . your daddy," he says.

From the other side of the bed, Ethan unfolds himself from a chair. "I'll do it."

I don't have time to worry about my parents' reaction to a strange man waking them up. I scribble the number and my parents' names onto a piece of paper. Cold, fluorescent light from the hallway floods the room as Ethan slips out. He could have used the phone in the room, but he's leaving me alone with Grandpa. In peace. I sit down on the edge of the bed and hold Grandpa's hand. Together, we watch the sky. It's beginning to take on a blue and purple color. The snow must have gone with the night.

"Always trust yourself, Nicci," Grandpa says. The words are clear and strong, spoken with a voice from healthier times. His eyes close. His breathing stops.

I panic, squeeze his hand. "Grandpa!"

He sucks in a deep breath. I let one out. He's still breathing. Just reserving the last bit of his strength. Waiting until my parents and Kristie get here.

The undersides of the clouds are pink when the door opens again. I squeeze Grandpa's hand for the last time, and let Dad take my place. Mom and Kristie are on the other side of the bed, but I can't join them. Can't stay here. I've said goodbye. One step at a time, I walk the tunneled length of the room and open the door.

Ethan is sitting on the padded bench in the hallway. Across six feet of white tile, we look at each other. His face is exhaustion-thin, spikes of brown hair falling over his forehead and into his eyes. He looks like heaven. Nebulous made solid. I cross the hall and stand in front of him, look down into his eyes. So much strength. He reaches for my hand, and I crumple down beside him onto the bench and hold on as if his hand were the only thing keeping me from falling.

And maybe it is.

We sit for a long time. Nurses go in and out of Grandpa's room. Then a doctor.

I take the first deep breath of the day and hold it before letting all the pent-up air inside out in one, long, shuddering sigh.

"All right?" Ethan asks.

Looking over at him, I can see my reflection in his eyes. "Yes," I say. "The rest is just details."

In the Philippines, children are not protected from funerals. And funerals are not a simple affair. What kind of affair a funeral might be depends on whether or not it takes place in the mountains or in the lowlands, is Christian or Muslim or animist, is traditional or Spanish. . . . The options are endless. Where I grew up, the option was Catholic and Protestant lowlander. The night before the actual service and burial, the family holds a wake. Sometimes it's called a visitation, but it's basically a wake. The first one I really remember going to was when I was about seven. My friends and I quickly abandoned the adults and went outside to play. *Do you know what's going on?* asked one friend in a hushed voice. From her secretive tone, I figured it must be something better than what Mom and Dad had told me. I shook my head, sure that she would tell me. She leaned in. *"We're waiting for the ghost. The dead person's ghost."* Unfortunately, I thought this was exciting—what seven-year-old wouldn't?—and completely ruined her attempt to scare me. Midnight came and went, and nothing happened. It was one of the most disappointing episodes of my childhood.

The rest is just details.

What I said to Ethan is true. Once all that's left of a person is an empty pillowcase, the rest is just details. That doesn't mean I don't hurt inside, but now I'm strong enough to hold myself up. It's a good thing, because Ethan has to go back to the city if he wants to keep his job. I put on my coat and walk him to the bus station. We stand around for a long time, waiting for the bus. I don't know how to thank him. Thanking him might even be insulting. Because at some point, I think at the point when he looked up from the snowy mat and opened his arms, politeness became idiotic.

When the bus pulls in, he touches my face. I can feel his heat through the gloves covering his fingertips.

"I'll keep the teapot warm," he says.

Then the bus pulls away, and I'm left with the details.

Following the trail we made walking together to the bus station, I walk back to the hospital alone.

By evening, it's snowing again.

Four days later, the cemetery's "Perpetual Care" employees lower the traditional casket and spray of roses into a hole. All around the green canopy tent, the snow is white and thick—it covers the drive and is piled in rounded caps on the tops of the neighboring gravestones. Beside me, Kristie leans her head on Matt's shoulder. Nathan and Philip are with a baby-sitter, but I've convinced Kristie that it won't scar them psychologically to be at the traditional church-basement noon dinner the Baptist matriarchs are cooking.

I wonder if the kids will want to build a snowman.

The pastor says something that sounds like he's wrapping it up. I'm grateful. My feet are frozen inside the borrowed snow boots. But there's still the traditional final viewing of the body. No one notices when I slip a western into the casket.

Details. Everything is only details.

Kristie hands me a tissue, and I realize my face is wet.

*J*uggling the stack of bills that have been breeding in my mailbox during the last week, I fumble with the lock on my apartment door. My fingers are clumsy. Hell, everything has been clumsy since I slipped the western into Grandpa's casket yesterday. I give up and set my bag and the mail onto the floor before bending over to try and find the lock in the hallway's gloom. The lightbulb overhead is perpetually burned out. I've told my landlord about it, but he scratches his belly and goes back to his TV. If I had a ladder, I'd change it myself.

I finally get the key in the lock, twist it, and shove the door open. It takes the last atom of energy I have to pick up my bag and the bills. Slamming the door shut with my foot, I drop everything. Then I drop myself. And sliding down the closed door until I'm sitting on the floor, I let all the details go. I'm too tired to hang on to them right now. My chest caves in, and I go through an entire box of tissues before the tears give in to sniffles. Only these tears don't cleanse, they just leave me empty and depressed.

No amount of crying or wishing will bring Grandpa back.

Outside my window, the neighbor's outdoor Christmas

lights still cast a multicolored glow across my ceiling. Bare tree branches sway back and forth, and the stick shadows and colored lights chase each other around and around my light fixture. No one wants to let Christmas go. But the lights will be gone by the weekend, and the city will be drab and gray for another ten-and-a-half months.

Right now, gray seems unbearable.

The red, green, and gold shadows highlight a cream envelope lying on the floor. It isn't one of the bills I picked up in my box. After a few fumbles, I switch on the table lamp beside the door. I don't have the energy to stand up yet, but I need a distraction. Using the toe of my boot, I pull the envelope toward me. The upper left corner has a printed logo. A sailboat made out of a crescent moon.

Dream Sail.

Rob.

I rip open the envelope and squint at the cream sheet of twenty-four-pound bond with the sailboat letterhead. Even without my glasses, I can read the message, handwritten and in blue ink: "Where are you? We need to talk."

Folding the sheet back into thirds, I slip it into the envelope.

We need to talk. It's another way of saying, "You don't agree with me yet, and this conversation isn't over until you do."

I don't have anything to say to Rob. Even with Nicci's code of ethics, I don't owe him any more hot air space.

Wadding up the envelope, I toss it in the general direction of the trash can.

Anger-fueled adrenaline has me on my feet and I'm almost out the door for a run around the block when the adrenaline drains away and leaves me more tired than I was before. I want off this roller coaster.

I want my life back.

Only I can't have it back. The rent is going to be due next month, and I don't even have a job. In the space of a month, I've lost everything.

Always trust yourself, Nicci, Grandpa's voice says in my ear.

Okay, I haven't lost everything. I'm still here. I was here before I was even old enough to have a job. Or my own apartment. Or be foolish enough to let loneliness push me into a relationship with all the meaning and substance of a bundt cake.

After putting some water on to boil, I pay attention to the blinking message light on my answering machine. Fifteen phone calls. After listening to five calls from Rob, each sounding more frustrated than the last, I erase the whole mess and make tea.

E-mail isn't much better. A note from Kristie saying she's going to stay with Mom and Dad for a little bit to help go through Grandpa's things. Do I want anything? I write back and tell her to keep all the westerns for me.

Five messages from Rob.

Five strokes of the delete key.

The last message halts me in my computer tracks.

"Here are a few pictures," Ginger writes. "I hope you had a white Christmas. I'm so happy!" followed by about fifty exclamation points.

My fingers are trembling. I can barely type a two-line reply telling her about Grandpa. After sending her the message, I shake my hands out, then reach for the mouse and click on the first attached photo.

A night scene. Neon buildings thrusting up from Victoria Harbour. Hong Kong's lighted glory doubled in the water, with mountains darker than the city-lit sky rising up behind the buildings. The salt-fish scent of the water reaches me. It's mixed with oil, rust, heat . . . the smells tumble out of the picture.

I quickly click the next attachment. The view from Victoria

Peak, the red tram car in the foreground. I remember the rocking ride to the peak, Ginger pointing out her parents' apartment building.

The next. A group of laughing people eating at an outdoor table. Ginger has pasted a heading over the top of this picture: THE LUNCH GANG. The gang is leaning in close, and over their shoulders I can see the narrow alleyway of a market. Wooden signs, heavy baskets of fruit and vegetables, plain and striped canvas hanging over the alley, people—hundreds of people. A dog scratching its ear. And now I can hear the drone of a hundred voices, the high-pitched cackle of an old woman rising above the buzz. A baby cries. The dog barks.

Shit.

I exit everything and shut the computer down.

Are you happy doing what you do? Grandpa asks me.

I'm scared. I'm shaking.

I strip off my clothes and take a shower, keeping the water as hot as I can stand it.

It takes me part of the night and all morning to work up the nerve to go down to Graphics and Design for my things. Not that "my things" consist of much more than a few pictures, a calendar, some bendy toys, and a plant, but I feel like a bad mother just leaving everything behind. I'm explaining my situation to the security guard at the front desk when he shakes his head.

"You're still on the roster as an employee," he says. "Might as well go on up."

I'm confused, but what the heck? I sign my name.

"Happy New Year," the guard says as I turn toward the elevator.

Looking back, I catch the tail end of his smile. He looks like he really means it.

"Yeah. Happy New Year to you, too," I say.

Eerie déjà vu.

The first place I go is Carol's office. She isn't around, so I leave a note on her desk. A stack of empty copy-paper boxes sits in the hallway, waiting to be recycled. I recycle one by using it to carry my things home. I've never been fired before and I'm not sure where they might have put my stuff, so I wander down to my cubicle. It seems as good a place to start as any. Some of the people I pass in the hall I actually recognize. I would never have believed it was possible to work at a place for nearly a year and be able to walk away so easily.

My cubicle is exactly the way I left it when I walked out over a week ago.

From what I've heard, this isn't common business practice. Maybe they haven't found a new copy editor yet. I shrug, and start taking down my pictures and putting them into the box.

"Hi," says a voice.

I turn around. Carol is standing in the doorway holding two cups of coffee. She hands me one.

"Hi." I take a sip and then sit down, pushing the box over so I can see her. It feels like the last two hundred or so mornings I've spent talking to her. Give or take holidays and those few weeks she wasn't speaking to me.

"What's with this?" I ask, waving my hand to indicate the cubicle. "Why is it all still here?"

"What's with *you*?" Carol asks in response. "I heard about the fight with Rob and you walking out. I've been trying to call you. Are you quitting? Did you get fired?"

I feel a little guilty for deleting all the messages on my machine. I'm not sure why I assumed they would all be from Rob. I wonder if Melissa is one of the voices I consigned to oblivion.

"Rob wanted me to marry him," I say out loud, as if this explains everything.

Carol frowns.

"And my grandpa died."

Her frown turns to sympathy. "I'm sorry."

I nod. "And I went off on the boss."

"Oh!" She starts to say something, but I interrupt.

"Rob isn't happy unless everything is his way." Somehow, I don't think I'm explaining anything. Condensing the past few weeks—*weeks!*—into four sentences . . . But Carol seems to understand. Maybe the thing with Bill has changed her perspective on relationships. I remember the pink-and-white bag. Her frustration with Kevyn. Maybe not. Or maybe Kevyn isn't just a relationship for her. Maybe he's a culmination of a long journey toward understanding.

Now I really am being metaphysical. I wonder if I could stand the food at a Buddhist monastery.

"Did you guys have anything in common?" Carol asks.

It takes me a moment to realize she means me and Rob.

"The sex was pretty good," I say.

She laughs a little. "That's what I said about Bill."

"Good sex doesn't have to turn into . . ." *Bill.* I'm trying to be fair to Rob because I don't think he's a cheat or a liar, but I've almost put my foot in my mouth. I don't want to hurt Carol, either. Or worse, insult her.

She figures out the missing word, but she doesn't look hurt or insulted. "No," she says.

We sit in silence for a minute. "Why did it take me so long?" she asks.

So long to what? Discover Kevyn? Figure out that Bill was a jerk? I don't know which question she's asking, but it doesn't matter because I don't have an answer for either one. There but for the grace of God and all that. If only a few things had been different, I'd have a shackle of gold and pressed-coal on my hand right now. Just a few details missing or added and there I would be.

It's frightening.

Carol is waiting for an answer. I don't know what to say, but I've got my mouth open to say something when the boss appears in the doorway. He clears his throat. I swear he looks guilty and embarrassed, but maybe that's just wishful thinking.

"Ms. . . . ah . . . Bradford?"

Can't he even remember my name? I raise my eyebrows.

He glances at Carol, then sighs. "I'm sorry for insinuating that you were carrying on a"—he glances at Carol again—"an improper relationship."

This isn't what I was expecting. And I don't know how to respond. I almost laugh. There aren't any guidelines for this sort of thing in Mom's *Guide for Girls*.

Maybe I should write my own guide. I'd call it, *Nicci Tells It Like It Is*. The answer for situations like this would come in Chapter 12—"So You've Just Accused Your Boss of Fucking His Executive Assistant"—under the subheading, "The Rat Apologizes."

"I've held your job," the boss says. His Adam's apple bounces a few times. "You've done good work, and I understand if there have been some . . . ah . . . *family* things you need to work out." He's hinting. He wants me to make up some excuse—lie—to keep his nose clean. Funny. In this case, the excuse wouldn't be a lie.

I'm just about to say thank you and I'll stay on. After all, jobs are hard to come by. Then I realize what this apology is all about. Fear. His fear. He's scared I'll say something about Melissa. He didn't think anyone knew. He's blackmailing me with a job I already threw in his face.

It would be funny if I weren't so angry.

Are you happy doing what you do?

No.

Standing up, I turn the anger into a polite sound of regret.

"I'm sorry," I say without a hint of apology. "I can't take you up on your offer at this time." He starts to frown, and I add the punch line. "Besides, I'm not the person you should be apologizing to."

He has the grace to flinch.

I think of Melissa hunting for a new job and I push a little harder, blackmailing the blackmailer. "Perhaps if you should give that person a letter of recommendation—a *helpful* letter of recommendation—it would work as well as an apology? That would end the matter, I think." I smile, all fangs.

He smiles. It wobbles a little, but he smiles. He's got mud in his eye, but he knows he's getting off easy. I've told him that I'll keep my mouth shut. I'm leaving. Melissa's gone. All he has to do is write a glowing letter.

The snake.

Still smiling, he slithers off to "just tell my assistant you won't be staying on." I hope the new assistant is less lonely than Melissa.

Carol's mouth is hanging open. "What the hell was that all about?" she asks as I sit back down.

"Loneliness." Looking down I see the Christmas list I was doodling the day Ethan took me out to lunch. A lifetime ago. "Grandpa—a set of cap guns?" the first line reads. I wad the list into a ball and toss it into the trash.

"Are you going to need a job?" Carol asks. This is such an understatement that I'm forced to laugh.

"Quite possibly."

"I may know someone," she says. "I don't know. I'll have to call."

Is there anything this woman can't do? I reach up and take down my calendar. "If I were a lesbian," I ask, "would you be able to set me up?"

She's quiet. I glance over at her. Her face is rumpled, eyes glazed over with shock.

"You . . . you're a . . . ? I mean, maybe. I . . ."

My foot's in my mouth again. I forgot that Carol takes everything literally. "No. What I'm trying to say is that you're always setting people up, always finding someone who can take care of a friend. One time, I thought what if I were . . . never mind." I toss the calendar into the box. It's time for a topic change.

"How's it going with Kevyn?" I ask.

At first it looks as though she's going to protest the abrupt switch, then she sighs. "He says we should wait until we get married."

It takes me three full minutes to figure out what she means. "No sex until you're married?" How . . . quaint. "Have you told him how historical that is?"

Carol nods. She looks miserable. The black lace thingie must be burning a hole in her dresser.

"So marry him."

"I'm still married," she says.

I always wondered what a wail would sound like. Now I know.

"What's taking so long? Have you tried one of those four-hundred-dollar divorce things they're always advertising after midnight?"

She shakes her head. "Those only work for uncontested divorces. The house—"

"You're holding out for *stuff?*" I stare at her.

Carol blinks. "All Kevyn has is an apartment. . . ."

"So?" It's my turn to shake my head. I do it gravely, slowly. "I always thought you were kinda smart, you know? Now I find out you're an idiot." I'm teasing her, but I'm serious, too. Why waste happiness for a bunch of things you'll give away at a garage sale five years from now?

Carol starts to laugh. "You know, I think you're right."

"Of course I am." I drop the rest of my pictures into the box. It's amazing how little you can accumulate in a space you're not comfortable with. Eleven months and I can't fill a single box.

"I used to think you were mixed up," Carol says. I look up at her in surprise, but she holds up a hand. "Not a lot. Just not very happy. Unfriendly and lonely all at the same time. But of the lot of us, maybe you're the only stable one here."

I mentally add a new chapter to *Nicci Tells It Like It Is*. I call this one: "So You've Just Gotten a Compliment Because You're Good at Bullshit."

Box under one arm, I step out of the office building for the last time. The sun is shining.

Sunshine in the winter is an insult. Unless it's in the woods somewhere, glittering on new-fallen snow. But in Boston, winter is gray, and sunshine just makes it grayer. Sunshine is yellow, and reminds you of green leaves and singing birds. Instead we've got crapping pigeons, exhaust, and some kind of dirt-brown sand that used to be snow. Once upon a time, I thought I was a city girl. Now I think it depends on the city.

I'm not going to think about *The Lunch Gang*.

There's an outbound bus in five minutes. I can take it or I can walk to the coffee shop and take another one.

I'm not ready to see Ethan. Not yet. And I'm a coward. I take the bus.

Leaning against the cold window, my worldly office possessions in my lap, I realize I'm frightened of the details. I've always taken comfort in details—used them like a shield. But being a few details away from disaster? It changes a person.

I can play a twisted version of the "Six Degrees" game with

my life. Let's call it the "Six Ifs." If Carol hadn't had that break-down. If Ginger hadn't decided to go back to Hong Kong. If Jimmy hadn't died. If Melissa hadn't asked me to help her. If I'd never met Ethan. If Grandpa were still alive. Six ifs. Six degrees of details and I probably would have married Rob. And had the Labrador, the two-point-four, the minivan, Julie and Rich movies, and the house in the suburbs. Everything I've never wanted. And then one day, I would have woken up—just like Ginger. Or maybe not. Maybe I just would have kept on going, making the best of a bad situation. I'd like to think I'm smarter than that, but I know it isn't true.

And Carol thinks I might be the stable one.

What a joke.

Because I don't believe in me anymore.

And that takes all the living out of life.

Chapter
21

$\mathcal{T}$ wo days later, Carol calls me to say that she's set up an interview with her friend for Monday. And I get a letter from Grandpa.

There are probably creepier things than getting mail from a dead person. I can't name any offhand. I know Grandpa was the last person to touch the letter inside, to lick the envelope, and that makes it hard to open the darn thing. I set it on my table, lean my chin on my arms, and look at it.

It looks back.

I get up to make tea.

It's still there.

Finally, I give in and carefully slit it open.

Inside is a folded sheet of lined paper. It's from the tablet by the phone in my parents' kitchen. Inside the folded sheet of paper is a money order. Made out to me. For six thousand dollars.

My hands are shaking. I set the money order down on the table and read what's written on the lined paper.

"Dear Nicci," it says. "Find what it is you want to do, and do it. Always trust yourself. Love, Grandpa."

I look at the postmark on the envelope. The letter was

mailed the day after Christmas. Maybe the storm delayed it. But I don't know what to do. Even if Grandpa were still alive, I would never have been able to take this money. Now . . .

I call my parents. Mom answers. I explain about the letter and the money.

"I knew about that," she says.

Talk about a fist to the stomach. *"What?"*

"Grandpa talked about doing something. . . . At Thanksgiving, honey, you seemed so unhappy. And frankly, I don't think Grandpa liked Rob all that much."

"Italian loafers," I say.

She laughs, but I can hear how choked up she is. "Something like that. Then at Christmas . . ." She pauses to blow her nose. "After you left, he insisted on going in to the bank and then the post office. When I asked, he just shook his head, but I watched him address the envelope. And there's a withdrawal of six thousand dollars from his account. It was the last thing he did, honey."

Oh, that makes me feel a *lot* better.

"But now?" I ask. "What about now? I mean, don't you guys need this? For funeral expenses or something?"

"Even if we did, we wouldn't take it back. He wanted you to have it."

I don't know what to say. Then she adds the punch line:

"Use it wisely."

I hang up the phone. Sitting back down at the table, I trace the patterns on the money order with my finger. As it settles in, the first thing I feel is relief. I can pay the bills. Next month and several months to come.

Use it wisely.

Somehow, paying the bills doesn't seem wise.

A loud knock on my door sends my hand and the money order under it skidding across the table.

It's a tired guy from FedEx. I'm surprised he walked all the way up to my door until he hands me a clipboard to sign. Closing the door after him, I look down at the legal-sized package. From Hong Kong. I have to use a knife to open it—Ginger hasn't outgrown the love of wrapping things in a roll of strapping tape.

Inside the box is a lot of tissue paper and a piece of wood. About four inches wide and twelve inches high, and painted with red lacquer. Raised gold characters adorn the front. I'm confused for a moment, then I realize what I'm holding: a funeral plaque. Digging farther into the box, I find a card from Ginger.

"I'm so sorry about your grandpa. I know you were closer to him than anyone," she writes. "You probably remember seeing these in front of the altars. The characters on this say 'Grandfather,' 'Friend,' and 'Immortality.' I think. I'm still lousy at reading characters, so hopefully it doesn't say something nasty. I'll burn some paper money next time I go to the temple."

Dropping down among the tissue paper, I hold the plaque in my lap. Half a world away, this plaque would sit on an ancestral altar along with lots of other plaques and incense and candles and ceremony. Here I put it on my coffee table, and wrap my arms around my knees.

Even without the ceremony, I feel comforted.

And I'm beginning to understand something. Finally.

Once upon a time, I thought I needed to get by on my own, make it on my own, be happy with just me for company. But friends—real friends—aren't just people to walk the halls with so you don't look like a lonely loser. Real friends are . . . life preservers. Without them, you sink. I've been trying to swim alone, sail alone, even when the loneliness almost crushed me. I even—

Another knock on my door.

—I even took bundt cake over the real thing just to prove I

didn't need someone to lean on, someone who could make the loneliness go away.

I open the door.

It's Rob.

We stand on either side of my threshold. I'm wondering if I conjured him up out of my self-analysis. He's surprised.

"You're here!" he says. All smiles.

"I'm here."

He steps forward, but when I don't move aside to let him in, he stops.

We look at each other a little longer. Then, "I'm sorry I've been such an asshole," he says.

He might be sincere. He might just be saying what it takes to get past me and into my apartment. The trouble with Rob is that I can't tell the difference.

"I'm not going to marry you," I tell him. "Not now, and not in the future, either."

One corner of his mouth jerks.

"Can I come in?" he asks. As an afterthought he adds, "Please?"

I push the door open, letting it bang against the wall, and walk back into my apartment. The lock clicks as he follows me and shuts the door.

"Why?" he asks.

"I've already told you." I sit back down on the floor in front of the coffee table.

He takes off his coat and sits down in the chair across from me. Leaning forward, he lets his hands dangle between his knees. "Can we just go back to being . . . you know . . . like it was?"

The look on his face tells the truth. He's hoping I'll change my mind after a few more months of sex on boats, meeting his parents, becoming entrenched in his way of life.

"What do *you* think?" I ask. I'm reining in the sarcasm. Maybe I do too good of a job, because he takes the question at face value.

"I think we could," he says, eagerness burning in his eyes.

I look down at the funeral plaque. I've worked myself into a corner.

Rob doesn't want *me*. He wants the girl that won't have him. But this isn't the kind of thing you can say to a guy. It's insulting. It insinuates that he has a brain the size of a pea. No, less than the size of a pea. Because if he actually *used* a pea-sized brain, he'd figure it out for himself. So I come up with an argument that would make Socrates proud.

"It won't work," I say.

To use a western analogy: "That ought to fix his wagon."

Ha. Ha-ha.

It might just be the bad overhead lighting, but Rob's face turns a shade of yellow.

"What do you mean?" he asks.

"It's over, Rob. What more can I . . . *do* I have to say? There isn't any relationship to go back *to*. I don't think there ever was."

He stands up, bumping the coffee table with his knee. The funeral plaque teeters and falls onto the floor. I'm reaching for it when his next words stop me.

"So basically you were just being a slut," he says.

Ouch.

I pull my hand back and look up at him.

"I was lonely," I say. "You asked me out. So if I'm a slut, what does that make you?"

Rob wrenches his coat off the back of the chair and stomps out, slamming the door in his wake. I don't know if he meant to, I don't want to say it was deliberate, but on the way out, he steps on the funeral plaque—

—and snaps it in two.

Broken pieces. Broken lives.

Find what it is you want to do, and do it.

Always trust yourself.

On Monday, I cancel the interview with Carol's friend. After cashing the money order, I buy two tickets to Hong Kong. One of them leaves in forty-eight hours. The other is open.

Kung Fu movies aren't big on denouement. The climax is always the big fight between the villain and the hero. The hero wins. The movie ends. Oh, sometimes some bystander will say to the hero, "You're a good man," or the girl will run after the hero crying, "Take me with you." Occasionally, it's really odd. The hero will knock the stuffing out of the bad guy, and a watching monk will raise his hand and chant, "Buddha bless you." I think it's because Kung Fu movie writers understand the realities of life. These movies are a tiny slice of time, a few compressed incidents. The big fight isn't the end for the hero. He's going to go on, have other adventures, live the next seventy years of his life.

I lean in to pay the taxi driver, then watch him pull away. The hot, brown smell of coffee is strong, even out here where I stand on the sidewalk. Looking up, I can see a few flakes of snow drift down through the glow of the streetlight. More snow. That's what Mom said on the phone when I called to tell my family I was leaving.

My parents are stoic about the whole thing. But the world is a lot smaller now than it was in the late sixties when they set off for a country on the other side of the globe. Of course, they could just be annoyed that I mailed them all the stuff from my apartment. I figure Mom and Dad's attic is a good place to store old memories while I make new ones.

Everything that was too big to mail and didn't have any

memories I sent home with Carol and Kevyn. Carol was all smiles and walked like she was wearing uncomfortable underwear. The black see-through thingie must be getting a workout. They didn't want the futon.

But they did haul it and all the rest of the furniture to the Salvation Army.

And thus disappeared all the pieces of Nicole Bradford's drab, gray life.

Except for the Kung Fu movies. And the broken funeral plaque. I'm taking those with me.

I open the door to the coffee shop, then drag my suitcase and the cardboard box full of videos and DVDs inside and set them by the door. The bell overhead chimes as the door swings shut.

Ethan is wiping down the glass case. Little ceramic burlap sacks filled with coffee beans litter the top of the counter. He stands up straight and looks at me. His hand is still absently swishing the rag across the glass.

"Hi," he says.

I bury my fists into my coat pockets. My heart is beating so hard the lapels on my coat shiver in tune to the beats. "Hi."

We could be strangers. Almost.

He's taking in the details. My oversized suitcase. The box wreathed in tape, and bearing my name and Ginger's address in black, Sharpie relief. Me. His face is blank. But he sees everything and he knows I'm here to say goodbye.

Not quite.

Leaving my luggage, I walk up to the counter. We're separated by glass and coffee beans and conflicting thoughts. He drops the rag behind a few faux burlaps with tags advertising Jamaican and Costa Rican.

"You're leaving?" he asks, leaning his arms on the counter.

And I'm tossed back to the first day I saw him. Grinning

Boy. *"You two have a fight?"* A lifetime ago. I think of Jimmy and Grandpa. Two lives ago.

"Yes." I barely get the word out.

"You're not taking much." He reaches for the rag again, rubs the side of the nearest ceramic bag. Espresso Roast. The skin around his eyes has gone tight. He's not cleaning the coffee shop. He's grinding his thoughts in his head.

I try to laugh, but it comes out too high. "I can barely lift the suitcase. I thought I was bringing too much."

"Not for a world tour."

He thinks I'm running away from my life. Just like his mom.

"I'm not taking a world tour."

The rubbing stops, and he tosses the rag away.

"Coffee with cream?" he asks.

I nod.

Digging out my wallet, I can barely separate the money and the smooth, hard piece of paper that's been the object of hope, ridicule, and fear ever since I bought it.

He sets the waxed-paper cup on the counter in front of me and rings up the bill. I slide the money—including an extra twenty to repay his loan—and the open ticket to Hong Kong across the glass. Not looking, he reaches for it, and I catch his hand.

His hand jerks.

His whole body jerks.

He thought I was leaving. Just like everybody else in his life.

The back of his hand is hard, veined, and hot under my icy fingers. My heart is about to smash a rib. On the wall, the clock has ground to a halt, dragging time with it. He looks down, and his eyes widen when he sees the airline ticket.

"I'll buy you a cup if you'll drink it with me on my break," I say.

He looks up from the ticket, and I can see myself in his eyes.

"Where will that be?" he asks.

"Hong Kong. Somewhere in Hong Kong."

Under my fingers, the tendons of his hand move. The clock ticks. He takes my money.

And he takes the ticket.

"Hong Kong's a big place," he says as he puts the money in the cash drawer. He leaves the twenty on the counter, but he's still holding the ticket.

I reach over and open the ticket. Inside is a Post-it note with Ginger's phone number and address. "Not so big," I say.

He looks up from the Post-it and smiles for the first time. "Maybe not."

A car horn blares from the street. It's my taxi. Call me a coward, but I paid him to drive around the block a few times, then come back for me. I didn't want any witnesses to possible humiliation.

I pick up my coffee and walk back to my luggage. It will be impossible to carry everything and the coffee, but I don't want to give the coffee up because he made it for me.

"Nicci."

Ethan calls my name, and turning around, I see him lift the partition and step out from behind the counter. He walks toward me, not stopping until only inches separate us. My heart starts thudding again and my ribs quiver.

"Nicci." He reaches out, hesitates, then puts his hands on my shoulders. I can feel his warmth through the layers of my coat and sweater. His eyes are dark. So dark I can only see myself in my own head.

"Nicci." My name is the barest brush of air against my lips. Then his warmth is my warmth, and our lips touch. Separate. Touch again. And cling.

"I'll see you in a few days," he says into my mouth.

"Yes."

The taxi driver presses down on his horn.

Ethan picks up my suitcase, and I pick up the box of Kung Fu movies. After he settles both my luggage and me in the back seat, he touches my cheek. "Be careful."

"Yes."

I kiss the tips of his fingers, and watch as he goes back into the shop.

"Where to now?" the taxi driver asks.

"The airport."

KAREN BRICHOUX was born in the Philippines between the time Kennedy was shot and the day Nixon resigned. She saw her first Kung Fu movie, *Five Shaolin Masters*, when she was eight. Obviously, this warped her forever. After spending seven years as a graduate student in European history, she realized that she might actually have to take a job as a professor, so she left the too-real world of academia in order to write fiction. She lives in the U.S. with her spouse and various species of fur-bearing house mammals.